In The Act of Flight

by Christian Pitts

ISBN 978-0-578-47368-0
(paperback)

ISBN 978-0-578-47369-7
(ebook)

To my amazing, brave, parents.

Acknowledgments

I would like to thank my parents, Allen and Peggy, for all their hard work, and for having the boldness and follow-through to create this amazing voyage.

I would like to thank my husband, Robert, for proofing this book, and for putting up with me for the many hours I buried myself in writing leaving him to wrangle two little boys and two rambunctious dogs.

I would like to thank Jessica Boling for editing and formatting this book, the creation of the book's cover, graphics, advertising and the bazillion other things she did to ultimately get this project off the ground and into print.

Foreword

This novel is based upon the true story of my family's three-year adventure living in the Sea of Cortez aboard a sailboat. I hope that by the end of this book you are able to fully comprehend the awesome feat of watery travel that my parents pulled off. They used their incredible work ethic and grit to overcome a variety of obstacles that came their way before we even left the United States, and made an incredible adventure come together.

I have chosen the genre of a novel to recount our tale, because after thirty-five years, memories are already in the novel form no matter how true to reality one tries to remain.

Table of Contents

Prologue

The Volante was in the act of flight...

Isabel put down her pen. 'No,' she thought, 'there is more than just getting loose from gravity, and taking flight, there is the *how* people become airborne, freed and able to escape from merely existing. That is my story.'

Isabel picked up her pen. *I am exhausted, she continued, and horrified by all the excuses I have heard over the years for bad behavior and bad choices holding people back. If there ever was a person who made bad decisions and had plenty holding him down, it was my father. But if there was ever a human who struggled on a minute- to-minute basis to climb up out of the mire of his own faults, then that man was my father as well.*

The oldest of seven children, my father left home at the age of fourteen to take a jobs as a night watchman aboard a tall-ship and a commercial fisherman at the piers in San Francisco. He did this to help support his family. On the commercial fishing boat he was governed by a wonderful captain, Joe Alioto, who instilled in Joe a love for the sea and a strong work ethic. Aboard the Balclutha, where he was a night watchman, he let his friends hang out and drink so long as they did not damage the ship. Soon it became the after-hours hangout for his friends, and fellow Sea Scouts. Teenagers swinging from the rigging, making out below deck, and smoking in the cockpit could be counted upon from midnight to four AM every Friday and Saturday night, with an occasional Thursday thrown in for good measure. But Joe's boss never would have suspected, for every morning the Balclutha stood spotless and shining in her berth.

It was on such a night that our main character, Joe, offered to drive a friend's sports-car home so his buddy could stay aboard with his girlfriend. Everyone thought that Joe wanted to drive the car because it was a beautiful, cherry red, little sports car with chrome that shown in even a hint of light. No one really seemed to grasp that Joe wanted to drive the car because he had submitted a sports-car design the year before in a contest run by Chevrolet and won second prize. This car bore a remarkable similarity to his design and he wanted to see how she ran, but he probably should have done his little test drive while he was sober...

A Chance Event

The 1954 Triumph TR3 hit the guardrail of the Richardson Bay Bridge at top speed. The little, red, convertible flipped over the suicide barrier with Joe drunk and unconscious in the driver's seat, his foot leaden upon the accelerator. With a tremendous *BOOM!* the car smashed into the bank under the bridge and exploded.

Without his seat-belt, Joe was thrown around the interior of the car. The windshield disintegrated into malicious splinters and jagged edges. Metal twisted and tore. Bones crushed into each other. Tissues ripped and bled. The gas tank erupted and all except for Joe's face was covered in gasoline. Within milliseconds his body was engulfed in fire. Profoundly inebriated, he made no effort to awaken.

A mustard yellow VW bus filled with hippies saw the explosion and screeched to a halt. The sliding side-door flew open and a large cloud of marijuana smoke billowed out. Two tie-dyed clad hippies jumped through the pot-cloud, fire extinguishers in hand, and ran toward the blaze.

The good Samaritans emptied their extinguishers into the flames, but it merely tamed the height of the fire.

"Holy shit, man! I can see the driver! He's on fire!" The man looked a little closer, shielding his face from the heat with the barrel of the fire extinguisher. "Shit! I think he's moving!"

Pure adrenaline kicked in. One of the men ripped off his shirt and used it to protect his hand as he tried to open the driver door of Joe's car, but the door had already transformed into a congealed mass of heat-softened metal.

They hoisted the fire extinguishers to smash the driver's window, which oddly remained intact, and reached inside to pull Joe from the burning wreckage. Flesh caught and tore on the jagged, glass, window fragments, but there was no other way to save him. They dragged him away from the inferno and fell into a panting heap next to him some fifty yards away from the wreck.

Lying on the hillside, a pile of charred flesh that had already started to melt from the bone, Joe awoke. He could not see through the smoke that rose from his own body.

"Man, you OK?" asked an unfamiliar voice.

Joe tried to focus on the voice and failed as he once again fell unconscious.

***

It took two whole days before Joe recovered semi-consciousness in the Stanford Medical Center's burn unit. Unable to see, and only able to hear muffled sounds, Joe had the acute sense that something terrible had changed for him, but he could not be sure what. The painkillers deprived him of his senses and he fell in and out of mild coherence.

Ignorance was bliss. Both legs were burned. The right leg, where healthy ankle and foot had once been, was now a deformed, stiff, club-foot. The left leg would need two square feet of skin grafts. Second and third degree burns covered seventy-five percent of his body. His singed lungs let him breathe only in short, agonized gasps and his eyes were cauterized by smoke. The only three places he had not sustained second or third degree burns were his face, palms, groin, and a ring around his head in the shape of a crown.

The doctors had wrapped him from head-to-toe in layer after layer of white gauze, soaked in medications. Only his mouth was visible. A clear endotracheal tube poked out of his mouth between blackened lips swaddled in white gauze. The tube shoved down his throat pumped oxygen to any surviving lung cells. A urinary catheter hung out of his penis, and a slow drip filled the bag at his side with dark brown urine. Three IV bags hung over his head and pumped fluids, antibiotics and morphine into him at precise rates.

Joe lay in a bed that looked like a gigantic gyroscope. It flipped him over every two hours in a huge motion that seemed designed to throw him onto the floor. Many of Joe's burns were deep enough to have caused nerve damage, and these he could not feel, but the other burns let out enough pain to make Joe think he was still on fire. No position was comfortable. Every time he so much as twitched he felt like a cheese grater ran up and down his entire skin.

The doctors kept him in a twenty-four hour drug-induced stupor, but Joe still had the sensation of being in an agonizing Hell that he could not escape. The smell of his own burnt flesh assaulted his nostrils for weeks. The pain never relented. Underneath the layers of gauze and agony he could not even blink an eye. Not even when they anesthetized him every two days to change his dressings that turned a purulent green and oozed the stench of dying flesh could he find a respite.

He lay immobile, vulnerable, as the medical teams poked and prodded, cleaned and changed him. The sounds of peeling stuck bandages, the pucker and pop as the layers were pulled off, the scratch of metallic instruments on fleshy, decaying debris and the flush of saline as the wounds were cleaned were all Joe could sense. The sound of the metal instruments thrown down on the surgical tray jolted him with their loud crash of metal on metal.

He lay in his bed of torture, unable to move, forced to take in every awful sensation.

***

Joe's family came to visit him and stood around the bed. His six brothers and sisters made room for his father and short, round mother. She would forever remember how he looked wrapped in all those layers of bandages, like a medical mummy.

"Well, John," his mother said to his father, "what are we going to do?"

His father stood at the foot of the bed staring at his son from a safe distance, and winced, but said nothing. Joe's mother just shook her head sadly, unsure if he was going to live or die.

"We will be back tomorrow, Joe," she said and walked away, afraid to touch her own son with even a pat on his bandaged hand.

The rest of the siblings stayed with Joe for a while longer. These were not unintelligent people, but the six of them standing at Joe's bedside, slack-jawed and sorrowful, had no solution for what to do next. Shock and despair have a funny way of sucking all hope right out of a person's head.

"What *are* we going to do?" his youngest sister asked.

"There is nothing we can do but wait," his brother replied.

As the eldest child, Joe's role was the protector, the breadwinner, the referee of sibling squabbles. As they looked on, his siblings knew that Joe no longer existed.

The brother they remembered was gone.

Or so they thought.

***

It is not easy for a young man who had left home at fourteen for jobs as a night watchman, and a commercial fisherman, and who had helped support his family, been a leader among his friends, and who despised the helpless as lazy, to become dependent himself.

A strong, active, stubbornly independent, young man never imagines needing other people to help him with the simplest of human functions.

Sipping water from a straw became a three-nurse endeavor, that usually ended with Joe swearing in pain. He could not sit up. He could not scratch his own nose. Such a sense of helplessness makes a man slide into that alternate-dimension of reality known as depression, where with the merest flick of a thought, a bad situation turns the strong and proud into a heap of rejection and self-contempt wrapped in a thick covering of hopelessness.

Depression is the scourge of mankind. Depression takes someone who would have fought the devil to cherish a flicker of hope and makes him give up, lay down, and let himself be tormented. In the stead of the warrior stands a puddle of semi-congealed self-pity and loathing just waiting to evaporate. A man who once dreamed of singular greatness and adventure, a man who thrived on living and joy, gives himself over to becoming part of a great nothing, and hopes for an immediate sublimation of self.

***

After three months, Joe's saviors visited him. He did not see them through the gauze shroud, nor hear them through his narcotic haze. But if he had known who they were he wouldn't have thanked them - he would have beaten them senseless. He would have pummeled them until their faces were missing. He would have hollered and raged in absolute anguish straight through to their souls and left them shattered and standing in a pile of bone dust.

Joe knew they had put him in the position of never being able to find peace in this life. Because of their actions he would have to endure decades of pain from crushed vertebrae, burns that would never heal and countless surgeries to attach skin grafts that never took. At only seventeen years old, and only three months into his recovery, he knew this without a doubt.

Infection after infection would keep him on high doses of antibiotics that made him nauseous so even the simple act of eating would never again be enjoyable. Not to mention the interminable, unbearable pain that emanated in jagged stabs and wretched, monotonous, pangs and throbs from every aspect of his being. No amount of drugs could kill the pain. Even when he was anesthetized he dreamed of agony. How could he feel gratitude towards people who had placed him in a living hell?

He longed to be outside his skin, free from pain. He longed to be in the act of flight, soaring above it all, free from torment.

The Change

For six months Joe lay in the hospital bed and waited for death, for if this was not Hell, he was certain this was good preparation for what surely awaited him in the afterlife. Skin cells that normally take fourteen days to appear, take months to come alive in burn patients. The intelligent, little cells seemed to fear laying down their matrix where such major trauma has occurred. They crept, seemingly one at a time, into place. His body seemed to send the weakest cells first, as sacrificial scouts. They died the moment the wounds were cleaned, or were eaten up by infection. Ever slowly, the next set of cells would come and meet the same fate. Six months into his recovery, Joe remained bloodied and full of large, oozing ulcers.

Joe's bones healed well. But the main pain came from the burns. By this point, Joe was addicted to his pain killers. Now, not only did he need them to keep his pain at bay, but also to keep him from getting nauseous and twitchy. He did not know he was an addict yet. The nurses kept the painkillers coming as a part of his three times a day medicine routine. To him he was just just following doctor's orders. Daily he sucked down his opioids with no idea that they did more than just dull the pain.

Depression took its hold of Joe and wrung him until the last atom of his self hung by one thread of magnetic energy. It flickered and strained, fighting the extinguishing lack of hope. With the energy left in that one atom a tiny, desperate, spark went off inside of Joe's head.

He opened his eyes. The anger flooded in. He grabbed his bed by the rails and shook until he broke off the bars the kept him from falling out. He threw the bars at the wall. The depression ran from the torrent of hate he unleashed upon it. Who the fuck was this agony to deny him his life? In that split-second change he no longer submitted to the pain. He stood tall in his mind and he challenged the pain every moment. He dared the pain to become worse. He challenged it to torture him more. He dared the pain to hold him back from a life he could enjoy.

He felt for the bar he knew to be hanging over the hospital bed. He ever so slowly raised his right hand. His bandages pulled and cut into his arm. He held his breath and kept stretching his hand ever closer to the bar above his head. Blind folded by the wound dressings, he felt the air with his hand hoping to bump into the bar he knew to be hanging there, bumping it several times before he could grab it. Grab tight he did.

Joe tried to pull himself up, but he was too weak. His right arm throbbed, but he did not let go of the bar. He willed his left arm into action. The digging of the bandages into his skin felt like razors cutting him to ribbons. Finally his left hand grabbed the bar.

He pulled, millimeter by millimeter, for a full ten minutes, sweating and cursing the entire time. And then he rose.

Joe sat fully upright. He felt amazing! He savored his victory over the horizontal and prone position he had held for the past six months.

"Hah! Fucker, you thought you had me."

He had won the first battle in his private war.

A few days later he demanded that the bandages on his head be altered to allow for openings for his eyes. A few bleary blinks later he had sight. Sight plus sitting up equaled progress despite still being wrapped top to bottom in white bandages.

Joe's mother came to visit him daily. His resemblance to a mummy so affected her that up until the day she died she would get a far away look in her eye when she spoke of her son in the years after his accident. The constant melancholy she felt for her son going through the rest of his life in pain was a testament to her depth of empathy. She would never lose this sadness. But every day she showed up, cheerfully relating to Joe the goings on in the world, never once touching his hand.

***

Day after day Joe stared at the TV, watching the details of the lottery and the war in Vietnam. Slowly, fewer and fewer of his friends came to visit as they were drafted and sent to their own private Hell. He saw glimpses of fatigue and loss in the soldier's faces on the news and for the merest flit of a second he was happy to be where he was.

Then he thought about the man he would never know who had to take his place in the war, a despicable war, and he was ashamed. A tidal wave of pain flooded over him, and as he fought it off, and concentrated all of his strength and focus to be rid of it, he wondered if this flood of pain was what the men in the killing fields felt as they were torn apart by bullets and napalm. Anguish and boredom are not good company for a man is his position to keep.

He watched the ants that traipsed past his window. He made mental notes about how they greeted each other as they passed in line, saw they only traveled a path laid down by other ants and would not divert, and that they sent out scouts. He noted how many times they touched antennae in greeting. He would toss a crumb into their vicinity and see how they coordinated their efforts to bring the crumb back to their nest. How bored must a man be to watch ants?

He received short respites from boredom when his family came to visit. At first they brought deli sandwiches for him and magazines. And then they brought beer, which they poured into empty Seven-Up and Coca-Cola containers. And then they brought friends. The glory of friends for an eighteen-year-old. There is no better medicine.

When he had visitors he often played cards. He would try to find games the other person did not know how to play so he could win. Either that, or he would invent games and then change the rules as the game went along so he could win. He was a not a liar, and he certainly did not have an ego that needed to win everything, but he did need the mental stimulation. Cheating was a way to keep himself entertained. He relished when someone caught him cheating and called him on it. He hated it when he knew his opponent knew he was cheating and would let him get away with it.

Letting him misbehave was just a form of pity, and Joe wanted no part of pity. Pity was for the weak and small children.

Now that Joe was able to sit up, Friday nights from eight to nine p.m. meant a party in his room. Laughter escaped from the closed door and the nurses would come and tell them to keep it down.

The family hid single doses of vodka and rum all around his hospital bed; under the pillow or mattress, or rolled in a pair of socks they left on the bed within Joe's reach. Sometimes his friends snuck in a little marijuana, even though he could not smoke it inside the hospital. He stored it up and waited until he was free to do what he wanted. He waited a long time.

Most of the time his roommates were cool with the hour of chaos; they all welcomed the distraction from staring at the ceiling all day. Once in a while, however, some poor soul would be in agony and the noise would be excruciating. On nights like these the party would silence, carefully pack up the food and booze and creep from the room.

They waved little, quiet good-byes and blew Joe and his roommates kisses. With sad smiles the patients would watch the family leave all the while pushing the button to call the nurse to get their comrade in pain some help.

***

As an uninsured person, Joe was forced to sell every possession, down to his twelve- inch black and white TV, to pay for his treatment. When he had nothing left to sell, but a pair of jeans his mother could put on consignment, the government's Medicaid program kicked in and took care of him. He was grateful when the assistance came through, but it was yet another moment when he had to accept more help. Furthermore, he literally had nothing that the hospital did not supply him, or that friends did not bring him. As a young man who let his independence define his manhood, the forced dependence on others shamed him and became another burden to bear.

After the first year in the intensive care burn unit, he was able to roll through the hospital halls in a wheelchair for twenty minutes at a time. Still wrapped in gauze, but with holes cut out for his eyes and mouth, he finally began to feel a bit of freedom. His friends and family continued to visit, bringing him marijuana even though he had over three pounds of it stashed in the plastic bag that was supposed to hold his clothes.

In the twenty minutes of liberty allowed to him every day, he would wheel past the nurse's station with a radio in his lap and tell them he was going to the roof to listen to music. From high above the city he would survey the skyline, remove the pot hidden in the battery compartment of his portable radio, and smoke his hippy cigarettes. From his perch on the top of the hospital he dreamed of flight. He felt the gauze fall away and feathers cover his scarred skin. He felt his bones lighten as they hollowed out, and his vision sharpen as his body readied to take to the skies.

Too soon the effects of the marijuana dissipated and a nurse would come up to the roof to tell him to return to his room. He would lower his head a bit and roll his way to the elevator.

The hospital's surgery residents, working on only a thread of sanity after their lack of sleep, found out what Joe did up on the roof. Far from dissuading Joe from smoking marijuana with his scorched lung tissue, they not only joined him but soon gave him money for the privilege. Soon he had a little nest egg. A miniscule amount of independence returned.

He watched them fall asleep standing up and was horrified to think that a doctor who was so tired that he could not remember his own name would operate on him when he came in for debridement surgery once a week. He could not comprehend the ridiculous hypocrisy of a profession which taught that sleep was a fundamental of good health, but did not allow its practice amongst its' own - the medical students. Joe had already grown to fear anesthesia, but knowing that these zombies of medicine would have him under their control every seven days made the thought unbearable.

When they came to take him to surgery, Joe wanted nothing more than to run away from them. Sitting in his bed he watched them approach and swallowed the bile as it rose in his throat. Even while sedated, he would clamp his jaw shut and suck air in through his teeth in terror as they transferred him onto the gurney and rolled him down the hall to the surgical suite.

When the nurse would lean over to ask if he was OK, he would lie and tell her he was fine. He listened to the rasp of the tape as it was peeled from the sterile surgical packs. He heard the loud clunk of metal-on-metal as the instruments were dropped onto the tray table. He fought to maintain his senses until the last bleary second as they injected the anesthetic into his vein. He could not resist their anesthetic control. Although not a religious man, Joe was certain he was in the seventh layer of Hell, and that he had been there for some time.

Ellen

Ellen saw Joe for the first time after he had been in the burn recovery unit for eight months. Still covered in gauze, she thought of him as hiding inside a cocoon, waiting to become himself again. She was careful to not even move the air as she walked around him for fear of causing him pain. It would take her five minutes just to pull the sheet back so as not hurt him. She did not dare to speak for fear the vibrations of her voice would trigger his overactive nerve bundles into a spasm of pain. She held her breath waiting to hear the slightest sound that she was hurting him. His persistent silence intrigued her. Not even a mumble of recognition floated through the gauze mask to her ears.

Ellen was a medical technologist. She came in to take samples of Joe's infections. With the gentlest touch possible she would dip her culture swabs into his wounds. Now that his bandages were off his face she could not bear to look at him for fear he would wince when she gathered his samples. But Joe stared at Ellen with the intent of a hypnotist the entire time she was in his room. He marveled at her delicate hands. Her quiet nature, and her obvious care to not cause him further suffering touched him.

With his face now fully revealed he said his first words to her.

"Thank you."

Ellen jumped backwards. It took her a few moments to realize that he had not yelped in pain. She looked him full in the face.

"You're welcome?"

Joe grinned. Ellen was mesmerized by the transformation in Joe's face when he smiled. The lines of agony faded and the warmth of joy spread from his chin to his forehead in a soft wave. He lit up from the inside and she basked in his glow.

"See you in three days."

Ellen gathered up her supplies and tripped over herself as she left the room. Joe liked that he made her off balance. Joe knew it meant that she liked him. With his brain occupied by the possibility of love, his pain subsided a degree.

When the three days had gone by, Joe sat himself up in the hospital bed and waited for Ellen to arrive. He watched her walk in balancing her tray loaded with jars and swabs. He let her set down the tray and take her samples. He did not speak to her until she went to leave the room and then he asked her to join him for lunch.

She took a moment to respond. "OK," she finally said. "Where would you like to go?"

"Right here is good for me," Joe chuckled. "I'll have room service bring us two tubs of Jello."

Ellen blushed, realizing how silly it had been to think that he could go anywhere.

"OK, tomorrow noon. I like strawberry," she said as she left, a big grin on her face.

When she returned the next day, she arrived with two sandwiches made of homemade meatloaf. When she opened the sandwiches, Joe thought he was mistaken, but there it was. Real food! Food made in an actual house by hands not covered in plastic.

He wolfed his sandwich down in about three minutes - nirvana! He realized he did not notice his pain, just the sweet satisfaction of a home-cooked meal.

Then he began to question Ellen about herself. By the end of her lunch hour, Joe knew all about her. She had a nice childhood with a little sister, riding bikes with friends and studying so hard she had been awarded a full scholarship to Stanford. However, her parents made her turn in down because they could pay for the college themselves and they told her should leave the scholarship for someone who really needed it. These were hardworking folk with spines of steel. By the end of lunch Ellen still knew nothing about him.

When she pointed this out to him, Joe replied, "Well, I guess you will have to come back tomorrow to find it all out."

Ellen came back the next day, and every day thereafter.

***

One day, Ellen and one of the nurses invited Joe and one of Joe's roommates, Steve, over for dinner.

With help from the orderlies, both Joe and Steve were set into wheelchairs. As they passed the nursing station, the nurse on duty wagged her finger at Joe and Steve.

"Be back in one hour."

"Yeah, we know," Joe muttered.

They were rolled down the hospital hall into the elevator, down the street one block, into an apartment building and into an apartment. Thankfully, the nurse's apartment was on the first floor.

Joe and Steve rolled into the apartment and inhaled the scent of a living room free of rubbing alcohol, bedpans, medical waste, or stinky people. The two men exchanged commiserating looks of glee.

As the cooking smells of heaven came to the two men they inhaled deep and relaxed. Pan-fried steaks, mashed potatoes with Parmesan cheese, garlic bread and a large green salad with Italian dressing. Neither man had seen a fresh vegetable or a complete piece of meat that looked like what it actually was in over a year.

As the ladies set down the large plates filled with glorious food, another tantalizing smell hinted to them from the kitchen. Both men inhaled deeply again, making the ladies laugh.

"That's fresh peach cobbler coming your way after dinner," Ellen said, "with ice-cream."

Joe thought he might cry. The amazing nutrients and warmth of good, well prepared food came to him, and filled him up. For the first time since coming to the hospital he began to not just feel an improvement in his physical condition, but he began to feel Well. He had been in the burn unit for twenty-three months, and was coming up on his twentieth birthday.

Two days later Joe called a friend and requested the first favor since his admission into the hospital; he asked for a bouquet of flowers to give to Ellen and the nurse. Finally! To finally feel alive!

Joe and Steve felt so invigorated by life on the outside that they then followed up that nicety by dragging their gurneys out of their room by pushing against each other and the walls, and having races down the hall in the middle of the night. When the nurse came to chase them down, they tried to hide in the elevator, but the two gurneys would not fit. Instead, they were wheeled back to their rooms, sulking like ten year olds until the nurse left and they burst into uncontrollable laughter.

***

Another year came and went. After three years of claustrophobia, surgeries, setbacks, infections, Joe's doctor came to him.

"Joe, now that you are of age, you need to make the decision about your leg."

Joe looked at Dr. Kudler with apprehension.

"Which decision is that?"

Dr. Kudler paused for a moment. "Your parents haven't talked to you yet about amputating your club foot?"

Joe's thoughts froze. Cold dread seeped into his bones. The rush of betrayal that the doctors and his parents had obviously had this discussion about him and never mentioned it to him in the three years he had been in the hospital floored him as much as the news that his foot needed to be amputated. If Joe could have backed out of the room through the wall he would have. He attempted to compose himself.

"So, my foot needs to be amputated?" Joe tried unsuccessfully to keep his voice from wavering.

Dr. Kudler let out a deep sigh. "I tried to get permission from your father a year and a half ago, but he said that amputation was a decision you needed to make for yourself. We probably would have had you out of here by now if he had given us permission. As you know, that foot has been a tremendous source of setbacks due to infections and ulceration. I think the foot will always be a major problem and a worse handicap than having no foot at all. I really think you would be better off with it amputated."

Joe looked at Dr. Kudler. While he understood that this was a difficult discussion for Dr. Kudler to have with him, and that he tried to be as nice and kind as possible while delivering the bad news, Joe couldn't help but hate him for it.

Joe set his jaw in a grim clench. "Do it."

Dr. Kudler scheduled him for surgery the next day.

Just as abruptly, three weeks later, as Joe lay in his bed in his hospital room, Dr. Kudler came in. He sat down in the chair next to Joe's bed, looked at Joe and burst into sobs.

Joe looked at the doctor in alarm."What's going on?" he asked.

It took Dr. Kudler a few moments to control himself enough to hand Joe a medical journal. Joe turned to the dog-eared page and read, *"New technique to repair clubfoot has proven most effective…"*

"Joe, I am so sorry." the doctor said softly. "I thought the amputation was the right thing to do. I picked this article up at lunch today and… I am so sorry."

Joe looked straight ahead. In the coldest tone possible he said, "Dr. Kudler. It is not your fault, but it is time for you to go." He thrust the medical journal into Dr. Kudler's shaking hands.

Dr. Kudler left the room.

Joe did not speak to anyone for ten days.

***

The second he got medical clearance, Joe went straight to the prosthetics department and was fitted for a new leg. He was kind to the orthopedist who made his prosthetic limb, but Joe angrily made his steps as he learned how to walk in the prosthesis.

The nurse in the physical rehabilitation department did not have to push Joe at all. He gripped the stabilizing parallel bars as if he were going to strangle them to death.

The nurse in the physical rehabilitation department did not have to push Joe at all. Whenever she tried try to give him a rest, he would push past her and keep working. After the first day she gave up and left him to his own methods.

In four days he learned how to walk.

The next day he checked himself out of the hospital without asking for a medical opinion as to whether or not he was ready. The nurses gave him a huge bag of bandage supplies, ointments, bottles of antibiotics and painkillers.

Before he left, Joe made his way to Ellen's lab. They had spent the last year talking about their lives, hopes, and desires. They revealed everything to each other, even the things that shamed them the most. He told her he was a high school dropout, she told him that she had been sent to modeling school because her mother felt she was too awkward.

For the past year, amidst the lovely words about each other and nurturing hand holds, they built a dream of flight from their stifled reality; an adventure. A full-blooded adventure upon the high seas. They would buy a sailboat and travel around the world. Joe's experience with boat repair and sailing would carry them through their adventure. Ellen would take classes in navigation and survival skills. Together they would be an unbeatable team upon the sea.

Amid the laboratory glassware, with her goggles in hand, Joe asked her to marry him.

"Yes," she said.

Despite all his faults, Ellen had fallen in love with Joe. She loved his wild ways and how they were so different from her own scheduled, uptight, manner. Joe seemed to tackle life with vigor and spontaneity. He promised a life of adventure and romance; a life where they could just follow the whim of the winds and their own desires. They would be tied down by nothing, not even the Laws of Man. They would be free to govern themselves and be accountable only to each other and Mother Nature.

Joe left the hospital wearing only a huge grin, the hospital issued gown, a canvas bag around his neck with all the medications he had been prescribed, and a massive roll of gauze that wound around his body and down his right leg. Any money he had made from the extra marijuana, he had given to his family to help them get by. His only other earthly possessions were his portable radio and a pair of crutches.

***

Joe needed to work to rebuild his economic life. He could not have his bride moving into his parent's house with him. He took a job as a marine carpenter at a boatyard during the week, and painted houses on the weekend until he had a good suit of clothes and enough money for first and last month's rent on a decent apartment.

He did all of this wracked by pain, and in the narcotic daze that had become his normal mental state. His trademark wince and then suck air in between his closed teeth maneuver became standard at this time, and was a trait he would keep for the rest of his life. He worked to keep his mind off the pain, but mostly he worked to achieve his dream of flight. The harder he worked, the lighter he felt.

He did all of this on his own. His did all of this with one leg. He did all of this in constant pain. He did all of this fighting infection after infection, and procedure after procedure to repair holes in his skin. The one help he accepted was from his mother to buy him a pair of pants, a shirt, and underwear, but only because they would not let him into JC Penny's wearing only an open backed hospital gown. He had tried and was turned away at the door.

He made sure he visited Ellen every night. Sometimes he would show up on her doorstep with sawdust and paint in his hair because he would rather spend those minutes with her rather than in the shower.

He brought flowers and nautical charts of the Pacific to court her imagination. Soon all they spoke about was the sea and escape from the mundane. Their imaginations rose and took wing, fleeing the known, creating wide-open spaces of adventure and discovery. Escape was such a real possibility in each other's presence. Their tender, downy wings began to sprout flight feathers.

The *Volante*

Joe and Ellen got married, and after a one-week honeymoon in the paradise of Hawaii, they re-entered the grueling reality of work and physical rehabilitation.

Between doctor's appointments and long hours on the job, Joe and Ellen looked for a sailboat. They tried yacht brokers and builders to no avail.

They wanted a sailboat that had good craftsmanship, and a good character. They did not want any of these new boats made of plastic and resin that got blisters on the hull, and whose aluminum masts would bend in half in a stiff breeze.

These boats tended to be sold by people who resembled bad used-car salesman. With greased back hair and plaid pants, these supposed nautical peddlers did not know a stern from a bow. They seemed to think the fact that a boat was only being kept afloat by the dock it was tied to a minor detail in the sale of a vessel.

After three years of search they had still not found *The Boat*. A slow despair descended upon Joe and Ellen. With despair came desperation. A traditional, lackluster future loomed in front of them, filled with short road trips across the state to camp and roast marshmallows, see the national monuments, and visit a few domestic friends. The prospect of adventure and travel that they imagined did not exist without *The Boat*.

Their tender wings of flight molted and left weak feathers of despair in their wake. They could not accept such a normal existence after having created such a vivid vision of escape. Like men trapped in the desert, they plodded along with their search, holding out hope, but their energies faltered. The discussions of adventure became fewer, and the tendency to just go straight to bed after work became greater. Depression knocked on their door, hard.

Then one day, Joe received word that his orthopedist had been diagnosed with cancer and wanted to see him. Although he hated Dr. Kudler for bringing him the news about his leg, he also admired him for having the guts to tell him the truth. He held a true respect for him.

Dr. Kudler had always come to visit him the night before a surgery with a file of papers three inches thick filled with diagrams and descriptions of the procedures and aftercare, how the medications worked and why Joe had to take the medicines he did. Dr. Kudler explained everything to Joe with a clear eye and a sense of humor, which helped set Joe at ease… until the medical zombies came to take him to the operating room.

Most importantly, however, was the simple fact that Dr. Kudler did not betray any signs of sleep deprivation, nor did he seem to do any illegal drugs. When he shook Joe's hand, Dr. Kudler looked him straight in the eye. He was the only doctor Joe trusted. Dr. Kudler made sure he was the doctor that saw Joe for every appointment, because not only was Dr. Kudler concerned about Joe's condition, but he really liked him. The feeling was mutual.

It felt strange to Joe to go to the hospital to visit Dr. Kudler, the patient. Joe entered the white room with the shyness of a child. He peered at the man who had saved his life, now shrunk to half his size, his skin deadly pale and paper thin, the medications killing him as much as the disease. Joe had been palpated and probed every day by this man until he became a functional semblance of himself again. He felt Dr. Kudler had rebuilt him inch by inch. Joe wished he could do the same for the doctor.

Joe sat down and patted Dr. Kudler's hand.

Without any preamble he looked at Joe and told him, "I want to sell you the *Volante*."

Joe looked hard into Dr. Kudler's face. They had spent many a hospital visit discussing sailing while the doctor inspected Joe's wounds and adjusted his medications. Dr. Kudler measured Joe's capabilities as a human being every time he shook his hand hello. He gripped Joe's bear-paw and felt the calluses and muscles hard from manual labor and judged him to be an honest man. Dr. Kudler did not trust people with soft hands, hands soft and squishy from disuse. He thought the lack of strength in the hand matched one's softness in the head, and he would cite some of his colleagues as venerable examples.

He knew from their talks that Joe was a purist and a romantic when it came to classic wooden boats. Joe spoke of wood as most men would speak of a beautiful woman. His voice caressed the grain and texture of gorgeous hardwood as he described a well-finished slice of mahogany. Joe could tell the type and quality of a piece of wood from its smell alone. Joe's dream to circumnavigate the globe in a classic wooden sailboat filled Dr. Kudler's head and transported him beyond the white walls of medicine and into the vivid world outside.

He watched Joe speak of his dream as though he were watching a master craftsman create a work of art. He saw impossibility roll out of Joe's way as he healed, and the red carpet of welcome escape unfurl before him a little more each day. Dr. Kudler relished his role in Joe's recovery. He felt like he had the ability to make Joe's adventure happen by piecing Joe back together. Dr. Kudler watched Joe's wings spread wide and the skies open up, blue and expansive, before him. A feeling of overwhelming tenderness invaded him every time they conversed. He came to love him like a son, and Joe's dream of flight became his own.

Joe had seen the pictures of the *Volante* on the wall in Dr. Kudler's office. Her cabin sides were made of a single piece of teak that had been split so the pattern of the wood grain matched on each side. All forty-two feet of her were planked with fir sanded to a smoothness that let her slip through the water like a well-oiled fish. A chiseled arrow down the length of each side of her white hull, filled in with cobalt blue paint. The varnish on the *Volante's* cabin sides and toe-rails made it look like they were formed of polished gold. Her mast was sixty-five feet from deck to sky, allowing for a massive expanse of sail that scooped up the wind and hurled her forward.

Besides being an impeccable example of craftsmanship, the *Volante* had a place in Bay Area history. She manned the submarine nets under the Golden Gate Bridge in World War Two with a crew of six men. Every man who crewed aboard the *Volante* pumped up his chest when he spoke of the experience. She won all her post-war races and made men champions. It was a Bay Area honor to have sailed aboard the *Volante* and the few who had the privilege felt they were a little above mere sailors.

Joe was taken aback at the doctor's offer. Dr. Kudler urged Joe to take his boat. He was sure the *Volante* would be in good hands with Joe. He needed Joe to take the *Volante*. Joe *had* to take the *Volante*. He tightened his enfeebled grip on Joe's hand. The tone of desperation that came from the doctor tightened the knot in Joe's throat.

"It would be my honor, Dr. Kudler," Joe accepted.

Dr. Kudler sunk back in his bed in relief. "Do you know what it means, Joe?" Dr. Kudler asked. "*Volante?*"

Joe shook his head. "No," he said softly.

"It means," Dr. Kudler said, "to be airborne, or in the act of flight. We both seek to be free, to seek something extraordinary in ourselves. Our own version of immortality."

Dr. Kudler broke into a fit of coughing. When Joe rose to call the nurse, the doctor waved him away.

"Just promise me, Joe, when you cross the Tropic of Cancer, you will think of me."

"Of course." Joe smiled that sad smile people do when they know they losing a beloved friend. "And thank you for making this dream a reality."

Dr. Kudler patted his hand and started to cough so hard he needed a tissue to catch the blood. He waved Joe out of the room.

***

Later that evening Joe walked in the door to his home, triumphant. He picked Ellen up and swung her around. He set her down and jumped up and down with her.

"Joe," she said between smiles and laughter, "what is it?"

"We have her, Ellen! We have her! We have *The Boat*! We are on our way!!!!"

Ellen shrieked with joy. "Yahoo, we are on our way!"

They jumped up and down together and grabbed each other tight. They smiled huge, radiant smiles at each other. Joe gave Ellen a long, long kiss.

Ellen stopped a moment. She spun on her heel and grabbed for a pen and a piece of paper. "We have so much to do!" she exclaimed. "Wood, sandpaper, varnish, groceries…"

Joe looked upon Ellen in pure joy. He felt ecstatic to watch his wife, who had stood by his side from the very beginning, become so fired up about their shared dream. He was beyond elated. He had made his wife happy. He felt that he was finally going to achieve his full potential in this life. In a whirlwind of activity, the preparations began.

Joe began immediate work upon the *Volante*. He spent every free second molding wood, repairing dry rot, painting, sanding, and installing new electrical. He purchased a new fifty horsepower Perkins diesel engine that he painted a bright blue. He made a new set of sails by hand. Bit by bit Joe rebuilt and refurbished every inch of the *Volante*.

Joe taught Ellen how to sand and varnish wood until it took on the luster of well-polished gold. She learned how to grease stuffing boxes, thread rigging, and just about anything else that had to do with boat repair and maintenance. She even painted the bilge with a violent orange colored lead paint.

Joe and Ellen looked at each other covered in the love of their efforts, dust pouring off of them, hands stained with varnish and grease in their hair. There was an intense connection of accomplishment.

Although the *Volante* had an impressive forty-two foot length, she was very narrow and the living quarters were tight, particularly by more modern building standards. One entered the *Volante* through the main hatch just forward of the cockpit with a tiny staircase, known as a companionway, that lead into the living quarters below decks.

The galley was on the immediate left. It consisted of a small, stainless steel split-sink, a camper-stove with a tiny oven, and a little area to chop vegetables. The 'running' water had to be pumped by pushing a little lever up and down with one's foot. There were several short shelves to store canned goods, but no refrigerator. All of these accoutrements were elegantly arranged into a space the size of a telephone booth, and trimmed in teak.

To the immediate right was a small navigation table. There was a settee, an upholstered bench that pulled out and could become a bunk, and a built in one-man bunk on either side. A fold out table, bolted to the cabin sole sat right in the middle of the salon with a large skylight overhead that kept the inside from being too claustrophobic. You could always look up and see the sky.

Just past the salon, on the port side, was the head. The head held a tiny sink and a toilet that had to be pumped by hand to flush, and just enough room for a body to turn around. A tiny hanging locker stood to starboard. Joe and Ellen's double berth was up in the bow where another large hatch sat directly over their bunk.

All these basic necessities were squeezed neatly into eighty square feet of perfectly varnished living space.

***

It took eight years of preparations to make the *Volante* as perfect as Joe wanted. During that time Ellen and Joe welcomed a baby girl whom they named Isabel.

At two weeks old, they took her sailing. At two years old, she fell over the side while the *Volante* was tied to the dock. Joe merely stepped onto the wobbly finger pier and plucked her by her life jacket, laughing, from the frigid water. When Isabel was five years old, they decided to move aboard the *Volante*, because they were certain they would leave any day now.

Every weekend they would announce to their friends, "Good-bye! We will not be here in the morning." And every Monday they would find Ellen and Joe trudging up the dock to work, and sending Isabel off to school.

Isabel grew up covered in the smell of salt and mildew. The warm clutch of the closeness inside the *Volante* bolstered her confidence, and she knew safety. There was no heating aboard the *Volante*, and no hot water, so she grew a hearty constitution and ruddy complexion. And, due to the constant roar of sanders, power saws and testing of the diesel engine, she learned to sleep through anything.

Despite the closeness of quarters, Isabel grew up as an extremely modest child. She would lock herself in the head to get dressed, a formidable task considering that the space was so tight that a grownup could not bend over to pick up a piece of soap if he dropped it. Nonetheless, Isabel crammed herself and her clothes into the head every day to dress in the morning and to get into her pajamas at night.

Her parents tried their best to immerse her in what they had hoped would become her new native culture; travel. Isabel learned about the travels of her parents' dreams. She learned about the Panama

Canal, Hawaii and crossing the Tropic of Cancer before she learned about her native Golden Gate Bridge or even Bodega Bay. In addition to learning a new word of Spanish at dinner every night, she ate spicy foods and listened to Mariachi music so that she would be prepared for her first international port of call. She built dreams of eye-popping color while she slept.

Stagnation

Isabel did not move from her place in front of the TV. Her mother moved between Isabel and the TV.

"Scrambled or hard-boiled?" her mother asked.

Isabel did not reply. She leaned to the right and looked around her slender mother at the tiny TV screen.

Finding it to be the norm that her seven-year-old daughter be lost in TV Land, Ellen returned to the stove and cracked eggs into the frying pan with a resolute sorrow. She could not remember the last time they shared a joke or even each other's attention. Ellen took a second to pull her long, bushy, brown hair into a ponytail with a plain elastic rubber band, and continued to scramble the eggs with her spatula until the phone rang. Ellen picked it up.

"Hello? Yes? Shit! I'll be in right away." She slammed the phone down and pulled on her rain jacket. She grabbed her keys and headed for the main hatch.

"Joe!" she yelled, "I have to go in early! The eggs are on the stove! Bye!" She brushed a quick kiss onto Isabel's forehead.

Joe was in the head on the can.

"Love ya," he yelled after his wife just as she pulled the hatch closed after her.

Knowing her father was likely still reading his morning paper and wouldn't be out anytime soon, Isabel stood and walked towards the frying pan without taking her eyes off of the TV. She grabbed the spatula and poked the eggs a bit. She turned off the stove and sat down in front of the TV again. Ten minutes later Joe came out of the head.

"Hey, kid," he said and walked over to the TV and turned it off. Isabel looked at the screen until the afterglow was gone, sorry to see it go, but she knew better than to argue.

Joe put the eggs on a plate and set them in front of Isabel. She stared at the gooey eggs. She hated eggs. Joe sat down next to her and stared at her pouting at her eggs. He chuckled at her apparent disgust. He hated eggs too.

"Look, kid, this is what you do."

He put the eggs on a slice of bread and smothered them in catsup. Then he rolled the bread up like a burrito. He handed the breadarito to Isabel. Catsup poured out the ends. She took a bite.

Catsup splattered on her shirt and poured out onto her hands.

"That's pretty good, right?"

Isabel nodded. She pushed as much of the breadarito into her mouth as she could, covering her mouth and chin in catsup. She held up her catsup-covered hands as she chewed with her mouth so full of food she had to chew open-mouthed. Joe handed her some paper towels and she wiped her hands and face.

"Hair time," Joe said.

Isabel stood up. She handed her hairbrush to her dad with a trembling hand. She gripped the table as her little head was yanked to-and-fro and the tangles were ripped from her scalp. Tears snuck out of her eyes, but she knew not to make a sound. Her hair was pulled tight into two even ponytails high on her head.

"All done. Blow your nose."

Isabel looked in the mirror as she blew her nose and saw the familiar look of a girl in a permanent state of surprise because her ponytails were pulled so tight. It was difficult for her to blink. She put on her coat and grabbed her backpack. Joe was already outside.

He lifted Isabel off of the *Volante* and onto the wet dock. The stink of Bay mud at low tide assaulted them with the ultimate stench of decay as rain pelted them.

Crabs skittered out of their way as Joe and Isabel walked to the long ladder at the end of the dock that lead up to the pier. The ladder hung well over Isabel's head. The lowest rungs were covered in mud, seaweed and barnacles. A few mussels dangled there as well. The rain ran off the muddy ladder and onto her face.

Joe lifted Isabel up and she grabbed the slimy lower rung. The mud and sludge oozed through her fingers. She swung her legs over her head to the next rung and then righted herself. She climbed the remaining twenty rungs of the ladder like a monkey. She was covered head to toe in mud and sea sludge by the time she reached the top. Only her ponytails remained intact.

Her father, on the other hand, managed to make his way up the ladder getting only his hands dirty. He stopped to wash his hands at a hose bib on the pier then washed Isabel's hands, too. He noticed, but made no mention of, the barnacle-induced gash in the palm of her left hand. Instead, he grabbed that hand and held it tight as they walked to the car.

They walked the length of the pier to the parking lot. The pier was lined on both sides by piles of wood, hauled-out boats with unpatched holes, garbage, fragments of rusted machinery and large chunks of general junkyard chaos.

Along the way, faces and arms came out of spaces unknown to the common eye as homes. Fifty-gallon drums served as doors, and old windshields as windows. Rarely did an actual door serve its intended purpose. People waved hello and good day to the father and daughter as they passed through in the heavy rain. Joe and Isabel waved back. They leaned into the wind and took the rain square in the face in defiance of Mother Nature.

The pier housed the remnants of the vibrant artist community for which Sausalito was known. The gaiety and freedom of thought practiced by the bohemians and hippies in the sixties and seventies drew the yuppies to Sausalito where they hoped to lose some of the uptight ways they were known for by association with actual beatniks and flower children. However, condominiums were soon built and the rents for the small, summer cottages that the artists had leased for decades skyrocketed. The hippies and their artistic compatriots were pushed off the land and onto the deserted shipyard docks.

They set up homes where they could, and paid rent to happy landlords who had not made a cent since World War II had come and gone, leaving their shipyards empty.

The yuppies, however, were not content to create an artistic diaspora from the land to the sea. For now when they looked out their expensive windows they no longer saw just water, but houseboats and barges set up for living. They began to complain and enlist the help of the law to 'clean up' their views.

Had they been yachts of a particular style there would not have been any conflict of interest, but as it was the conflict started. The bohemian hippies who had created Sausalito stood up for themselves, and the tyrants from on high still have to look at their houseboats and barges.

Joe and Isabel heard a muffled yell and stopped near the base of the pier. They both looked around searching for the origin. They stood upon a large sheet of metal that covered a hole in the pier.

Joe called out, "Anyone down there?"

"Yes, Goddammit! Get me out of here, ya bastards!"

Joe pulled the metal sheet back. Rainwater poured into the gaping hole. Joe squinted his eyes against the wind-driven rain and peered downward. There, below the pier, in the darkest, filthiest, creepy-crawliest place in Isabel's world was a short, cranky man, with a face shriveled up like a prune. He spoke so far out of one side of his mouth that Isabel could not see his lips move when she stood right in front of him. He stunk not only of rank mud and ancient salt, but also of stale alcohol, urine and human excrement. Tattered fabric hung in threadbare disintegration on his crooked body. The remnants of his clothing wished to dissolve into nothing just to escape their filthy fate. The pouring of rainwater on him was the closest thing to a shower he had had in his recent adult life.

Joe reached his arm through the sizable hole and grabbed the man by his shoulder. He pulled him out in one quick motion and flung him onto the pier.

"Dammit, you bastard! I got stuck down there last night and only now are ya pullin' me out! A man could die down there in such weather. There is no care in ya, ya selfish bastard!"

With this last remark he leaned in close enough for Isabel to be able to make out all of the tiny red blood vessels in the yellowed whites of his eyes.

"I can put you back in if you prefer, Willy." Joe took a step towards the little man as he spoke.

Willy backed up a pace. "You and your devil child, get along! I have no place for ya here!"

"OK, Willy, have a nice day."

Joe and Isabel turned and resumed walking.

"That's right, keep walkin'. Walk right back to hell where you and the devil child belong!"

Willy deviated from the regular residents of the pier in that he was not an artist, actor, musician or carpenter. He was not even a man who worked with his hands. Willy was just a lost-soul. The residents of the pier looked after him the way kind-hearted people look after a mangy, stray dog. They gave him handouts of food and clothing, and made sure he had a blanket on cold nights. Sure he would bite, no one ever invited him inside.

Joe chuckled as he pulled Isabel along behind him. Isabel knew better than to look back at Crazy Willy. He had once chased her down the pier just for being in his line of sight. Instead, she kept her eyes glued forward into the raindrops that threw themselves into her eyes. She smiled to herself, proud that her father would help such a mean old man and not be scared of him. This was her father's lesson number one; smile in the face of fear. She would learn to do this often in her future.

***

The gunmetal blue, 1969 Cadillac Coupe de Ville, complete with large tail fins and red rocket tail lights awaited them. Joe leaned against the driver's door and breathed in the cold morning air while Isabel struggled to get the huge passenger door opened. She had to brace one leg against the car to leverage the door, but as she got it open a bit the door gained momentum and swept her off her feet. She managed to keep her upper body from hitting the ground by hanging onto the door handle as her legs were swept out from underneath her.

She pulled herself up and threw her backpack into the car. Now she struggled to get the door shut. She could only reach the door handle if she had one leg out of the car, so she got the door moving and pulled her leg in at the last minute. She managed to close only an edge of her jacket in the doorjamb. Relieved that she had not smashed her leg yet again, she left her jacket stuck in the door. Her tennis shoes were soaked and covered in mud. She shivered in the front seat and waited for departure.

Joe leaned against the car with his back to his daughter until he heard her door shut. Then he whipped the driver door open and jumped in so fast it looked to Isabel that the door had opened of its own volition and Joe had magically appeared in the seat next to her.

Joe turned the key in the ignition and the engine purred to life. He stepped on the gas and gave the engine a good revving. Joe took his time, pumping the accelerator up and down, letting the car warm up. He gave Isabel a knowing look and she grabbed the door grip as tight as she could.

Joe stepped on the gas with such force that he sent mud, gravel and water spewing out behind the Blue Bomber. With a squeal from the power steering, the Cadillac lurched and fishtailed its way out of the pothole-infested dirt parking lot at top speed. The windshield wipers did not keep up with the rain, but Joe did not slow down. Isabel was on her way to school, and he did not want her to be late.

Utter, Slogging Reality

Joe dropped Isabel at school. He returned to his boat repair shop at the foot of the pier. It was colder inside the shop than it was outside. Small puddles formed on the floor where holes in the corrugated metal roof let in the rain. He let out a deep breath of frustration. Two boats stood hauled out on the ways waiting for his attention, but he could not work on them in this weather.

He tried to think of a project to do in the shop, but the boat's owners had only requested to have the bottoms of their boats painted. There was no wood working project he could do inside to make money. He cleaned the sawdust out of the table saw, and oiled the blade on the band saw. He sorted the sandpaper by grit, and took inventory of the bottom paint. He swept the floor, and put out coffee cans to catch the water from the leaking roof. He sat by the phone until one o'clock waiting for it to ring.

When no one called, he pulled out a beer, and nursed it as he looked with longing at his Latitude Thirty-Eight magazine. *"We go where the wind blows"* was printed under the title. He opened the pages and skimmed the articles on sailing in

Mexico. The happy daydream of flight came over him.

Meanwhile, Ellen wandered her white maze at the hospital. She clothed herself in white scrubs and covered her shoes with sterile white wraps. She stuffed her hair into a sterile white hat and locked herself into a sterile white room. She worked alone with her arms under a hood to prevent the virus she was working with from infecting her if she spilled it. The only sound was the whir of the centrifuge on the counter.

Although she found her work as a microbiologist stimulating, she was isolated from everyone. No one came in to ask a question or to see how she was doing, even though she was a fairly popular person in her department. She left the room only at lunchtime to walk through cramped white hallways to the white cafeteria.

She looked around the cafeteria to see if she knew anyone. No one. She gathered her lunch and carried her tray to a table. She pulled out her Latitude 38 magazine and read. Her head filled with warm breezes and the sounds of waves splashing on the *Volante*'s hull. After she ate she scurried back to the laboratory and locked herself inside until quitting time.

The Decision

Joe had drunk three beers by the time he called his wife.

"May I speak to Ellen, please?"

"Just a moment."

While Joe waited for his wife to come to the phone he traced the picture of the sailboat on the cover of his Latitude Thirty-Eight with his finger.

"This is Ellen."

"Ellen, it's me," Joe said. "Pick up some groceries on your way home. We're going to Mexico."

There was a long pause on the other end of the line. Ellen, as a logical human being, let her mind race through the many things that would have to be put into order if they were to go to Mexico. She thought of her job, Joe's business, Isabel's schooling, and their house they had rented out two years ago. But they had dreamed and planned for this trip since before they had married. It was to be their adventure of a lifetime. Adrenaline ran through her body thrilled to finally be released.

"I love you, Joe."

"I love you too."

Joe hung up the phone relieved. A burden lifted from his shoulders. They had tried to leave several times before, but delays came from all around. Joe needed more surgeries. Money issues made Ellen decide she needed to stay at her job a while longer to prepare their bank account for departure to the same degree they had prepared the *Volante* which lay sedentary at the dock, heavy and slumbering.

It seemed that every time they had a real chance to leave Joe would get drunk to the point of oblivion and end up sick for a week recovering. He had several other bouts of drunkenness that lasted for more than a week each, which caused doubt in both Ellen and Joe. And then there were the painkillers. He could not function without them. But this was in an era before being addicted to prescription medication was even seen as a problem. In that time it was just deemed a necessity.

***

Their most real attempt at departure had occurred when Isabel was three. They had rented out their house in Sausalito, and Joe had negotiated a deal with his friend Peter to buy his boat repair business. Ellen took Isabel to the laundromat to do their last load of laundry before they left. Isabel had found another little girl to play with and the two girls raced excitedly around the laundromat.

The other girl showed Isabel how to swing from the heavy Formica folding table. It looked like fun. Isabel grabbed onto the table to swing just as a lady set down an extra heavy basket of laundry on the edge of the table. The folding table immediately flipped over and crashed on top of Isabel. Ellen, who had her head in a dryer, heard the crash of the table and the subsequent yell from Isabel. She ran to Isabel and lifted the table off of her. The side heavy metal edge of the table had impaled Isabel's skull and crushed the left temporal bone of her skull and brain. A large chunk of Isabel's skull protruded out of the skin of her forehead.

Ellen picked Isabel up and dashed to the car. She pushed the accelerator to the floorboard and ran every red light as she raced to the hospital. She left the car running as she whipped Isabel off the front seat and ran with her into the emergency room.

Isabel had stopped crying and was able to see where she was. She watched a large woman dressed all in white came out from behind the tall desk to take her from her mother's arms. Isabel took one look at the huge stranger coming at her with arms outstretched and fainted.

After the initial medical assessment, Joe and Ellen were told that their daughter may be mentally challenged and/or epileptic. Isabel's parents decided to have a surgery to repair the lining to her brain and to have the bones in her skull put back in place. Her parents waited with baited breath to make sure she recovered in full.

The doctors told them it would be years before they knew for sure if she would have problems. Isabel had to endure several months of going to school in a construction helmet in case she had a seizure, which of course, made her the laughing stock of all her preschool and kindergarten classes. Ellen quizzed Isabel daily on her learning and retention skills, routinely asking her pop quiz questions over breakfast or dinner. Isabel's answers to these questions dictated how Ellen's day would go.

Isabel answered the same questions every morning for four years. Over and over and over. If there is anything that will pull out your flight feathers, it is excruciating repetition. Even if the repetition does not happen to one directly, it's worse than second hand smoke in its ability to permeate the people around it.

Besides Isabel, Joe had his own tedious daily repetition; clean the leg, bandage the leg, take the meds, feel nauseous, drink away the pain, hobble and work hard through this tedious, repetitious life. There is no cure for frustrated, repetitive, flight-feather loss other than willful abandon. Willful abandon is all Joe had left when he called his wife that day. This time they would cast themselves free.

Joe made a survey of the *Volante*. He took a case of varnish, four gallons of paint, several sheaves of sandpaper, some lumber, tools, paint brushes and rigging wire and brought it all down to the *Volante*. He called his friend Peter and told him the shop was for sale. Peter was happy. He had been after Joe for years to sell him the shop.

By the time Joe went to pick Isabel up from school at three-fifteen he had all his business affairs in order and fifteen thousand dollars in his pocket from Peter.

Ellen arrived at four-thirty with her arms full of grocery bags. She looked at the lumber lashed to the handrails, the dinghy flipped upside down on the cabin top, the life raft strapped next to the main hatch, and the waterproof survival bag next to it. She hurried to put the groceries away.

"Holy Christ," she thought, "we are really doing it this time."

A huge smile came over her face. She made a call to a real estate management company in

Sausalito that she had researched two years prior, and hired them to collect the rent on the house and pay the associated bills while they were away. Then she disconnected the phone and threw it onto the dock. She unplugged the TV and set it on the dock for someone to take. This was the first step; they were off the grid.

Just about the time that the second thoughts showed up, Peter showed up to shoo the family aboard and cast them off. He threw the dock lines onto the *Volante's* decks. He wanted to be sure Joe did not change his mind. Then he tossed Isabel a Composition Book.

"Izzy! You'll need to write don everything you see and tell me all about it!"

Izzy waved goodbye to Peter.

For good measure Pete gave the bow of the *Volante* an immense shove away from the dock before Joe even had a chance to start the engine. Drifting away from the dock, the family was on its way to adventure in Mexico.

Freedom

The *Volante* was in the act of flight as she passed under the Golden Gate Bridge. She soared through the waters in a smooth, deliberate manner. Joe headed her for the open water of the Pacific Ocean. He felt no pain at all. He turned up Jimmy Buffett's "Mexico" and tightened the jib sheet. The *Volante* picked up speed. Every second she escaped closer to Mexico.

Ellen felt safe in the cozy tenderness of the *Volante*. Although she had become an avid sailor since meeting Joe, the grand scale of the open ocean, and the vastness of endless possibilities overwhelmed her at first. She had, of course, been out on the Pacific before, but now that she had left all she knew it seemed bigger and more imposing.

She did not think of turning back, but as the *Volante* passed through the gigantic, black shadow of the Golden Gate Bridge, she realized how small and vulnerable an entity they were. Millions of tons of orange steel hung over her head, held together by an act of balance, engineering and multiple tons of bolts. In comparison they were just a dot, capable of being crushed by the slightest provocation of nature. Although it was just as possible, it had never occurred to her to feel that way on land.

Think about that for a moment. A woman who loves and marries a man who has been burned alive, and has a daughter who crushes her own skull with a table does not stop to think of the infinite possible ways that there are to be hurt, maimed or killed while on the land where these things actually happened to her family. But throw her in a boat on the open ocean and all of a sudden she has this formidable clarity about the veritable plethora of ways her family could be hurt, maimed or injured while aboard a forty-two foot sailboat in the middle of the vast Pacific Ocean. Thankfully she quickly came to her senses and put this avalanche of fears out of her mind, or it would have been a much less interesting voyage.

Isabel, now seven years old, sat apart from her parents up on the *Volante*'s bow. The crisp wind pulled her hair back and allowed her to face the future head on. A real live adventure was afoot and she relished being a part of it. She took in the salt spray as it washed past. The wind was strong enough that when she faced directly into it she could only hear the rush of air past her ears. She looked ever forward, straining to see the future and what it held for her. Even though all she could see for now was an immense expanse of dark green water, her mind searched for that next point of land where the next adventure awaited.

Yesterday the weight of normalcy crushed all of their shoulders so that they moved as though the Earth's gravity was tripled for them. This day they were the birds of freedom flying for warmer skies, fueled by adrenaline and the dream of escape. They were finally in the act of flight. Ellen looked forward and loved her daughter's lack of fear. Ellen, freed from fifteen years of wondering the white hospital maze, had the door to her life blown wide open. She gulped the cold, fresh air as it flooded over her. She took one last look back at the small town she had called home.

Nope, no regrets.

***

For his part, Joe refused to acknowledge the place they were leaving. Any progress he had made there was a result of his sweat and blood. He thought of the pointless manner he had kept his boat repair shop clean enough to satisfy a health inspector, the futility of painting a boat in the rain, and the stymied manner in which no matter how hard he worked he never got ahead in life, at least not how he saw it.

He forgot that he had cheated death and been a successful owner and operator of a boatyard. He forgot that he had designed and built beautiful boats for years. He forgot he worked until exhaustion consumed him, sacrificing bits of his fingers to sanders, and had even been scalped by a band saw. But the gods of success were never satisfied by his offerings and did not allow him to advance in the smooth manner of most workaholics.

No more rat race, no more selfish neighbors who complained to the police about where he parked his car, or people who yelled at him when their boat was not finished on time or to perfection, nor crummy people who only looked out for themselves. He looked forward with a determined glint of glee in his eye, positive he had finally outsmarted fate.

Half Moon Bay

The *Volante* spent her first night in Half Moon Bay. The family lay in the cockpit after a dinner of canned soup and looked up at the stars. They mapped out their destinies in the constellations. They were happy to feel the cold night air and the rolling of the waves under them. They enjoyed the silence. Their freedom was now complete.

Ellen felt safe and serene. She trusted Joe's abilities as a captain and navigator, and she was happy to do whatever he asked of her. He came from a long line of navy men. Although Joe had not been in the navy himself owing to his missing leg, he had been in the Sea Scouts and worked on boats his whole life. From the Scouts he went on to be a commercial fisherman and then a maritime carpenter. There was no situation Ellen could predict that scared her with him as their guide. She knew he was her protector. He was the master of the wind and waves, and the *Volante* moved under his hand as if an extension of his person. The *Volante* stretched to catch the wind and turned in tight circles when he commanded.

Ellen marveled at Joe's skill as she made the Big Dipper out of Orion's Belt. In the midst of their calm constellation reflections Joe bolted upright and flung open the seat locker he sat upon and ripped out the contents. Ropes, fenders and winch handles were flung behind him. Ellen and Isabel sat up in alarm.

"I can hear a rat! It's right under my head!" he shouted.

He peered into the now emptied seat locker and looked around for evidence of a rat. But there were no chew marks, no telltale droppings, no quick dart of movement. He turned and pushed Isabel off of her locker and emptied it as well. She huddled up against the cabin, her arms around her head to protect herself from the onslaught of flying life jackets and coils of rope.

Ellen watched her husband with her mouth open. Just a second ago she was marveling at his skill and calm, and now he moved like a man possessed. Joe, for all the beer he drank, was a slow moving thinker and artist, not a violent madman. She had never seen this anxious, freaked out person in front of her.

Joe's search revealed no rat. He refilled the seat locker with angry motions and sat down. Ever hopeful the fury was over, Ellen went to get a piece of chocolate for everyone for dessert. As she went down the companionway into the boat, Joe dashed past her on the deck up to the forepeak where all of the sails were stored.

He heaved heavy sail bags out of the deep locker and checked them for chew holes. The chocolate forgotten, Ellen and Isabel watched from the cockpit as he hurled insults at the invisible rat and threw the sail bags out of the forepeak onto the decks. With all the sail bags littered around him he sat on the cabin top and shook his head.

He knew he had heard the chewing noise again. He envisioned a shitty, waterlogged, rat nibbling away on his beloved boat, his masterpiece, and he was filled with rage as if the rodent gnawed on the *Volante* with malicious intent, as if this rat was sent by the fates to ruin his plans of flight.

As Joe heaved the sails back into the forepeak he heard it again. Chew, chew, nibble, nibble, snap, snap, pop. Chew, chew, nibble, nibble, snap, snap, pop. He left the sails scattered on the deck and ran down below. He lifted the floorboards and inspected the bilge. The bright orange bilge sparkled. A small amount of water sat in the most aft section of the bilge where the bilge pump was located. There were no rat marks to be seen anywhere. And yet the sound persisted. Chew, chew, nibble, nibble, snap, snap, pop. Joe smashed his fist into the cabin side in frustration. He held his hand in agony.

"Shit, fuck, damn!" he yelled.

He stomped the three steps to the galley and angrily rummaged in the tiny cabinet. He yanked out a fifth of Jack Daniels, knocking the rest of the contents onto the cabin sole. He removed the lid without looking at the bottle, ears peeled for the sound of the rat, and took a swig. Ever so slowly he screwed the lid back on the bottle, straining to hear the rat's sounds. Nothing.

He put the floorboards back in place and went to lay in the cockpit. Isabel and Ellen watched him. They held their breaths to listen for the rat noises hoping to hear the rodent for their sake as much as for Joe's. They heard nothing that sounded like a rat.

Ellen feared for Joe's health.

Maybe, she thought, *his drinking has gone to delirium tremens. Or maybe he took too many of his pain relievers at once and he is hallucinating.*

Either way did not bode well to be stuck in the middle of the ocean with a man not in his right mind.

Joe put his hands over his ears and turned on his side in the cockpit, trying to sleep. When she heard his snores, Ellen put a blanket over him, and she and Isabel went below to their bunks.

Doubt filled Ellen. Their initial peace shattered. She went to her bunk and lay awake, waiting to hear further sounds of madness from the cockpit.

Isabel passed her father's ravings off as just another one of his displays of temper. She was oblivious to the fear that brewed inside her mother. Isabel lay down in the cockpit and listened. All she could hear was the barnacles feeding. Chew, chew, nibble, nibble, snap, snap, pop. Surely her father, the master of all things maritime, knew the sound of a few barnacles. With the blissful ignorance of a seven-year- old, Isabel fell into a peaceful sleep and looked forward to a new day of adventure.

Monterey

In the cold, morning fog, the *Volante's* diesel engine fired up and they were off to Monterey. The *Volante* left a swirly wake of white bubbles as she cut across the glass topped gray of the calm ocean. Ellen poked her head out of the main hatch and was relieved to see her husband reincarnated as the master of the ocean she loved and trusted. Joe threw her a smile and she warmed.

Isabel was already up on the bow, a piece of bread in one hand and a cup of cocoa in the other. Ellen found a mug of cocoa on the stove for herself. She held the warm mug to her chest and inhaled the sweet chocolate and cinnamon scent. She smiled to herself over her daughter's thoughtfulness.

In the four hours under power to Monterey the family didn't speak. It was not an angry silence, but a silence of reflection, taking in the monumental task they had set, to go around the world, starting with Mexico as their first foreign country.

In a wooden sailboat.

Without radar.

Without a Satellite Navigation System or a satellite phone.

Without a Ham Radio or a buddy system of any kind.

Just themselves, some paper charts, a pencil, and a sextant as old as navigation itself.

***

When they pulled into the harbor at Monterey, Isabel was struck by the sameness between Monterey and her old Sausalito. How could one travel for two days and arrive at a different place of such similarity?

The buildings on the waterfront needed repainting, their pale gray coverings hung in strips. They teetered on brown pilings covered in seaweed, barnacles and slime. Saltwater flowed in and out of the harbor past the pilings in a dull green-gray slosh of sea foam. The cloud cover never lifted. A few gray and white seagulls flew overhead and screeched their yelling gull cry.

Isabel pulled on her white fleece jacket and looked around. Decidedly underwhelmed, she pulled out her journal and wrote: *Monterey. Different place, same place.*

Ellen, however, loved Monterey. She had studied at Hopkins Marine Station when she was in graduate school and remembered her time there with fondness. She did not see the gray Monterey in front of them. Instead she saw the first time in her youth when she had been free. Away from her family and Stanford life, she had been able to unfold her wings for the first time. She dove, sailed, and researched the tide pools. She made friends from different walks of life and she felt for the first time that she was a grown-up in control of her life and her destiny.

"Monterey is amazing!" Ellen exclaimed. "There is so much life in the waters here! Let me show you the wonderful tide pools!"

"Ellen, it is freezing," Joe chided."No one wants to hang out at the beach today."

"It's so gray, Mom. I want to stay aboard and read."

"I think we should head for Santa Barbara." Joe said.

Ellen looked at her husband and daughter. How could these two not see what was in front of them? She sighed.

"You are going to like it here," she promised. "Now, get off the boat. I have things to show you."

If there was a way to drag a man and a little girl off a boat and across the water, Ellen would have done it. As it was, she was limited in her abilities, and instead had to resort to making a thermos of hot cocoa, throwing it into the dinghy and plying them with it as they rowed to shore.

Cannery Row awoke before them. Storekeepers threw open their shuttered windows and rolled up their metal doors. A magnificent carousel full of wild horses started its first run of the day and spun Isabel in a flurry of rainbow colored horses. One t-shirt shop stood on a lonesome corner. This was the time before the Aquarium was built and conquering hordes of weekend tourists filled the streets of Monterey like locusts and blocked the naturally beautiful view of the town with their shopping bags filled with snow-globes and stuffed animals.

Freddie the Freeloader was the resident sea otter attraction and he lived in the Monterey Bay. The sea otters swam through the harbor on their backs with large rocks on their chests to break open the shellfish they had found. They smacked the shellfish on their chests with rocks so hard that one could hear little 'bangs' all over the harbor.

Ellen used the binoculars to watch the sea otters wrap themselves in kelp to keep from floating away, and pointed out their behavior to Isabel and handed her the binoculars.

"Oh, Mom, I want to pet one!" Isabel said excitedly.

"You can try, but their teeth are sharp enough to take your hand off at the wrist."

"Oh." She put her eyes back to the binoculars. "They sure look soft and friendly from here."

They walked past the Hopkins Marine Lab. Sad to see it closed, Ellen took ten dollars from her pocket and put it into the donation bin at the doorway. She cast one last wistful glance at the entrance and lead the family back to the dinghy to go home for lunch.

Joe too thought the otters were wonderful; elegant swimmers, that glided through the water without apparent effort. However, any admiration for them dissolved as soon as one tried to use the side of the *Volante* to open a clam.

The sound of a hard clam shell as it made contact with the side of the boat had Joe dashing outside to scare the pest away.

"Get out of here!" he roared.

The otter did not even lift it's eyes to Joe as he yelled. The otter continued pounding away with all his might on the hull. Joe shook with frustration.

"Gaah! First it was rats, now it's sea otters!" he yelled. "Go away, you parasite!"

He chucked his ceramic coffee cup at the otter and missed its head by a centimeter. The mug sunk below the the dark green water and disappeared. Unperturbed, the otter continued to open his clam, banging the clam on the *Volante's* hull.

"God dammit!"

Joe hauled up the anchor with the windlass, and as he pumped the handle up and down he glowered at the sea otters that glided past on their backs without a care in the world. He turned the *Volante* away from Monterey and headed for the open ocean.

San Diego

San Diego; the big stepping off point for sailors going to Mexico and beyond. The point of no return. The point where one would leave behind life as he knew it and take a blind leap off a cliff of faith and hope all his preparations would sustain him in the years to come.

San Diego was the last place to do repairs at a boatyard and buy necessary equipment. It was the last place to get a real, all American dinner of steak and potatoes. It was the last place to go to an American hospital or visit an American dentist, or even drink water safely from a tap. Stories ran rampant in the marine community of Mexico's butcher doctors, bandidos, deaths from contaminated water and the lack of marine supplies.

While Joe and Ellen had chlorine for the water, and knew that antibiotics were considered over the counter drugs in Mexico, they were not without any fear. Out of all the scary things people could bring up, bandidos seemed to be the biggest fear of all.

"They murder people in their sleep."

"They take what they want and will leave you to rot."

"You can't trust the police down there. They're the worst thieves of all."

"They'll steal your dental fillings for the precious metal."

A friend had told Joe a gruesome story of torture to remove gold from a fellow sailor's mouth. Joe, who had all gold fillings and three, front, gold teeth, took a quick trip to the dentist and undertook the precaution of having all of the gold in his mouth replaced with ceramic. With all the fillings and gold teeth he had, it is hard to say if it was really less tortuous to have this done by a dentist or a bandido.

Ellen and Joe knew people who had survived for years in other countries, but the nervousness of the unknown sat upon them. Thieves were the only thing that did not scare them as they figured they had nothing to steal except the *Volante* herself. They hoped that her technical inferiority compared to more modern cruising vessels would make her low on the list for bandits.

The *Volante* did not possess sonar, radar, or even a powerful engine someone could easily steal. Furthermore, the task of turning on her engine required a series of random steps that a skilled mechanic, let alone a random bandido, would ever have been able to decipher. She had no bright and shiny pieces of metal decorating her, nor any fancy equipment.

The *Volante* lay at the docks of San Diego's Silver Gate Yacht Club for weeks, captured in ropes, a wooden Gulliver imprisoned by three puny Lilliputians. She appeared impatient to get out and tackle the open seas as she surged and pulsed with the tides.

Joe fussed over the *Volante* and made many improvements to her halyards and paint. Ellen noted that a stressed look came over Joe's face any time she asked for their departure date. He would answer not with a time, but with a list of the many things left to do to make sure the *Volante* was ready for extended ocean travel. She helped him finish projects with her calm and quiet manner intact, trusting in his expertise and knowledge.

Over time, however, Joe had done and redone many projects over again. As Ellen helped him she realized that this repetition was just a stalling tactic and that they were using their money to fix things that weren't broken. And there is nothing that will get a demure, hardworking Protestant to leap into action as the waste of time and money.

When Ellen asked Joe again for a departure date and got the usual answer, she looked Joe straight in the eye and told him, "Cut the crap. We are leaving at the end of the week."

Joe set down his wrench and left the *Volante* without a word. He headed to the Boll Weevil, the closest bar and hamburger joint.

For her part, Ellen went about her evening as normal; cooking dinner for Isabel and playing Go Fish. After Isabel went to bed, Ellen waited up for Joe in the cockpit.

He finally staggered aboard at midnight, looked at Ellen and said, "OK."

Then he went below and passed out.

Ensenada

The family left the security of the known the next day and headed for Ensenada. The romance of an overnight sail overcame Joe and Ellen's feelings of doubt and frustration. They held hands under the stars as the *Volante* pushed through the ocean's top. The sparkle of the moon on the ocean's black waters and the warm, southern breezes set them to dreaming aloud.

"I can't wait to see all the flowers. And the art," said Ellen.

"And the beaches with the clear, blue water! I can go swimming!" said Isabel.

"And eat the amazing food. Fresh tortillas, mmmm," said Joe with closed eyes. Then he sat up suddenly. "And the beer!"

Ellen shot him a disapproving look. He shot her a big, toothy grin.

"We should see some good fishing," he said hopefully.

Isabel listened to her parents and her imagination watered in anticipation. She imagined crystalline turquoise waters over white beaches filled with the finest sands, beautiful women with long, dark hair wrapped in jewel-toned ribbons wearing colorful, long, flowing skirts with white blouses covered in floral embroidery. Handsome men in tight navy blue suits with silver buttons and shining black boots lead dancing horses through her head. Pastries filled with vibrant yellow pineapple and orange mango, and cookies filled with spicy ginger sat in piles in brick bakeries waiting for her to eat them.

She looked over the cockpit's coaming and strained to see the lights of the dreamed of land.

***

A wall of boulders fifteen feet high and ten feet thick protected Ensenada's harbor. There was a break in the wall eighty feet wide that allowed the *Volante* to pass into the calm waters of the harbor and take refuge from the immensity of the ocean. They arrived an hour before daybreak, set anchor and slept.

They awoke at eight o'clock excited to see the foreign land it had taken them so many years to get to. Joe opened the main hatch slowly from below. He grinned at Ellen and Isabel then motioned for Ellen to go first with a gallant wave of his arm towards the companionway stairs. Giddy with delight she tore up the stairs. She surveyed the scene around her and let out a gasp. Joe and Isabel smiled at each other, sure Ellen had just seen a view of undeniable beauty.

Isabel climbed out next to her, prepared to take it all in for herself.

What she saw was the dirt brown of the harbor's water. At least an inch of diesel fuel floated on the water's surface and spread as far as she could see. Pale rainbow patterns floated meekly on top of the dense brownness.

Looking at the shore they saw a waterfront of decrepit industry. Rusting steel buildings and gray, crumbling concrete lined with dirty streets met their gaze. Joe pushed past his wife and daughter and their disappointment. He took a quick look and sucked in some air between his teeth. That was the most voice he gave to his negative thoughts.

Ellen watched in horror as a man who unloaded fish from his boat at the neighboring pier threw a lit cigarette into the water. She grasped the handrail in anticipation of the burning impact she knew would rush towards them. Isabel could see the thought that the harbor would burst into flames and burn them all to cinders shine in her mother's eyes. The impending inferno soup was a far cry from the crystalline blue waters they had imagined.

Joe prepared the dinghy to go to shore, determined he would find the Mexico they imagined. It was here somewhere. With trepidation Ellen and Isabel sat down in the dinghy. He rowed them to the beach full of good humor and without any apparent worry that the harbor would explode at any minute.

They went to the Captain of the Port and then to Immigration to check in, as every vessel traveling internationally is supposed to do in every port that they enter. It was funny to the family that the two offices were clear across town from each other. They had to return to the Captain of the Port for a signature after going to Immigration because only at the Immigration office could they verify the validity of the tourist visas.

Isabel cringed to think that this daylong process would be something they would have to do in every port. She smiled when spoken to, but otherwise she sat and fidgeted in her chair while she waited for her papers to be reviewed and signed. She could not understand a word of what the smiling man in the uniform behind the desk said to her.

As they crossed town on foot for the second time she complained to her father, who shrugged and pointed out that they did get to see the entire town as they crossed it twice that afternoon.

"Kid, you are going to have to learn to see the silver linings to get through this life with your sanity intact."

"Yes, Dad." She sighed.

There was never a childhood complaint that was good enough for a man who had been burned alive and clawed his way back.

They celebrated their first official check in by buying authentic Mexican foods. At the local bakery the delicious aromas of fresh baked goods grabbed them by the nostrils and dragged them inside. Ellen picked up a large tin tray and a pair of tongs from the stack at the front of the bakery. She walked past piles of muffins, cookies, rolls, and pastries. Joe and Isabel pointed at each yummy treat they wanted and Ellen put them on the tray, along with two ginger pigs for herself. In total they took home three muffins stuffed with pineapple, two ginger pigs, two plain rolls, two pink and white coconut rolls and two chocolate covered bread rolls.

At the grocery store they also bought a package of chicharrones, chili covered peanuts, lime and chili chips, and two cans of Herdez red salsa and a bag of tostadas. They licked the drool from their mouths as they waited in impatient anticipation of the buffet to come.

Joe also picked up three cases of his favorite beers. He stacked the heavy boxes on his shoulder and did not seem to mind walking with it for the two miles it took to get from the cervezaría back to the harbor. He already had decided to store the beer in the bilge to keep it cold and two cases should be enough to get him to Cabo San Lucas, with one back up, just in case.

The first sight of the Mexico Isabel had imagined came to them several blocks up from the harbor. The buildings were painted in every possible color of the rainbow. The square adobe and concrete buildings came in shades of magenta and green, yellows and oranges. In the outdoor market there hung bright vegetables, fowl, meat, kitchen utensils, tools, clothing, and souvenirs.

Isabel lead the way through the market with shouts of joy, pointing at every new item she saw, making sure her parents took in everything she did. One stall was filled with plastic products of every kind–buckets, bottle-brushes, storage bins, brooms, and dishes in every jewel tone color invented. One corner glowed from the neon oranges, yellows and greens of broomstick handles. The store appeared to be a festival of rainbows. Isabel had to look hard to realize that there weren't any toys for sale in the shop. There was just shelf after shelf of magnificent neon hues in plastic.

Isabel's head swirled with tie dyed images of all the magnificent colors she had seen. Never before had the world been revealed in Technicolor to her. She saw the green, yellow and blue in her father's eyes, the intense coffee brown of her mother's hair, the red in her own sun kissed cheeks and nose. Her brain opened to fantasy and fairy tale. Reality as she had known it in her previous gray, concrete, and electronic existence ceased to be. Light flooded in and covered the dull pigments with magic. Stories full of make believe flew into her head. She had entered the age of fantasy. She could not wait to return to the *Volante* and write in her journal about the day's adventures.

Hours later, with their arms full of Mexican snacks to add to their provisions, they headed back to the *Volante*. Dark clouds blotted out the lowering sun as they rowed home. A strong wind had picked up, and angered the waters around the *Volante* into spitting piles of white-capped foam, that slapped at her hull in irritation. The dinghy bobbed in a precarious manner as Joe landed her in the frothy chop. They climbed aboard the *Volante* and went below to enjoy their goodies, happy to be home.

Ellen laid out the baked goods on a plate and cut each one into threes.

But before they could eat anything, the anchor dragged. Joe went above deck and tried to reset it multiple times without success. He tried dropping the forty-five pound anchor with a hundred feet of chain attached to it, and backing the *Volante's* engine to get the anchor to grab into the mud below. But every time, the anchor could not find a grip and had to be hauled up covered in slimy mud that felt more like Vaseline than wet dirt. Joe tried to set the anchor until the engine started to overheat.

Joe looked around him and decided to pick up one of the official moorings for rent in the harbor. With the *Volante* now secured, Joe and Ellen went below. Ellen fixed dinner, while Joe got into his loungewear, which is to say that he sat on a settee in his underpants, and plugged in his earphones to his portable tape deck so that he could listen to the soothing tunes of Chuck Mangione ricochet through his ears. He sat in happy repose with his eyes closed and a half eaten chocolate covered bread roll in one hand.

Isabel ate a bright yellow, pineapple stuffed muffin and looked out of a porthole, hoping to see a postcard sunset. She scanned the sky for a hint of red or orange flame, but saw none. Instead, forbidding dark gray and charcoal hues threatened from the heavens. Massive white thunderheads pulsing with electricity and mares' tail clouds stretched long by hurricane force winds high up the atmosphere lay in wait above her head.

Isabel ignored them. She looked around the anchorage and saw a man on a boat about thirty feet away who waved at her. She waved back. Joe saw Isabel wave and pulled off his earphones.

"There's a guy in the boat right next to us waving at us." she said in response to her father's curious look.

"Right next to us?"

Joe got up and took a casual glance out the porthole. Then he pushed Isabel out of the way and ran up the companionway to the cockpit. He grabbed Ellen by the shoulder on the way. Ellen's muffin fell to the floor and the dinner was left to burn on the stove. In a matter of seconds, the engine roared to life.

The man on the other boat had not been waving in greeting, but in warning. The mooring had not held, and the *Volante* was headed straight for the boulder breakwater, pushed by the strengthening winds.

The second Joe turned on the engine the heavens opened up and dumped rain on Ellen and Joe. As Joe hurried up the deck to untie the *Volante* from the mooring, golf ball sized hail pelted them without mercy, stoning Joe and Ellen in their underwear. The wind howled, turning the rain into vicious, stabbing needles.

Joe cranked on the windlass trying to raise the mooring buoy so that he could untie the *Volante* from it. He looked around briefly and realized that the *Volante* was not the only vessel in distress. Of the hundred boats in the harbor, only the ones tied to the dock appeared to be safe from crashing into each other or the breakwater.

"Shit! This place is turning into nautical bumper cars," he said.

Ellen, who was at the helm, yelled below for Isabel to bring them their foul weather gear. Isabel ran and grabbed the waterproof jackets and pants from the hanging locker. It was then that she realized the danger they were in. The breakwater loomed only twenty feet from the porthole. The rocks growled and became more jagged as they sharpened their teeth in preparation for their wooden meal. The angry water gnashed against the rocks.

Isabel grabbed the rain gear and threw it up the companionway to her mother. Ellen did not bother to wear the jacket. She held it up to her face to protect herself from the stinging rain that blinded her. Waves crashed over the breakwater, and a heavy spray landed on top of the *Volante*. Joe tried throwing the anchor over the side to slow down their advancement on the rocks, but it was no use. The anchor had nothing to catch onto.

Joe used the windlass to pull the anchor back up, but the chain kept slipping in the track and let more chain out putting the *Volante* closer to the breakwater. Joe threw the handle to the windlass over the side in a fit of anger and grabbed the chain, hefting it in hand over hand.

"Throw her in full reverse, Ellen!" he yelled over the wind and waves crashing over the sea wall.

"What?" she yelled back. She could not hear a word.

Joe threw his arms towards the stern as hard as he could, motioning as best he could to turn up the engine and go backwards.

Ellen threw the engine into reverse, and it died.

"Dammit, dammit, dammit," she yelled.

She fumbled with the key, her fingers slippery from all the water falling from the sly. The rain in her eyes blinded her. The rocks, with their gaping jaws drooled white, foamy spit.

Joe was so angry, that he did not stop to untie the *Volante* from the mooring when he got to the buoy. He kept pulling on the mooring line until he pulled up the 'mooring' itself, which turned out to be a Ford engine block. It landed with a crash onto the deck. Joe stared at it in paralyzed frustration.

"A god-damned fifty-pound engine block was supposed to hold the fifteen-ton *Volante* in place in the middle of a fucking hurricane?!" he growled to himself.

Furious, he cut the rope and threw the engine block and buoy back over the side.

Meanwhile, Ellen had finally coaxed the *Volante's* engine to life. A huge lump caught in her throat - relief. With shaky hands Ellen pulled the gear shift knob to put the *Volante* into reverse again. This time the engine maintained its mighty roar.

Slowly, she negotiated away from the breakwater backwards. Joe ran to the cockpit and grabbed the tiller from Ellen as the other vessels in the harbor descended upon them, pushed by the wrath of the storm. Boats slid all over the marina; the chaos of a hundred drunk drivers. Joe ran the engine at full-throttle and spun the *Volante* around narrowly missing a small fishing boat. This is no small feat for a vessel with a turning radius of no less than a hundred feet.

Joe headed the *Volante* out towards the open sea. Behind them the family could hear the crushing and crashing sounds of vessels out of control colliding with each other. Ahead of them fourteen-foot waves blocked the marina's exit. Joe turned up the *Volante's* engine and ordered all hatches locked. Below decks, Isabel secured them as fast as she could.

Joe headed the *Volante* straight into an angry wave filled with thousands of miles of momentum. Although terrified, Ellen saw the glare of anger in Joe's eyes. She knew there was no dissuading him from his plan. Like a caged animal crazed with confinement will throw himself against the bars of his cage, Joe needed to flee the claustrophobia and fury of the Ensenada harbor. He did not care the cost of escape.

Of course that was just what Ellen thought. In reality, Joe knew the harbor was the least safe place for them to be. As he saw it, they were far more likely to be smashed to smithereens by a tuna seiner not attached to a mooring in the harbor than they were to be obliterated on the open ocean. But such moments of decisiveness and determination are not always the best time to explain oneself, so it's really no wonder Ellen thought they were all about to die.

Ellen hunkered down as low as she could in the cockpit and held onto a winch for dear life. She knew she was going to die in her underwear. Her mother would have been so disappointed. Isabel sat on a settee below decks and talked to the *Volante* as if she was a person and the waves were her enemy.

"You can do it," Isabel encouraged and patted the *Volante*'s cabin side."Don't let them get the best of you."

The *Volante* climbed up, up, up the front side of the wave. An amazing roar emanated from the engine as Joe revved it up as far as it would go. Just as she was about to stop her forward motion she came over the top of the wave and slid down its backside into the open waters of the Pacific. The wave crashed into the harbor.

They had made it past the wave's break point.

As they looked back at the Ensenada sea wall, all they could see were gigantic walls of white salt water beating the boulders of the breakwater, exploding with terrifying force upon impact. The town appeared to be wiped out and replaced by a mountain of infuriated sea foam.

Onward the *Volante* crashed through the tempest.

Coming Upon the Tres Marias

After leaving Ensenada, the *Volante* made a four-day crossing to get to Bahía San Carlos. After twenty-four hours the winds died down and the hot sun that Mexico is known for came out.

The first three days at sea Joe would not sleep. He stood with his hand on the tiller and left it only to go to pee over the side. Ellen offered time and again to relieve her husband from his insomniac duties, but he put her off.

She could tell he did not trust her, even in broad daylight, even on a course he had charted himself, to steer the *Volante* and be responsible for their safety. She tried to persuade him of her skill by noting aloud the course he followed, the wind speeds and the fathoms of water under the *Volante*. She cajoled and petted, threatened and fumed, to no avail. She fell silent from lack of trust on the second day. Joe was silent from lack of sleep and the heat beating down on him.

Isabel, however, wrote vivid stories about sea creatures in embroidered dresses in her journal. She did not know of her parent's silent feud.

On the morning of the third day they came upon the Tres Marias Islands. As their name indicated there were three islands in a row. The first and second ones were thought to be deserted, but the third was a penal colony.

Ellen and Isabel sat on the deck and watched the islands go by. The islands were just close enough together that one could make out an island on the horizon, just as the last one disappeared from view. Joe decided not to stop at any of the islands fearing a chance meeting with some foreign criminal in the middle of the ocean, hundreds of miles from civilization where the VHF radio was out of range to call for help if they needed it.

Joe, in his exhausted state, stood like a statue next to the tiller and refused to give up his post. Ellen tried again to convince him to at least lie down in the cockpit for a rest. When he refused she stood stubbornly at the stern looking at the trail the *Volante* left in the water, angry that her husband would not allow her to help. She muttered half words of hate under her breath. She looked out on the horizon, and wished to be far enough from her husband that she could disappear over the line of sight. She searched all around looking for a way out.

And then she saw something, a blur of orange color in the distance. Ellen grabbed the binoculars. Through the lenses the orange dot became a boat full of men waving long weapons over their heads. It sped towards the *Volante* growing bigger by the second.

"Oh, my God, Joe!" Ellen yelled. "Bandidos!"

Joe, who had dozed off standing up, jerked to life. With his seafaring eyesight he did not need the binoculars to know that a speedboat filled with eight armed men raced towards them. He turned up the *Volante's* engine and grabbed Ellen and Isabel and literally threw them down below. He locked the hatch after them.

"Joe! Joe!" Ellen pleaded. "Let me out so I can help!"

She shouted at Joe as she tried to muscle the hatch open. When she could not open it she shook it with all her might. Ellen ran to the skylight and tried to push it open, but Joe stood on the latches. Ellen and Joe rushed to the next hatch, she to get out, and he to lock her inside where he thought she would be safest.

She ran back to the galley and looked out the porthole. She could see the speedboat gaining on them. Ellen dove her hand into a drawer in the galley and pulled out her long, carving, knife. She pulled Isabel close to her and they hunkered down close to the cabin sole, waiting for the approach of the escaped prisoners. Ellen waited with impatience for the inevitable.

The speedboat pulled right up next to the *Volante*. Ellen and Isabel flattened themselves onto the cabin sole so the men could not see them when they looked in the *Volante's* tiny portholes. Ellen and Isabel hung in the infinite moment of uncertainty as she listened to the words being exchanged between Joe and the men.

"¿Tienes cerveza?"

"¿Cerveza?" Joe said.

"Sí. Si no tienes cerveza, ¿tienes ron o tequila? Podemos darte langostas."

Langosta, Ellen thought. *I know that word. Damn, why can't I remember what that word means?*

After this brief discussion with Joe, the hatch unlocked and opened. Joe saw Ellen poised with her knife in hand. He motioned for her to put it down while he turned and smiled at their new friends behind him. He flashed Ellen a toothy grin and laughed.

"They're fishermen," Joe explained. "It turns out the second island is a fishing colony. They want to trade us lobsters for beer," he said, waving a live lobster at her.

Langosta is lobster, Ellen thought. *I will never forget that word again.*

The fishermen were lucky this day, because Joe was a great aficionado of beer. He had been taken by the cheap prices of his favorite Mexican brands in Ensenada and had stocked up. He had a case each of Tecate, Pacifico, and Dos Equis, which he kept cooling nicely in the bilge. Only a six-pack was missing from each case.

The fishermen were so excited to hear not only was there was beer aboard, but that there were vast quantities available, they upped the offer from lobsters to guns. With a nervous smile Joe gently pushed the gun back at the fisherman.

Another fisherman raised his arms towards Joe with a lobster in each hand. Ellen looked at the lobsters with longing and Joe saw the look on his wife's face. He knew how much Ellen loved lobster. Furthermore, he knew she had never been fond of how much beer he drank. It would set him in good stead to make this trade for his wife.

He turned from his wife to the fishermen and made a deal. He traded all of his beer for twelve lobsters. The trade was a true act of love on Joe's part. He had a violent allergy to shellfish, a fact he discovered at their wedding reception when he bit into a crab canapé and developed such a bad case of hives that he stopped breathing. He spent their wedding night in an intensive care unit on a respirator. And then checked himself out the next day as soon as he was coherent enough to find his pants.

Let's not forget his love for beer. He did not rise in the morning nor let the sun set at night without a beer. For Joe to give up all of his beer for an evening of bliss for his wife was a huge romantic gesture. Ellen saw it as such and filled with joy and love. It was with no small amount of relief that she watched the cases of beer leave the *Volante* to be enjoyed by men other than her husband.

Joe was interested in the fishermen's boat. He had seen many of the long, narrow, fiberglass boats in the harbor in Ensenada. They were twenty feet long and six feet wide at the widest point. They had no cabin, just four benches that ran the width of the boat. The fishermen explained that the boat was called a ponga, and these boats were the fishing boats and maritime transportation of Mexico. They were good for short-range fishing as they were fast and could hold a lot of tonnage in relation to their size. They were useful as water taxis because one ponga could hold twelve people.

Because the boats were made with fiberglass they were easy to repair and required minimal maintenance. Joe marveled at the hundred horsepower outboard motor the men had attached to the stern of their ponga. It was no wonder they had been able to catch up with them so quickly.

The men opened their beers as soon as they got them. They thrust one into Joe's hand, raised their bottles and said, "¡Salud!" as a toast.

After a few more exchanges of camaraderie they turned their ponga back to their isolated island, and the *Volante* continued on her way. As Ellen cooked the lobsters, Joe ran the boat downwind so the shellfish fumes wouldn't harm him. The thought of impending death made him more alert for several hours, and he was coherent enough to explain some navigation basics to Isabel in the meantime, such as the use of a sextant.

Isabel refused to eat anything that had to be boiled alive. She became nauseous at the sight of the lobsters trying to push the lid off of the boiling pot of water to free themselves. When Ellen took a break from the cooking and went to the head, Isabel grabbed the last two living lobsters and threw them over the side. She prayed they swam home and warned their friends to stay out of lobster traps.

Ellen was relieved her daughter had a compassionate heart and did not chastise her for stealing her lobsters. Ellen spent the afternoon and evening indulging in an all she could eat lobster buffet. She slept that night without a thought as to her husband's lack of confidence in her sailing abilities.

She was too full and contented to care.

San Carlos and Bahía Magdalena

After four more days at sea, the *Volante* came to Bahía Magdalena. A wide shipping channel divided the bay. On one side of the channel lay the town of San Carlos. To the other side was a vast expanse of sand dunes. The channel was well marked with green and red buoys.

Confident that he knew what he was doing, Joe entered the channel at the *Volante's* top speed, which was only about eight knots or a little over nine miles per hour. However, with fifteen tons of mass, even at eight knots a boat could do a lot of damage to herself if she were to run into something. And, as luck would have it, a sandbar, whose presence only registered on the depth gauge after the *Volante* had run aground, halted their progress with a dull scraping sound.

Joe set the engine into reverse and tried to back the *Volante* off the sand bar, but without success. He decided to wait for the tide to come in and hope they would float off.

As they waited, two boats of fellow cruisers passed by the *Volante* without so much as a wave in their direction. The powerboat seemed to laugh at them as it careened down the channel, throwing flumes of spray and jarring the *Volante* with its wake, but not enough of a jar to shake her loose from the sandbar. The second boat, a sailboat, eased by under sail, and went past them in silent grace like a butterfly upon the wind

Joe and Ellen sat in the cockpit and stewed. They were shocked that the two boats went past without any offer of help. To not offer assistance was rare among sailors. A person had to either know you personally and not like you, or feel he would be endangering himself to not stop and help. Joe and Ellen did not feel either of these conditions applied and spent the next four hours fuming while waiting for the tide to rise.

When the tide finally lifted the *Volante* from the sandbar, Joe proceeded with extreme caution, as it was apparent that channels in Mexico were not marked like they were back in the States. Joe set anchor in a quiet cove off to the side of the channel, about a mile away from the other cruisers.

Huge sand dunes rose from the beach in smooth, gentle slopes of fine-grained sugar. They swirled and changed shapes in the wind so that the landscape the family saw as it awoke was not the same one it had seen the night before. The sand of the dunes was finer than baker's sugar, softly tinted beige. It caressed their skins in the gentle breeze and cushioned their falls as they took running leaps off of the edges of the sand dunes and fell fifteen feet at a time without a care, the sand sucking them in on impact.

Ellen, normally the grounded assessor of all things that might be dangerous, played with an abandon never before seen. Her big brown hair flew around her head as she ran full tilt and soared through the air, landing in sand up to her knees. It was the first time she let go of the Earth with happy abandon and took flight, the unbearable weight of concern gone from her body. Joe stood at the foot of the sand dunes and photographed her. He had never seen his wife uncaged before. He watched her, awestruck by her transformation. He had never been so in love.

The next morning, the boats that had passed the *Volante* when she was stuck on the sand bar entered the same cove where the *Volante* bobbed at anchor. Joe and Ellen watched them with contempt as they set anchor, still angry from the previous day. One was named the *Matilda* and the other named the *Georgina*, both after their captain's wives.

The *Matilda* looked like a much larger version of the *Volante*, she being seventy-five feet long to the *Volante's* forty-two. The *Matilda* was a varnish palace comparable only to the *Volante*. The *Matilda* glowed at sunset with that beautiful golden orange that only well varnished hardwoods exude. Joe rowed over out of curiosity to see how a man who was such a good seaman as judged by the beauty of his vessel's bright work could have been so rude as to not stop and help a fellow sailor in need.

The skipper of the *Matilda*, a balding man in his late sixties, greeted Joe with a cordial smile and invited him aboard. Joe took a tour of the big, beautiful sailboat and realized that the man was alone. He was single handedly maneuvering the large vessel down to the Sea of Cortez. His wife had died two years earlier. They had planned to travel the world's oceans in the *Matilda* when they retired. He explained to Joe that he felt much closer to his wife at sea, and therefore decided to stay off land as much as possible. He felt that by doing their dream trip even though she was gone he stayed close to her. He did not want to defile her memory by bringing another partner aboard the *Matilda* to help him complete their trip.

The man turned and said, "Isn't that right my love?" as if his wife was standing right next to him.

Joe felt uneasy being in the same space as a man who spoke to the ghost of his dead wife. Ha backed away and thanked him for the tour.

Joe returned to the *Volante* ashamed that he had been upset that a delusional man in his sixties who single-handedly skippered a seventy-five foot boat under sail hadn't stopped to help him. As any good man of the sea knows, when helping another, be sure not to harm one's self. The *Matilda* could have run aground trying to help the *Volante* and they both would have been in trouble. Although the *Matilda's* skipper was a man who lived in his memory, he was a true man of the sea, a man to admire.

The *Georgina* was much less interesting to Joe and Ellen since she was a motorboat. Joe and Ellen, and therefore Isabel, had become sailing snobs. They did not see the sport in sitting in a boat while a motor whisked one from destination to destination without having to calculate the wind pushing on the sails, without having to adjust lines here and there to keep the boat on course, or needing to think to keep the boat going.

They looked at the *Georgina* with her large radar dish and scoffed again, this time at the occupant's apparent inability to navigate, as a real sailor should, with a sextant and compass, the guide of the stars, and paper charts. They did not feel that people who traveled in motorboats were worthy of the term 'yachtie'.

However, all prejudices aside, Ellen was delighted to get a call from the *Georgina* inviting the family over for tea. Tea aboard the *Georgina* sounded like a highly civilized affair, as the *Georgina* was an eighty-five foot Grand Banks powerboat. Isabel never told her parents, but she thought that if she ever had to have a powerboat, a Grand Banks would be the way to go. Grand Banks were elegant. From the teak accented sun porch outside, to the bar inside made out of solid mahogany, to the fancy navigation system on the bridge with all of the flashing lights, the *Georgina* was a fully loaded luxury cruiser. They even had powered water and a hot water heater for showering.

Running water aboard the *Volante* was neither powered, nor was it hot. If the family wanted to shower, they filled a black plastic bag with water and set it out in the cockpit to warm up. They wrapped the boat cover around the cockpit and took a three-minute shower in a trickle of water that barely got their hair wet. The ordeal was a far cry from the sliding glass doors and sparkling fixtures aboard the *Georgina* that shot geysers of hot water from every angle. She even had a small bathtub.

Joe and Ellen were sufficiently impressed with the facilities that the hosts asked if they wanted to take a hot shower. To a non-sailing person, it might seem odd to offer one's shower to someone they had just met, but the lack of amenities aboard many sailing vessels was common knowledge in the yachting world, and it was considered rude not to offer a fellow cruiser a shower if one had a shower to offer.

Joe and Ellen accepted and rowed back to the *Volante* to get their soap and towels. Isabel was horrified. She had always been a modest child. From the time she could remember, Isabel refused to let her parents dress or bathe her because she did not want to be seen in the nude. On long crossings she would refuse to bathe because she was sure she could be seen on radar. She was horrified by the idea of taking a shower aboard a boat that belonged to strangers and sat in silent mutiny in the dinghy.

Isabel's parents finally talked her into taking a shower by showing her that the door to the head locked. Isabel undressed as fast as she could and took a frenzied shower that lasted a minute and a half. She didn't even bother to use soap.

In her hurry, she knocked a bottle of shampoo off a shower shelf. Isabel grabbed onto a handle in the shower to steady herself as she bent down to pick it up. The handle turned in her hand and the side of the shower gave way. Isabel, soaking wet and naked, fell onto the carpeted floor of the salon where her parents were having tea treats with their hosts. Horrified, Isabel scrambled to her feet and jumped back into the shower, slamming the hidden door closed after her.

They might not have seen anything embarrassing about her seven-year old body falling naked into their living room, but Isabel was mortified. She dressed without drying herself. She went out the real door to the head and went straight to the dinghy where she sat with her head down until her parents came to look for her.

"Come on, Izzy, come back aboard. It's no big deal. Everyone's seen a body before."

Isabel shook her head, never looking up.

"Isabel, you are being rude. Get up here now," commanded Ellen.

Isabel clamped her criss-crossed arms tighter across her chest.

"Fine, Izzy. You can sit there all night," Joe said. "I am not arguing with a seven-year old." He turned and marched back into the cabin.

Ellen's face tightened. She didn't want to make a scene where others could hear her. She marched back inside, too.

"Argh, kids," she offered by way of apology as she sat down on their beautiful, upholstered settee and took up her iced tea.

As her parents rowed the dinghy back to the *Volante* several hours later, Isabel still hung her head.

"Isabel, that was so embarrassing!" chided her mother. "I cannot believe you behaved like that in front of our new friends. That behavior is reprehensible! You are going straight to bed when we get home."

Isabel glared even harder into the bottom of the dinghy.

The funny thing about being sent to bed on the *Volante* was that Isabel's bunk lay right in the middle of the boat. There was no isolation, no confinement in a dark room. Nothing. Instead there was the pretending to be invisible as Joe and Ellen complained about her behavior as they tidied up. It was more like being sent to bed under the kitchen table while one's parents performed a post-mortem on the day, and the biggest event was not the cool people they had met, but their daughter's apparently unacceptable behavior.

She pulled out her journal and in her seven-year old scrawl, wrote a short story. 'A swamp monster ate a loud earthling. Ha, ha, ha. The End.'

She shoved the journal under pillow and turned her back to her parents and tried to fall asleep.

***

Two days later, Joe had a craving for beef, so he raised anchor and took the *Volante* across the channel to the town of San Carlos in the search of a *carnicería*. They entered the town slowly, looking for any signs of life. The streets appeared deserted. Their shoes left little clouds of dirt in their tracks. They saw the backs of people as they turned corners, or heard footsteps approaching like shadows from the past playing with them, but they did not see any faces until they arrived at the butcher shop.

The small stucco storefront was painted a brilliant blue with a bright red line framing the one window. A big brown cow stood tied in the back of a Chevy pickup truck outside the shop. People walked by and stopped next to the cow and gave her a once over. One man in a particularly large straw hat actually picked up his hands and made an artist's frame with them. He stood back a little ways and moved his frame from the ribs to the rump roast and finally settled on a space of tenderloin whereupon he lowered his hands and licked his lips. Isabel hoped the cow did not know what was in store for her. Looking at the cow in the back of the truck Isabel no longer felt hungry.

Joe entered the dark shop with enthusiasm. He did not mind the dusty floor, or the smudged glass on the display case. The old, metal cash register was tarnished and covered in a layer of grease splatter.

Joe overlooked the apparent lack of hygiene on the counter and looked to where they cut the meat. The butchering space may as well have been a hospital operating room. Stainless steel tables and hooks gleamed and white walls glistened. Joe asked for two steaks. The butcher informed Joe he did not have any steaks right now, but that if Joe came back "by three" - he shot a look out the window towards the truck - "no, maybe four," he should have plenty. Joe nodded and Isabel grimaced.

Ellen saw the look on her daughter's face and pulled her out of the butcher shop before she embarrassed them. She walked Isabel around the corner. She grabbed her by the shoulders and looked her straight in the eyes.

"We are in a foreign country now. Things are done differently here," Ellen said sternly. "It is not for you to judge the differences. You are to watch and learn. I don't want to see any rude facial expressions from you again."

Ellen let her words sink into Isabel's brain, and when she saw that Isabel understood she let go of her shoulders. They walked back to the front of the butcher shop and caught up with Joe. Isabel kept her face pointed to the dirt and watched the tops of her shoes as she walked.

While they waited for four o'clock to come, the family walked around the town and saw many small houses all with their front doors open so that a they could look in and see an entire domestic world spread before them -, kitchen, table, bed, people. All of it. The absolute openness of people's home astounded Isabel who had a tendency to hide even her simplest possessions from the sight of those closest to her, let alone a bunch of strangers wandering the streets of her town.

The family went to the local bakery and bought ginger pigs, Isabel's new favorite cookie. Not only were they delicious, but they were bigger than her two hands put together, a child's heaven in every sweet, gingery bite. Ellen and Isabel sat on a bench in the plaza and ate the cookies while Joe went in search of a case of beer.

Isabel loved the plaza. There was a bandstand gazebo in the middle, and sandstone tiles paved the large square. Ellen explained to Isabel that every town in Mexico, no matter the size, had a plaza. Some had bandstands where local musicians would play on the weekends or in the evenings, and others had tiny stands that sold shaved ice treats or barbecued corn on a stick. There were always people in the plazas except for during siesta, when entire cities in Mexico became filled with ghosts and tiny dust filled tornadoes.

Isabel thought that the Mexicans were sophisticated and thoughtful to have created a place for the entire population of a town to gather to enjoy themselves and socialize for free. She was happy her parents had brought her to such a friendly country. The social implications of the plaza were so different from her childhood notion of community.

In the States she needed a formal invitation just to go over and play at someone's house. But, as her mother explained it to her, here was a beautiful plaza with the specific intention of being a place for people to gather and hang out whenever they wanted, no invitation necessary. Such graciousness boggled her mind in the most wonderful way. She wanted, more than anything, to be a gracious Mexican.

While his family enjoyed the plaza, Joe went to the local depósito , which was a place where one could buy entire cases of drinks and return the empty bottles for a deposit that often cost more than the beverages themselves. Joe asked for a beer and the proprietor brought him two cases of beer. Joe insisted that he wanted only one case, at which point the man behind the counter became stern and told Joe that if he wanted beer he would have to buy the two cases. Joe looked at the forty-eight bottles of beer that had been thrust under his nose and laughed.

He bought the two cases, and opened a bottle for himself and offered one to the seller. All annoyance left the man's face as he judged Joe to be a gringo of generosity. The seller stopped men as they passed the depósito and asked them to join the gracious gringo for a beer, and that is how Joe managed to drink an entire case of beer in one hour; he gave a beer to every man who passed the depósito until he had none left to give.

Now Joe was left with a case full of empty beer bottles, which brings one to the most interesting aspect of the depósito economy. When Joe collected his deposit on all of the beer bottles, he ended up with more money in his pocket than he had originally paid for the beer. Joe picked up the case of beer and let the pesos jingle in his pocket as he walked back towards his wife and daughter. He was thrilled to find out that Mexico was a generous place that paid a man to enjoy his beer. He had truly found nirvana.

The family returned to the butcher shop. The cow and the truck were gone, and in their stead was a long line of people waiting to buy meat. When the family paralleled the main window the butcher saw them and motioned for them to come inside.

Outside, the dust seemed to know not to cross the threshold into the butcher shop. The flies flitted over the heads of the patrons outside. Inside, however, the entire butcher shop had been transformed into a sacred space of cleanliness and purity where no speck of dust or unruly parasite dared to tread.

The family watched as the checkout girl rang them up on a sparkling cash register and tallied off the number of steaks with a new red, wax pencil on a gleaming white piece of butcher paper on the counter.

The girl herself seemed to have been carved from a bar of honeyed soap, and rubbed smooth with a fine cloth until she gleamed. Her crisp white uniform let off the bluish glow of absolute clean. The smudges on the display case were gone and in their stead was a large slab of shimmering glass that shone so bright it was hard to see the meat inside.

So much light came into the butcher shop seeking the clean surfaces to reflect off that it was darker outside the shop in broad daylight. Isabel looked over her shoulder as they walked out to the street and saw a white glow emanate from the doorway of the butcher shop. Isabel was sure that she had seen the clean lights of heaven her parents had told her about.

That night Joe started up the barbecue. Earlier in the day, with meticulous attention to detail, he had massaged the steaks and then marinated them in a peppery brine. He placed the steaks upon the flames with the care most people use to lay their babies to sleep. He relished their aroma and slowly sipped a beer as he watched them cook to a smoky perfection, the drips of fat disappearing with a sizzle as they hit the hot coals. Finally his works of art were ready.

He placed his steak onto a plate and carved himself a perfect sized bite. He turned the piece of meat around on his fork and admired it from all angles. He stuck the meat onto his tongue and waited for it to melt with perfection in his mouth. He opened his eyes a second later and spat the meat out in disgust.

"It tastes like hay!" he gagged.

He tried another bite, as if unable to believe his rotten luck. He spat it out as well.

"Try some sauce," Ellen suggested, handing Joe a bottle of A-1. Joe drenched his steak in the sauce and tried again.

"Shit!" he yelled, and threw the steak, plate and all, over the side. Ellen dashed down below and tried to whip up an offering of tuna fish salad, but Joe was too disappointed to eat. He pouted in a corner of the cockpit and drank another beer. Ellen and Isabel ate their tuna sandwiches in silence.

Grass-fed beef was not yet fashionable in the States. Joe's taste buds had yearned for the fatty, grain finished beef of home. Here in the desert, the beef ate the hearty little grasses that managed to survive drought after drought. There was no corn for miles. In the desert, masa was shipped on trucks once a week to make tortillas for the humans.

Still sad about bad steak the family went down below and tucked into their bunks. Not too much later a small motorboat pulled up alongside the *Volante* and someone knocked on the *Volante's* hull.

Joe pulled on his prosthetic leg and went up the companionway. A man with a thick handlebar mustache told Joe that he was the harbormaster and that Joe would have to pay for the privilege of staying the night in the San Carlos Marina. Joe thought it strange for a harbormaster to be asking for fees at ten o'clock at night, not to mention the fact that they were not in a marina; they were not tied up at a dock. They were anchored off the shore in an area that was marked neither by buoys, nor by signs on the shore. Furthermore, there were no mooring buoys to signify that they were even in an official anchorage of any kind. However, he did not want to argue.

"How much is it per night?"

The mustache twitched a little. "Well, do you have any bullets for my revolver?"

Joe replied, "Let me go see," and he headed below decks. He knew he did not have any bullets, but he needed a minute to think.

Joe knew the man with the mustache had a gun or he would not be asking for bullets. Joe wondered what person would give bullets to a man whose gun was possibly unloaded, thereby ensuring the lethality of his weapon. On the other hand, if the gun was already loaded and Joe refused to give him the bullets, the man might just blow his brains out and rape his wife and child. He pushed the thought out of his mind. He had no bullets to give the man. All he had was a little money and beer. He figured if the man was willing to barter, he might be interested in beer.

Joe looked at Isabel as she slept in her bunk. He opened the bilge and took out two six-packs of Tecate. He carried them up the companionway.

"I am sorry, señor," Joe said. "I do not have any bullets. But I do have two six-packs of beer if you are interested," and he held up a six-pack in each hand.

The man shrugged a little, and then leaned in to take the beer from Joe.

"Gracias, señor," the man replied. "These will work fine. Buenas noches." And the man left.

Joe watched the man leave and did not return below until he was out of sight. Isabel grabbed her father's arm as he passed her again.

"Goodnight, Dad," she said in a sleepy whisper.

Joe looked at his wife. Ellen's face was buried in her pillow. She had not looked up the whole time the transaction was taking place.

"Good job, Joe. You kept us safe for another evening, honey."

In the dark Joe gave his wife an ironic look.

"Yep, that's twice in one week that beer has come to our aid."

Ellen chuckled.

The New Zealander

When Isabel awoke the next day, the *Sylvia* was anchored next to the *Volante*. When she went above decks to check on the dinghy she saw the *Sylvia's* crew having breakfast in their cockpit. Aboard was a couple in their late fifties and their twenty-year-old son. With them as crew was another twenty-year-old man from New Zealand. All four of them waved to Isabel. She waved back and went below to tell her mom and dad about their new friends.

About five minutes later, the young New Zealander sailed over in a small sailing dinghy called an El Toro and knocked on the *Volante's* hull. Introductions were made all around. The New Zealander put the *Volante's* crew under his charming spell as soon as his delicious accent rolled out of his mouth.

For a cruising child, anyone under the age of thirty is considered a playmate. Therefore, when he invited Isabel to go for a sail Isabel jumped into the El Toro before her parents finished saying yes.

Isabel and the New Zealander sailed all around the bay. They found an entrance to the small river that flowed into San Carlos Bay and went up it. They saw masses of pink birds that covered the low sand spits on which they stood, and then great crowds of bluish-gray birds with long yellow legs and beaks. A gaggle of stunning white birds blinded them with their brilliance while they stalked fish in the shallows or stood with one leg tucked up, dozing. They sailed past in silence; the twenty thousand birds looked at them unfazed. The New Zealander let Isabel steer for a while in an impromptu test of her yachtie abilities. He was impressed that she was able to sail a true course. He was pleased by her many questions about his little El Toro and the rigging and could tell she was a true child of the sea, and he felt instantly that she was a sister to him, bonded by sea salt and an adventurous spirit.

By noon their stomachs growled with hunger. The New Zealander took over the helm and turned the El Toro to leave the estuary. There was the crack of the small boom as it traded sides of the boat. This sound sent every bird they had passed into flight. The blue sky darkened and became a chaotic bramble of pinks and grays. The calm silence was replaced with the frantic squawks and screeches of terrified birds. As the flocks mixed into each other they took on a terrifying resemblance to a gigantic swarm of feathers. Isabel ducked her head under the impending pressure of so many birds pushing the air down around her. She covered her ears against the deafening racket of confusion. The New Zealander sailed forward, stoic, a mild expression of awe in his eyes.

As they returned to the *Volante,* Isabel knew that she admired the New Zealander for his bravery and skill. She was happy to have been asked to go sailing by such a skillful young man. It was Isabel's first experience with the equality that true yachties had in them. No previous judgment had been made of her based on her age, race or sex. He thought of her not as a seven-year-old girl, but as a fellow adventurer and capable sailor.

Isabel would only realize how special this instant trust and respect found among her fellow yachties was when she returned to the States. But as the future remained unknown to her, for the meantime, she reveled in her abilities and the peace of mind such equality of treatment brings.

Cabo San Lucas

As they rounded the tip of Baja, the family crossed the Tropic of Cancer. Joe looked up and gave a silent thank you to Dr. Kudler. As they dropped anchor in the Bay at Cabo San Lucas, Joe realized that of all the little milestone markers he had consciously made, this one, the Tropic of Cancer, was the most meaningful. Without Dr. Kudler, there would be no Joe to go on an adventure. Joe smiled up at the sky, hoping Dr. Kudler could see him.

They saw the classic symbol of the arch in the rocks at the tip of Baja. It was just as amazing in real life as it was in the pictures they had seen. Before them the beautiful beige beaches stretched for miles around the bay. Seals barked at them from the rocks. Isabel watched as the water changed from the gorgeous navy blue of the deep Pacific, to the crystal clear light green of the more shallow water as they neared the beach. At three fathoms the water was so clear that she could see all the way to the bottom, and could tell which kind of fish swam there. She could tell the bottom was the same beige sand as the beaches.

On the beach sat a lone hotel, the Hacienda. The terracotta tile roof and whitewashed adobe walls of the hotel stretched out wide, but were dwarfed by the immensity of the beautiful, clean beach, and the sweep of waters of the Pacific upon the shore. A deep purple bougainvillea climbed up the shady side of the two stories of the hotel. The verdant green and bright flowers of the bougainvillea contrasted deeply with the desert of Baja; dark brown rocks, beige sand, Joshua trees and cacti.

A huge sailfish, about eight feet long, hung upside down by his tail in front of the hotel. A man stood next to it having his picture taken. Then the fish was lowered down and a man in a white apron with two long knives came out of the hotel to filet the fish. A few minutes later people started showing up to watch the fish be filleted. Then he handed off large pieces of fish to the people who came prepared with plastic bags.

"Why isn't the guy who caught the fish cleaning the fish?" Isabel asked her parents.

"It's a big fish. You can pay a guy to clean the fish. Or, sometimes, people just want to catch the fish and they don't actually want to eat the fish…"

"Then why would you catch a fish?" Isabel interrupted.

"For fun, maybe," explained her mom.

"That seems really wasteful, mom," Isabel said.

"Well, at least this way, the fish is getting passed out to the community and is being put to good use."

Isabel seemed to contemplate this idea for a moment, but was distracted by a little rowboat coming out to the Volante. The rowboat came alongside the Volante and a mom with four kids handed over a bag of sailfish fillets.

"When you get settled I'll send the kids over to play," she said. She smiled at Isabel. Isabel watched as they made their way back to their own sailboat, anchored a few hundred feet away.

Sure enough, true to her word, about an hour later the little rowboat returned full of kids.

"Hey! Come ashore with us! We're havin' a beach day," said the twelve-year old boy in blue swim trunks.

"Yeah, jump in," encouraged the thirteen-year old girl in the red swimsuit.

Joe looked over the side at the bunch of smiling, sunburnt faces.

"Yeah, jump in," the youngest two chimed in.

Isabel looked to Joe for permission. With a length of rope in his hand he motioned for her to go with the other kids.

She climbed into the dinghy.

"Swim home when you're ready," he called after her, and went back to coiling the jib sheets as if he had just sent her play at the neighbor's house, and not just sent her off with complete strangers in a foreign country.

This is how Isabel found out that children who traveled in the cruising world were very malleable and outgoing. They skipped the getting to know you phase and jumped directly into true friendship. From the days of seclusion on long ocean crossings, and the cramped confines of their floating homes they would emerge as extroverted sponges eager to soak up the stimulation and knowledge of their new surroundings. They were not shy because of newness; they sought it out and tried it on for size. They became perfectors of a chameleon nature as they blended into places and cultures where they did not speak the language by learning a new tongue in record time, and took on games that required skills of which landlocked children had never heard.

The moment a vessel came to port, the youngsters rowed, swam or windsurfed over to greet any new children. They became an instant band. Every day they went ashore. Some days they boogie-boarded or body surfed. Some days they sat on the beach and watched the waves. Other days they wandered the streets of Cabo San Lucas and saw what there was to see; palapa bars, loose dogs running the streets, kind humans, colors of all kinds.

One day they walked past a wall of posters showing masked men in long tights, capes, and full face masks. They stood proudly, chest out, chin raised, with their capes billowing in the wind behind them, one foot on top of another guy's chest, the victor.

"Who are those guys?" Isabel asked one of the gang, pointing up to the poster.

"Those are the Mexican heroes, righters of wrongs, purveyors of goodness," she was told.

"Wow," she said looking quite impressed.

And that is how Isabel was introduced to Lucha Libre, Mexican wrestling entertainment.

***

Isabel grew used to not having to explain herself. She grew used to the act of just being. She grew used to wearing what she wanted and chopping off all her hair because it was more convenient to have short hair. She grew used to the magnanimous nature of human beings. She forgot that intolerance and cruelty existed. She fell into a dream of discovery and contentment, free from the burdens of a traditional human existence.

She grew used to saying what was on her mind with vehemence and without repercussions. She enjoyed a good debate. She thrived with the other cruising children in the atmosphere of freedom of movement, freedom of speech and freedom of self. She felt herself lift off the ground in that act of flight known as being one's true self.

***

Back aboard the *Volante*, Isabel would think nothing of challenging her parents' ideas and engaging them in a good debate using her limited seven-year-old logic, except for when it came to math. Mathematics, the most revered of all educational pursuits to ocean travelers. Mostly because without math, one cannot use a chart, calculate how far one's gone, or know where one is in the middle of the ocean. Isabel was terrible at math that had anything to do with more than basic addition or subtraction.

Joe sat Isabel at the chart table, and opened the chart for their next destination.

"You open the pinchers like this," and he held the two tips of the pinchers up to the scale on the edge of the chart. "See, one inch equals a hundred miles on this chart. Therefore, how many miles is it between Cabo San Lucas and Isla Isabela?"

Isabel used ruler and a pencil, charted their course, and then measured the line with the pinchers. She added up the miles, "Two-hundred and fifty-seven."

"Good. Now when we are at sea on this next crossing, you will need to help me use the sextant to see where we are."

Isabel sat up a bit straighter and smiled. She knew she was as important as her parents now. So cool.

Los Arcos

By the time the *Volante* reached Cabo San Lucas, Isabel had become very strong and proficient in the family's rowboat. When she was in the little boat by herself she felt she could make it soar. She could maneuver around rocks and make perfect landings. She could ride the surf onto the beach and hop out on dry land. It was like having access to a car at age seven. She could take herself wherever she wanted to go and her parents were glad to be free of her for hours at a time. Honestly, even a perfectly well behaved child can seem stubborn and overly effervescent in such a small living space.

Isabel noticed the famous arches of Cabo San Lucas the minute they came around the point and entered the bay. The water would form a rising wave and then go crashing through the arch sending white foam shooting out the other side. From the deck of the *Volante* Isabel watched the waves cascade through the arch.

And that is when she conceived her plan. She would go through that arch riding on top of one of those waves.

Isabel got permission to go for a row. Her parents gave her the obvious warning to stay where they could see her. She figured that if she could see the arches from the *Volante,* her parents would be able to see her at the arches, so without a hint of duplicity she jumped into the dinghy and away she rowed.

She rowed along the towering wall of dark rock that made up the northern wall of an otherwise open harbor. She watched crabs as they scurried out of sight. Schools of brightly colored fish shone through the ocean's dark blue so that she saw the confetti of their shapes traveling underneath her.

Isabel was so focused upon the fish she did not realize that she had rowed up to a rock ledge filled with sea lions. The reek of rotting fish assaulted her nostrils. Some slipped into the water, others lifted their heads and stared at her, obviously miffed to have been awoken.

The sea lions in the water swam around the dinghy and tried to get a better look at her. Isabel was certain the sea lions would swim right under the dinghy and flip it over. She rowed as fast as she could towards the arch, hoping to outrun the sea lions. The sea lions popped their heads up next to her, keeping pace with the dinghy with ease. She rowed with all her might. She heard a sea lion back on the ledge bark and she knew he was laughing at her.

Exhausted, she slowed her pace. She watched as the sea lions bobbed in the water, inspecting her. She made herself as little as possible in the bottom of the dinghy and clutched the oars. She held her breath and waited for an assault of some kind. She half expected one of them to jump into the dinghy with her. Nothing happened.

Isabel peered over the edge of the dinghy and there were the sea lions staring at her. They seemed happy to hang out next to the little boat and wait for Isabel to provide them with a little entertainment. It occurred to her that the sea lions were just interested in watching her. She had surprised them as much as they had surprised her. She sat back down on the thwart and began to row towards the arches again laughing at herself.

The waves came through the arch with an enormous whoosh sound, and refocused Isabel to the task at hand. A spray of water hit her and Isabel realized she was in the direct path of the waves. She backed away and turned herself around to face her challenge.

Her father had taught her the theory of timing the waves. She figured that she would have to wait to get through the arch to the ocean side before she could come sailing back through it into the bay as she had imagined. She watched, waited and calculated. She rowed as fast as she could towards the arch, but before she could get up enough speed a wave came and pushed her out of the way. She was lucky the wave did not break over the top of the dinghy and swamp her. She sat and recalculated.

Meanwhile, Isabel's parents searched for her. They made frantic calls over the VHF radio asking their neighbors in the anchorage if they had seen their daughter. Her father picked up his binoculars and scanned the anchorage. He did not see Isabel anywhere. Struck by a sudden, horrible thought he turned his binoculars out towards the open ocean. He spotted Isabel as she waited and measured how to get through the arch.   Isabel was unconcerned that the arches were the point of land that separated the harbor from the open ocean.

Joe threw the glasses down and radioed a friend who had a dinghy with an outboard engine for help. The friend whizzed by the *Volante* and picked up Joe. They rushed to Isabel's aid.

At this point, however, Isabel did not feel that she needed any help. She had survived the onslaught from the sea lions, and the wave had done her no harm. She felt quite invincible and important. She calculated the ebb and flow, current, wave height and velocity in a manner comparable to a professional physicist. She looked as far down the wave's path as she could to gauge the set time and wave height.

She saw her father approaching in the motor-powered dinghy and she was suddenly seized by the notion that she had to get through to the other side before he could get to her, or she would never have a chance to surf the arches of Cabo San Lucas again. She squeezed her eyes shut so she could not see her father waving his arms to catch her attention and tell her not to do such a thing.

Swoosh! A great wave crashed through the arch just as Isabel was about to get the bow of the dinghy equal with the rocks of the arch. It sent her back towards her father covered in salt and spray as if to say, "No, no, little girl, listen to your father." She saw the foam form a finger and shake it in her face for emphasis.

Her father arrived on the scene. Isabel sat in the dinghy with her head down and waited for him to yell at her. But he did not yell at an intolerable instance of rebellion from his daughter. His eyes were merry, but Isabel did not notice because she was focused too hard on avoiding his gaze.

Joe thanked his friend as he climbed into the dinghy with Isabel. As his friend pulled away Isabel knew this was it, this was when the yelling would fall forth from her father's mouth in a deluge that would make the waves look as harmless as little squirts from a water pistol.

Isabel looked down into the bottom of the dinghy to avoid looking at him. He started to talk to her. She did not listen. She tuned out, blocking the yells she knew she would hear. But then it occurred to her that he was not yelling. He was calm. Not only that, he did not reprimand her, but rather he told her how to perfect her skills timing the waves, "… a skill every decent sailor should have," he said.

Isabel looked up at her father in shock. He motioned with his hands towards the waves and pointed at the crest and trough, telling her how the waves sped up until the point of impact, how to get to the other side Isabel must row into the whitewater and not wait for it to clear out because by that time the next wave would already be on its way towards her. Isabel was so amazed that she could only stare at her father.

Joe nudged her out of the way and took up the oars. He pointed the dinghy towards the arch and looked over his shoulder. He told Isabel to hold on, and then they charged.

Joe pulled the dinghy along with big strokes that pushed Isabel backwards. She hunkered down and got ready to go through the arch. Joe matched the water speed. They felt the wave come underneath them and raise them up. He stopped rowing and lifted the oars out of the water. The little white rowboat rode on top of the wave and shot through the arch. Adrenaline filled their bloodstreams. They passed through the arch in utter silence. They came out the other side. Exhilarated, Joe spun the dinghy around and looked back towards the arch.

"I have been wanting to do this ever since we got here!" he laughed. " Let's go through again, kid!"

He winked at Isabel in complicity. She blinked hard. Making her father happy was a far cry from the spanking she thought she would receive.

"YEASSS! Let's do it!" she yelled, ecstatic to be on a joint venture with her father.

Rested, Joe prepared himself. He watched a couple of waves, gauging them. Then he took up the oars and rowed as fast as he could to get up to the speed of the wave they were trying to catch. The wave came under them. They surfed the crest of the wave, hurtling towards the arch.

"Duck!" yelled Joe.

They ducked under the arch and were spat out the other side as if ejected from the mouth of a gigantic whale.

"We did it!"

Isabel threw a hug around her panting father and he hugged her back.

"Triumph and victory!"

They headed back to the *Volante,* not wanting to tempt fate again. Ellen waited for them on the deck. When they were within Ellen's earshot Joe started in on his lecture.

"…and the next time you try to sneak off and do something dangerous like that you'll be grounded. Got it?"

He landed the dinghy. Isabel climbed aboard the *Volante* and her mother grabbed her and gave her a hug.

"I hope you took your father's scolding to heart, young lady. We don't want you to pull another stunt like this or you'll be living up the mast for a week."

She gave Isabel another hug and added, "But I bet it was fun to go through the arches wasn't it?"

Joe and Isabel exchanged glances and she gave them both a wink. They all burst out laughing.

"Next time you two better take me with you."

And the next day they did. It was a great day.

***

It was in Cabo San Lucas that the family learned of the collective fun to be had every Sunday on the beach. First thing on Sunday morning there was the weekly radio net. One person would act as the mediator, and the cruising community would hit the radio waves to get questions answered about who had rigging to buy, who had the skills to fix sails, which doctor to ask for at the local hospital, if someone had a rowboat for sale, and so on.

And then there would be the announcement, "See you all on the beach at noon." And at noon all of the yachties would show up with a potluck dish to share and large blankets and towels to spread on the beach.

The palapa beach bars would send waiters around with trays loaded with cold beers and Cokes for sale. Massages were given, music was played and the usual game of volleyball would break out.

Some yachties would market their wares or skills at the Sunday picnic, and so blankets were spread out upon the sands and covered with sewing machines, sand paper, and woodworking projects. The seller's would sit drinking a beer, making no real effort to hawk their goods, but happy to chat about them if asked.

Isabel would boogie board or body surf while her parents talked to other yachties about where they would go next and if they could copy charts for that area. Opinions were made about the safest places to wait out the hurricane season that hit every summer, and whether the new Dacron sails really did hold up better to the salt and the sun.

At the end of the day everyone returned to their boats sunburnt and happy. They were filled with the special sense of community, that they were all in the world together, not as individuals kicking and screaming against each other.

The term 'mine' evaporated. In its stead came the words 'we', 'us', and 'our'. People were gracious and offered a seat and a drink when another approached. There was no jockeying for prime places to sit; they were offered up along with a drink without prior request. Nothing needed to be asked. When help was needed, it was given. When a person got out of line they were carefully put back into place with kind words that made the offender realize in an instant the harm he could cause with a violent tongue. With gentle care even the old curmudgeons forgot their bad behavior and strove to be better, kinder people.

Generosity lived in abundance. Kindness reigned.

Isabel's Changes

Isabel bloomed in the carefree nature that her parents allowed her in these foreign lands. Her stubborn nature softened and she became easier in some ways for her parents to tolerate. On the other hand, her tongue, freed from any previous constraints, went a mile a minute, and the number of questions she asked astounded them.

"Why is the water blue?" she would ask. Before they could answer, she followed up with, "What makes the wind blow?"

"Why do fish eat other fish?"

"Why am I not as brown as my dad?"

"If we are South, where do these birds fly in the winter?"

"Isabel, seriously, if you aren't going to let us answer, then you need to find these answers for yourself," her parents told her.

"Good idea," she said with a smile, and off she went, diving over the side of the *Volante* with a face mask and fins to watch fish.

She brought random strangers home for her parents to meet, often embarrassing her parents who had run low on provisions, and could not offer these impromptu guests more than a sip of water.

Other times she would tell her parents how she had lunch at the house of a family that had twenty-five children, and every one of them was beautiful and wonderful, and laughed with twinkling black eyes. Or she regaled them about how she ate corn cobs covered in chile and mayo on the beach.

She would think nothing of knocking on the door of a house that interested her and ask to be let inside. Oddly enough, no one ever turned her down. She marveled at the gigantic oven with a brick wall built around it that was the bakery, and asked to stick her hands in the dough for the bolillos. She liked to take off her rubber sandals and feel the dirt of the street "poof" between her toes. She walked past the little tin shacks where cruisers could pay twenty pesos for a shower. The plinkety-plink of the water against the corrugated metal sheet shower stalls made a happy sound, and she would lean up against the metal wall in the shade enjoying her aqua serenade.

There was no tourist melee in Cabo San Lucas yet. The native inhabitants outnumbered the foreigners five-hundred to one. A few sport fishermen came to Cabo San Lucas at the time to hunt giant Marlin. The one hotel, Hacienda de Los Lobos, took care of the tourists. One timeshare loomed, half-built at the far end of the bay, a harbinger to the future timeshare apocalypse of the the future. No timeshare salesmen pelted their sales-pitch at people who walked past in peace on their way to the supermarket. The alcoholic orgy-center of bars and nightclubs ready for Spring Break did not yet exist. A few shops and restaurants mingled here and there with traditional shoemakers and a pharmacy where shoes could be custom made and antibiotics did not require a prescription. Mexico was easy to see without all the tourist business blocking the native beauty. Tourist business is good for the local economy, but it really mucks up the view if one is looking for a natural reality.

In the town, the sound of laughter and loud, out of tune singing erupted out of windows and doorways. The vibrations of joyous life pushed at Isabel and made their way into her being as she walked. The gray, peeling paint of her previous life fell away. Beneath, an Isabel full of ideas and confidence erupted.

***

Old school busses were the main form of transportation up and down Baja, as well as in the cities. They were painted bright shades of blue or green. They rattled and thumped through the streets, causing an ear splitting commotion. The diesel monsters threw their horrible exhaust in the air and made Isabel cough. The smell of diesel exhaust would forever transport Isabel back to Mexico.

The first-class busses were far better than any bus Isabel had seen the States, however. They had leather seats with clean doilies on the head rests, individual foot rests and showed movies. There was no sign of the chickens and livestock she had heard about riding the busses, nor were there loads of vegetables filling the aisles. These busses were a little too neat and tidy for Isabel, who longed to ride a bus while petting a goat.

Without television to distract her, Isabel invented her own stories to amuse herself, and scribbled them down in her journals. Her imagination absorbed and changed reality so that she had to get into the habit of really looking and listening to her surroundings to be sure her senses had not been fooled yet again by an onslaught of the unconstrained reformation of facts.

She cut out pictures of wild turkeys and muscular men from the magazines her parents had brought to trade with locals and fashioned amazing tales of daring and adventure. In one story a young man managed to subdue a gigantic turkey that had escaped from the local secret chapter of Vicious Mutant Turkeys and ran rampant through the streets of Seattle. The man received a reward and the whole city had a free Thanksgiving.

Isabel would draw out headlines and paste the pictures onto paper so they looked like real newspaper articles. Ellen liked the stories so much that she sent the 'articles' back to the States for her family to enjoy.

Isabel took to writing almost every day, either in her journal or in some creative form such as writing jokes, made up news articles or long letters to her paternal grandmother. Thus, the family would spend its evenings with Ellen and Isabel curled up with books and pens and paper, and Joe plugged in to his music. They passed many evenings this way in happiness.

On the Way to Goat Island

As the *Volante* left Cabo San Lucas, Isabel rummaged in the seat locker.

"Whatcha lookin' for, kid?" Joe asked.

"I need a line big enough for this lure," she said, holding up a silver lure about a foot long with three huge triple pronged hooks.

"Hmm. You are going to need a heck of line for that lure," Joe said and he pulled an extra jib sheet out of the locker and handed it to Isabel.

The jib sheet was fifty feet long and half an inch thick. She tied the lure on to the jib sheet and threw the lure over the side, careful to let the line out slowly so that it would not become tangles in the Volante's propeller. Then she hooked the end of the jib sheet to a large cleat at the stern of the Volante. She brought out a book to read and sat at the stern to keep a distracted eye on her line. Joe chuckled. At least the kid was entertained.

Isabel looked up every so often and tugged on the line to see if she had caught anything. And then she saw the sailfish sail. She dropped the book and immediately started pulling in the line hand over hand as fast as she could.

"Dad! Dad!" she yelled to her father.

"No! No! Don't do it!" she yelled at the fish.

"What?"

"The marlin, dad, the sailfish!" she cried.

She had no idea how she would land a fish that size, but more importantly she did not want to. How would a family of three without refrigeration store a fish that big? His life would be lost for nothing.

Joe watched from the cockpit as his little daughter hauled in the wet line as fast as she could. He watched in utter amazement as the tip of the marlin's sword nose rose up over the edge of the deck, and the mouth opened wide to grab the huge lure as Isabel gave it one last mighty heave out of the water as she fell backwards onto the deck. The sailfish lowered himself back into the Pacific, and circled the Volante a couple of times looking for his prize.

Isabel lay panting on the deck.

"Is it gone?" she asked her father.

"Nope, he is right there," said Joe pointing to the stern again.

Isabel got up and looked over the side. She waved at the marlin as he swam past.

"Thank goodness I didn't catch him, dad. It would have been such a waste."

Ellen, who had watched the entire episode from the companionway smiled at her daughter. *Good kid*, she thought.

***

The *Volante* continued on her way towards Goat Island, traveling through the glassy water with confidence. Only the sound of her engine, a droning of security from under the cockpit, cut the silence. Isabel dipped her toes into the water and played at making different trails and swirls as the water pushed against her feet. The cool waters quenched her burning skin. She enjoyed the gush of dark blue water between her toes. She kicked the water away from herself into large sprays of foam. She tried to kick hard enough to get her parents wet in the cockpit. They did not mind the cool refreshment of a little salt-water spray; it was a hundred and ten degrees.

Attracted by the scattering water, a large, metallic blur swooshed towards her from the deep. Swift, like a behemoth butterfly, a manta ray flew right beneath her feet. Looming and gray, the manta ray paralleled the *Volante*. The manta was huge, half the length of the *Volante*, nose to tail.

Isabel was sure he was going to wrap his whip-tail around her waist and drag her under the ocean to his den. She sucked in her breath and pulled her legs into the safety of the *Volante*, hugging the cabin and she tried to make herself one with the wood. Isabel watched mesmerized with fear as the manta ray's graceful wings pushed through the water, keeping pace with the *Volante*. Then, in a magnificent leap, he was out of the water.

For a split second he hung in mid-air at Isabel's eye height.

They locked eyes.

Isabel imagined the dark rocks, the closeness of being swallowed by the sea, the water wrapped around every appendage and protrusion. She felt the pressure of the depths grow as she was pulled ever under. Fear gave way to wonder as she saw the rocks and sea fans that comprised the manta ray's garden. She saw the herd of seahorses that played in his yard. She imagined the dining table on the ocean floor where she was invited to dine from seashell dishes with the manta ray and his family. They would exchange jokes and stories over a dinner of seaweed and shrimp. She would tell her silly jokes to the manta ray's children.

Right before dessert, the manta ray would look up at his clock and say, "Oh, dear, so late already?" Then he would escort Isabel home, where he would catapult her back onto the deck of the *Volante* with a massive flick of his tail.

"Watch what you're doing, kid!" Isabel was jolted back into reality by her father yanking her by the elbow to keep her from falling over the side into the Sea of Cortez.

Isabel scrambled to her feet, still in her father's iron grasp.

"Go sit up on the bow and keep a look out for rocks. That should keep you from daydreaming."

Ellen handed Isabel a soda and a sunhat.

To the average person, being sent to look for rocks would probably be the last thing in the world one would think to tell a child to do to keep her focused. However, as every sailor knows, aside from storms, rocks, or anything else one can crash into, are the most feared occupants of the ocean. Isabel was thrilled to have the grownup job of Lookout. She ran to the bow of the *Volante* to take up her position with pride.

Isabel was relieved to be away from the loud diesel engine. She loved the feel of the wind in her face. She looked deep into the clear, blue waters searching for the dreaded rocks. She looked up at the coastline, about a half-mile away, and saw a beached trimaran, a type of boat with three hulls.

Isabel ran down the deck to point it out to her father, and as she ran she looked over the side and saw it - a massive clump of rocks - not more than three feet away from the *Volante's* hull, looming under the water.

Isabel screamed and pointed downward. Her father looked to where she pointed, and through the blinding glare on the water's surface he was able to make out the hulking, imposing forms of doom under the water's surface. He backed the engine, bringing the *Volante* to a full stop.

"Goddammit! Why didn't you tell me sooner?"

Isabel pointed to the trimaran on the beach.

Joe was quick to set bow and stern anchors to keep the *Volante* in one spot while he consulted his coastal guidebook on the area. He looked to see if the rocks were charted, and if so, how he might safely navigate around them in order to go in to see if there were any stranded people aboard the trimaran. He found the entry in the guidebook in small print, more of a footnote really.

He read carefully, "Large, submerged rock formations exist beneath the surface, extending from shore to a mile out."

He looked towards the shore. "We have got to be at least a mile out. This entry must be wrong."

Joe decided he could not risk the *Volante* to look for stranded people. He took out his binoculars and scanned the beach. He went below and pulled out an old foghorn and let go a few blasts. He hoped that if someone were stranded on the beach in the trimaran that they would hear the signal and make themselves visible. He gave a few more blasts on the horn and waited a precarious twenty minutes for someone to appear as he walked quick circles around the deck of the *Volante*, making sure she was no closer to the cragged rocks.

He scanned all along the coastline and was struck by the dryness and desolation in the place. Sharp, white rock glared back at him, throwing the power of the sun into his eyes. Through the curtain of heat ripples that wafted out of the ground he made out only a few cacti scattered here and there. Otherwise there was no sign of life nor any place to take shelter. Without water, in the dry, hundred-and-twenty-degree desert heat, he was sure no one could survive more than a few days.

He gave the air horn three more short blasts and decided to wait fifteen of the longest minutes of his life before extricating the *Volante* out of the hellish, rock infested waters. No one appeared. Joe rubbed the sweat from his brow. He did not want to be responsible for leaving people stranded in the middle of nowhere so he waited some more.

"You," he said pointing to Isabel, "watch the beach."

Joe paced the deck and kept his eyes on the rocks. Joe sounded the horn every ten minutes for two hours. When he felt certain there was no sign of life, he pulled up anchor.

Joe set Ellen and Isabel as look outs on either side of the *Volante*. He was thankful the waters were clear. But the strong sun cast such a glare upon the water that the friendly, clear waters turned into a blinding sheet of reflection. All they could see was great swaths of white that poked into their eyes forcing them to squint. Ellen had a pair of polarized glasses that helped to eliminate the glare. Isabel stood on the shady side of the *Volante* where she could use the boat to shade the closest water and allow her to see. All of their faces stretched tight with grim tension. Ellen's head pounded. Joe steered the *Volante* along at a snail's pace.

"Rock!" Ellen yelled and Joe veered off to one side.

"Rock!" Isabel yelled and pointed.

After an hour, Ellen's head ached from the concentration. Joe growled at his family to keep alert. They continued this zigzag routine until they felt they were in the clear. It took over three hours the clear the rocks they could see.

As the waters deepened, they relaxed a bit. Joe grabbed his chart and a red felt tip pen. He shook his head as he wrote 'ROCKS' closer to shore than they were shown. Then he opened his guidebook and rewrote the entry – 'Rocks extend up to a mile and a half from shore. Proceed with extreme caution – reduce speed, turn on fathometer and set outlooks on both sides of vessel.' Ellen brought cold sodas up from down below and gave her husband a neck rub. Joe let out a deep breath.

That night as they lay at anchor, Joe had a terrible nightmare in which he struggled through the desert unable to breathe in the desiccating heat. His family dead in the heat, the *Volante* in pieces on a craggy, rock infested beach and he buried up to his neck in the sand, unable to move. He felt the horrible misery of loss and the terrible loneliness that ensues. He rolled over and hugged his wife.

Goat Island

Dawn arrived and within a few minutes a very nice man in a bright blue ponga came out to greet them. He was the uncle of the island's goatherd, a young girl of fifteen years. From her perch on the hill the goatherd had seen Isabel. She asked her uncle if the family could come and visit. Doña Jejene, the matriarch of the island, granted her permission and sent the uncle to ask the family ashore. Delighted for an excuse to be on solid ground, Isabel put on her flowered dress while Ellen did her hair and Joe put on long pants to cover his artificial leg.

They beached their dinghy. The uncle greeted them and lead them up a steep path of sand so fine it reminded Isabel of baker's sugar. At a plateau, the family turned and looked back out at the *Volante* anchored peacefully near the beach. Their guide kept walking ahead without them and they ran to catch up. His blue shirt and cut off shorts were bleached from years of wear in the salt and sun. His skin was a gorgeous dark bronze and his eyes sparkled a jet black from under the brim of his faded lime-green baseball cap. He took the family to a modest village of ten to twelve adobe homes with thatched roofs that housed various members of his family.

Under the shade of a canopy made from a vibrant red bed sheet held up by poles of tall cactus sat Doña Jejene in a high backed chair made from driftwood. She held herself regal and straight even though her age wore as melted wax wrinkles down her cheeks. Her round body sagged from her straight skeleton and made soft billows of skin and flesh around her arms and middle. She was impeccably clean and wore a long, sun-bleached, cotton skirt of navy blue, and a bright white, short-sleeved button up blouse. Her long, white hair was pulled tightly from her face so there were no wrinkles in her forehead, and it piled high upon her head in a gigantic bun.

Her granddaughter, the island's goatherd, stood to Doña Jejene's side, a thin young woman with laughing black eyes. She wore sand colored pants and an earthen shirt. Her body was in camouflage against the earth's background. For a brief moment it appeared to Isabel that her head floated in the air.

Introductions were made by hugging each member of the family. Joe, Ellen and Isabel were turned around so they could be met from every angle. Their clothes were carefully pulled on to show the full extent of their patterns and colors. Compliments were made and they were shown around the village by having their hands held like intimate friends. Then the men pulled Joe along with them to the beer table, and the women took Ellen and Isabel to the kitchens.

Ellen and Isabel were asked to participate in a tortilla contest. They had no idea how to make tortillas and indicated as much in their poor Spanish. The islanders laughed at a such lack of ability, and asked Ellen and Isabel to be judges, not contestants. What ensued was a friendly competition between the grandmother and the goatherd as to who made the best tortillas.

The competition was heated enough that each made her tortillas in a separate kitchen and Ellen and Isabel were lead to each kitchen to have a taste. The kitchen walls were made of adobe and had been whitewashed inside and out. The kitchens were separate from the thatched roof houses so that when the fire was going in the wood burning stoves the heat would not affect the temperature of the houses and make them hotter in the already sweltering heat of the noonday sun.

The griddles the tortillas were cooked upon were pieces of sheet metal that were held up by stacks of cinder blocks with a roaring fire underneath. One could not stand directly in front of the griddle without getting singed shins, so the women stood off to one side and kept the cinder blocks between them and the flames at all times.

First they tasted the grandmother's corn tortillas. They were perfect spheres of uniform thickness. She made big points with Ellen by adding powdered milk to the tortillas for nutrition. The corn tortillas were crispy and loaded down with delicious butter. Ellen let every bite melt in her mouth. She felt instant satisfaction and calm.

In the goatherd's kitchen they tasted flour tortillas. Isabel preferred flour to corn tortillas no matter how nutritious the corn ones might be, and apparently indicated that the goatherd was the winner by eating four of her tortillas covered in butter and goat cheese.

Isabel and Ellen loved to watch the women make their tortillas by taking a round ball of dough and smacking it on the palms of their hands into perfect, flat, round tortillas. The dough hit the griddle with a sizzle. The metal let off the delicious smell of fried dough. Every few tortillas a big air bubble formed and the tortillas were blown up like balloons on the griddles. Isabel watched in awe as the goatherd flipped the tortillas with her bare fingers. She thought she must be brave to flip tortillas without the protection of a spatula.

Ellen and Isabel were both impressed by the roundness of the tortillas the ladies made. They took up balls of dough and tried to make their own round tortillas, but they came out looking more like amoebas with a case of the mumps that wouldn't get cooked all the way through no matter how long they were left over the blistering fire. Their inability to make tortillas was cause for great amusement among the island's women who considered making handmade tortillas as natural as having teeth.

The islanders laughed until they cried as attempt after attempt by Ellen and Isabel to make a round, flat tortilla was deemed insufficient and was thrown into the flames for disposal. The full body laughter was contagious and Ellen and Isabel shook so hard with convulsive joy they could no longer see what they were doing. Anyone from the real world would have walked by and seen a group of howling females with tears running down their faces and thought someone had died, but in the protected confines of the island kitchen, the women cried with laughter until their hearts bled honey and the ground was filled with syrup, their wrinkles vanished and they all became five years old, playing with dough for the first time, making figures of horses and deer to play with later.

Meanwhile, Joe and the fishermen talked about men's business. In this case they listened to the weather report. Anyone whose life depends on the sea had a deep interest in the weather. A hurricane warning had been issued for the Sea of Cortez. The good news about hurricanes and tropical storms was that there was generally a warning period long enough ahead of time to allow for one to protect oneself, either by putting plywood over the windows if on land, or moving to a safer anchorage if on water.

The men plotted wind directions and looked over maps of possible anchorages to run to, each trying to outdo the other with his plan of attack. There was a sort of reverence given to a man of the sea when he predicted the weather and outwitted Mother Nature. He might be able to say he saved a boat or a life and men would respect him for his knowledge and expertise. All throughout history, men have always been drawn towards leadership. The women joined the men and passed out beers. Isabel did not care for discussions of weather so she left them to their man-talk and scheming and went to see the herd of goats.

There were two hundred goats of all sizes crammed into a small pen whose fence was wholly composed of driftwood and lengths of saguaro cactus held together with pieces of bailing wire. They moved towards Isabel in one giant mass of hair and hooves as she approached. The whole fence stretched out towards her as they strained to see her. The goats in such quantity overwhelmed Isabel. She had seen movies with cattle stampedes and the way that the fence groaned and bent as the goats urged themselves into her direction she was convinced that at any second the goats would escape and do no less damage than the herds of TV cattle she had seen.

She hung back from the pen and was joined by her mother. The goatherd saw Isabel peeking out from behind Ellen and went up to the pen and removed a nanny goat and two kids. Then she took Isabel by the hand and made Isabel pet them. Isabel liked them instantly. The baby goats were the best. They were so little and friendly. When she crouched down to their level the kids came over to her. One tried to climb in her lap. He was black and white and had a soft coat. He liked to nibble on the collar of her dress. Isabel wanted to bring him back to the boat to be her friend. The goatherd thought it was a good idea and gave the baby goat to Isabel as a present. Ellen saw this transaction carried out in sign language and the occasional 'Sí' and put a stop to the goat moving aboard by bringing up the likelihood that the goat would fall overboard and drown.

Disappointed, but appeased by the idea that she was saving the goats life by letting him stay on dry land, Isabel left the goat in the far superior hands of the goatherd.

Goatless Isabel made her way back to the table where the men still discussed the weather. Ellen and the goatherd were pulled into a group of grownups, so Isabel was left again to entertain herself. Feeling sorry to be kept from the other's conversation, she walked around some of the outbuildings kicking at pebbles and trailing her fingers along the mud walls.

She looked up from her shoes for a moment and saw a deer no more than ten feet away from her. The deer saw Isabel too. Isabel tried to stay very quiet and watched her wiggle her ears and then turn towards her. The deer took a step in her direction. Isabel took a step back. She had a gorgeous, light and shiny brown coat. Her ears were huge in comparison with her head, and they flicked at the flies that tried to land on them.

She walked towards Isabel in a nonchalant way, without hesitation, sizing her up as she approached. Isabel stuck her hand out and the deer put her head forward so that she could scratch behind her ears. Then, like a cat, she moved forward and back, turning her head left and right so that Isabel could scratch her in just the right spot. She stopped for a second and she pressed her head against her hand to tell her to keep scratching. Isabel smiled and gave her a full head massage and ear scratch with both hands. She followed her around the buildings and Isabel tried to outrun her just for fun, but she kept up with ease. Isabel hid in a doorway and the deer found her.

Isabel's parents called for her. She was reluctant to leave the deer, but her parent's voices took on an alarmed tone so she returned to the discussion table. She was about to tell everyone about the deer when the goatherd said, "I see that Maria has taken a liking to you," and pointed behind her. Isabel turned to see the deer following just behind her left shoulder. Isabel was thrilled. She thought the deer was even better than a goat because she had never heard of anyone playing with a deer before. Maria nudged Isabel to get her to scratch her ears again.

An orange tomcat scampered onto the scene and went up to Maria shaking his head to entice her to play. The cat rolled over on his back and the deer pushed her nose into the cat's belly. The cat retaliated by batting the deer on the muzzle. The cat then got up and went over to the water bowl for a drink and Maria followed suit. The siblings drank for a while and then they went back to rough housing. They rolled and swatted, nudged and batted, kicking up dust and entertaining all. They played for ten minutes and then they flopped down next to each other to sleep, the cat's body serving as a pillow for the deer's head. Isabel could not take her eyes off the deer that thought she was a cat, or the cat who thought he was a deer. This was way better than television.

Isabel was told that a hurricane was brewing. They would have to make a run to safety because the anchorage they were in was wide open to the sea, leaving plenty of room for the storm driven waves to gather momentum and crushing strength. The most protected anchorage in the area was Isla Partida, about twenty-five miles away. Isabel, deprived of playmates for so long did not want to leave the island filled with creatures she saw as friends. Tears came to her eyes, but she tried to hold them in because she knew it was rude to cry in someone else's house.

Doña Jejene saw Isabel's sadness and pulled her close. Wonderfully crushed in her arms, Isabel smelled the clean scent of watered soil. She felt instant peace and calm. She felt such an intense flood of love and belonging that tender roots sprung out of her feet and rooted her into the ground. It would be the only time in her life that Isabel felt she belonged to any one place.

Her mother touched her on the shoulder to give her a gentle tug to come along and the roots recoiled and sucked themselves back into the soles of her feet. Isabel thanked Doña Jejene and the goatherd for the wonderful day. She gave the deer one last scratch and followed her family down the sandy hill to their dinghy. When they reached the beach, Joe gave the fishermen a hand pulling their pongas as high up onto the beach as possible and anchoring them there. Then Joe, Ellen and Isabel hopped into their dinghy and made haste to the *Volante*. They ran into each other as they lashed pieces of equipment to the deck and shoved loose items into drawers that latched closed. The skies darkened around them. They all put on their bright yellow foul-weather gear and took off for Isla Partida as the hurricane came for them.

Outrunning the Hurricane

The family of three was in the middle of the Sea of Cortez. Hurricane Bertha pummeled all forty-two feet of the *Volante*. It occurred to Ellen that hurricanes were named after people because they had the same violent nastiness and unpredictability inherent in even the noblest human being. Hurricanes made calm, inviting waters violent, and turned breezes that caressed the cheek roar past with a speed that burned the skin and left it raw. The waves ran fifteen to eighteen feet high, and as they crested and fell they became formidable walls of punishment.

The violent, white waters beat the *Volante* and shook her inhabitants. The waves made the *Volante* shudder and stuttered her progress. Rogue waves attacked from the quarter. These waves were the ones that threw the family off of their feet and whip lashed their necks. The *Volante* was pushed into precarious sideways tilts until she righted herself. There were no rules of engagement in the war for survival upon the hurricane-ridden sea. The family adjusted second by second for the onslaughts of wind and wave that belted them. There was no praying aboard the *Volante*. With teeth gritted they narrowed their eyes and dared the forces of nature to do their best.

Ellen sat in the cockpit with the *Volante*'s old wooden tiller clenched in her right hand and her feet braced against the opposite seat. Her eyes were set dead ahead daring the next wave to break over the *Volante*. The wave hit and Ellen was gone from view as the water crashed onto the cabin top and rushed over the top of her. Isabel watched her mother from the galley porthole that looked into the cockpit. She squished her face into the glass pane waiting for her mother to reappear.

When Ellen did come back into view she appeared unchanged and glared steely faced into the storm. Strands of her dark hair had escaped from her ponytail and stuck to her face with salt water. Every aspect of her being was drenched in salt. Isabel noticed the shiny object clamped to her mother's chest; a barf bowl. The family's future in the hurricane was being steered by a person demented with seasickness undergoing ferocious attacks by the elements. Isabel was afraid for a moment. Ellen saw her little daughter through the porthole and gave her the quickest flit of a smile just as another wave hit her and she disappeared again.

The *Volante* made headway with her engine running and the mainsail double reefed. Double reefing the main shrunk it down from its seventy-five foot height to a twenty-foot high triangle of material that reduced the force on the mast and prevented it from snapping in half.

The engine, normally a deafening roar of diesel motor, was unheard over the rage of the storm. The spreader lights were on to allow any ships to see them. Although they had a radar reflector already, Joe tied a rope around the pressure cooker and hoisted it up the mast to act as another radar reflector, because lights or no lights, the rain and waves made the visibility nil. He did not want to take any chances of getting hit by a ship.

Next, Joe was below decks with Isabel. Upside down in the bilge he tried to unclog the electric bilge pump. He swore as his sausage fingers struggled to grasp the delicate screws that held the pump together and swore again when he pulled a Barbie doll arm, a sock and a small screwdriver out of the limber holes that allowed the water to flow from the bow of the boat back towards the stern where the bilge pump was located. Beads of sweat formed on the bald spot on the back of his head. He sat up and Isabel could see his big brown mustache turned down in a grim expression.

Another sideways wave hit and Isabel's eight-year old frame was flung across the cabin. She was an upside down pretzel caught between the table and the settee. Her dad was face down in the flooded bilge. The porthole over Isabel's head opened and water poured onto her in torrents. Isabel scrambled to right herself and to close it. She pushed with all of her might against the massive torrent of water invading the *Volante*. Her dad pulled himself out of the bilge and helped her. They pushed the little pane of glass closed against the might of the ocean rushing into the cabin. There was a loud crack and a rip and Joe jumped in a new direction leaving Isabel alone to secure the porthole.

A new hole had formed where the forward hatch used to be. Joe disappeared up through the hole to the outside. There was an influx of water that looked like a personal Niagara Falls coming into the cabin every time that a wave broke over the bow. The bilge filled fast and the floorboards were afloat. Isabel climbed on top of the table in the middle of the cabin and held the metal rod that reinforced the skylight above her head for balance. There was nothing she could do to keep the water from coming into the *Volante*.

Meanwhile, outside, Ellen had seen her husband fly out of the forward hatch and fling himself onto the deck. She stood up to see if he had fallen overboard, but she was knocked backwards by a wall of water.

Joe managed to regain possession of the forward hatch cover by throwing himself along the deck like and all-star baseball player running for home plate. He caught the very edge of the hatch in his outstretched hand as it went over the side. He hung onto the lifeline and pulled himself back aboard, for at this point half of his body hung suspended over the hungry water. As he tried to stand his phony leg spun around on its stump and he ended up with the toe of his false leg pointing out behind him. Undeterred, he did not stop to straighten it out. He grabbed a coil of rope and tied the hatch into place. Blinded by the pounding waves that did their best to drown him with their repeated soakings and pounding, he strapped the hatch back into place while he cursed at the hurricane.

"Is that all you've got?" he demanded as he shook his fist at the elements.

Below decks Isabel was now more than a little panicked. The water was now to the height of the table she perched upon. She was not sure if her father was coming back or not. Isabel jumped into the rising water and sloshed her way to the galley.

She grabbed a saucepan and bailed pan after pan of water down the sink. She stifled her urge to cry. She did not want to be like Alice in Wonderland and add to the flood with her tears.

Joe reappeared in the main hatchway.

"Jesus Christ!" he yelled when he saw how much water they had taken on. He slid down the companionway and submerged himself below the floating floorboards and pulled out a handle and a hose. The hose he threw out the main hatch and the handle he fit into a slot for the manual bilge pump. He moved the handle up and down to prime the pump.

"Start pumping!" he yelled to Isabel.

Isabel flung the saucepan behind her and pushed the bilge-pump handle up and down splashing water everywhere as she flailed her arms.

Joe submerged again. A few moments later the electric bilge pump purred to life. Joe came up spluttering for air. Within a few minutes the water level decreased dramatically, but Isabel's adrenaline still jerked her arms up and down at a frantic rate. She wanted to see all of the water gone *now*.

Joe looked at Isabel working the pump handle like a child possessed and he burst out in a deep belly laugh.

"Pretty exciting, eh?" he said, and made a smile of large, wolfish, white teeth. He left Isabel to finish the pump out and went to check on Ellen.

Isabel splashed away at the pump. After half an hour, the floor boards no longer floated in the salon, and the electric pump seemed to keep up with the incoming water enough for Isabel to take a break. Her arms were exhausted. She couldn't lift them. She looked out the galley porthole and saw her mom and dad sitting one in front of the other, one hand each on the tiller, one leg braced on the opposite bench seat, her father's hand holding on the coaming in the cockpit.

Their eyes stared straight ahead into the storm, daring it to beat them. In the midst of all the rain, waves, pitching about and fatigue, Ellen still had her barf bowl clamped to her chest. It was then Isabel realized that she had nothing to fear. Not because her parents had full command of their situation, but because out in the midst of the sea and the storm they were doing all they could do to survive. If death were to come there was nothing they could do about it. Isabel no longer feared death and the scary unknown associated with death. If their lives were to be taken it was out of her hands. There was no point in worrying about something over which she had no control. Her father and mother obviously felt the same way. With the fear of death eliminated, the family rode out the rest of the hurricane in relative peace.

Ten hours later all three of the hatches along the cabin top had held up to the beating from the hurricane. The *Volante* finally made her way into the well-protected harbor of Isla Partida. When she rounded the point into the harbor the waves disappeared and the wind died down from a roar to a howl. They dropped anchor just as dawn was beginning to break. They were so happy to be free of the bullying waves. It was as if a massive headache had suddenly stopped pounding in their heads. They were deafened by the volume of the storm, and hoarse from trying to communicate over the storm's roar. None of them had enough strength to pull off their soaked clothes, so they piled into their sopping wet bunks and fell asleep. They did not awaken for twenty-four hours.

Isla Partida

When the family awoke, the hurricane had passed. Not a wave or whisper of wind remained from the hellish night. They hung the cushions outside to dry, along with every article of bedding and clothing they had. The cabin-top of the *Volante* was not visible for all the fabric. Thin, silvery lines of crystallized salt formed on every surface, including their skins. They took inventory of their food. Thanks to canned goods and strong plastic bags the family's pantry had suffered minimal losses. They rinsed themselves off with fresh water and put moisturizer on all the red spots and raw skin. Isabel looked at the beach with longing.

After a lunch of reconstituted mashed-potato pancakes, they decided to explore Isla Partida and rowed ashore. They left the dinghy at the beach and climbed the rocky terrain up to a cave. The mouth of the cave was large and allowed light to enter even into the farthest corners. Drawings of seashells and men with spears lined the walls. Ellen wondered why cave paintings on an island would not picture a fish. A pile of large, Chocolate clamshells sat next to a fire pit at the cave's opening and filled the air with the smell of rotting seafood. It was clear that the family were not the first modern visitors to the cave.

The view from the cave revealed a large circle of clear, pale blue water surrounded by rosy beige beaches and steep sea cliff walls of red rock. The *Volante* lay at rest in the middle of the peaceful anchorage. From their vantage point they watched a ponga speed past with four fishermen and realized there must be a fishing village on the far side of the island.

Isabel explored deeper into the cave and found a clump of crystals sparkling in a corner. She was excited to have found what she thought was a rare gem. Her parents did nothing to dissuade her.

Joe and Ellen stood at the mouth of the cave and let Isabel take their picture. They were calm and in a pleasant frame of mind after their hurricane ordeal. After such an ordeal one's picture of relativity is quite changed. Relative to surviving the night on the open seas in a hurricane there would not be much that would be more stressful or challenging. The family felt empowered. The hike up to the cave had limbered their stiffened joints. As dusk fell over the island, they were happy to return to the *Volante* for dinner.

However, when they walked back to the beach the dinghy was not there. Joe looked into the bay and saw the small white boat floating away in the breeze. Without a second's hesitation he ripped off his phony leg and dove into the water. He swam as fast as he could after the little boat. Ellen watched her husband in shock. Surely, she thought, if anyone should be swimming after the dinghy it should be the person with two good legs.

She pointed to Isabel. "Stay here."

She kicked off her sandals and dove into the water after her husband.

Isabel watched as her parents swam after the dinghy and made no apparent progress in catching it. She gathered up her father's phony leg and her mother's shoes and sat down on the beach. She watched as the dinghy outpaced them. She traced the outlines of her feet with a stick. She knew her parents weren't going to be able to catch the dinghy and she shook her head in that slow, bored way people do when they feel someone else is engaged in stupidity. In fact, she was quite certain the hurricane had driven them crazy and that they were going to drown in their attempt.

She remained on the beach and watched her parents swim. She resigned herself to the possibility of becoming an orphan. She mulled over her survival plan options. She thought she might be able to swim to the *Volante* and navigate back to La

Paz. From there she would be able to get a bus ticket back to her family in the States. She would explain what had happened and she would live with her grandmother.

Isabel watched as her father altered his course and instead swam toward the *Volante*. He pulled himself aboard, started the engine and hoisted the anchor. Ellen pulled herself aboard just as Joe turned the *Volante* to go after the dinghy that had floated out to sea. Now Isabel was far more concerned. Her escape route had been taken.

OK, she thought, *Time to think of a Plan B.*

If they did not come back for her she could always hike to the fishing village and hope that someone there would take her to La Paz.

But, she thought, *they will come back for me.*

Isabel decided she would stay on the beach and await her fate.

As the sun sank behind the cliffs, the tide rose and Isabel's beach became smaller and smaller. Fiddler crabs emerged from their burrows and skittered across the beach to scrutinize the intruder. When Isabel was still the crabs would come quite close only to scurry away when she moved. She was grateful the crabs did not have opposable thumbs with which to tie her up. They did, however, have a huge pincher claw that they carried in front of them as they scurried sideways across the beach. This snapping claw set Isabel on edge when they came near her and she used her father's leg to ward them off, shaking it at them.

The sky darkened. Isabel sat with her legs pulled up into her chest, and her arms wrapped around her legs. She had only a ten-foot square piece of beach left and the night filled with the sounds of water splashing, crab claws snapping shut and the persistent buzz of a cicada who had somehow come to the island aboard a fishing boat. She had to remind herself over and over what the noises really were. They were not girl-eating monsters come to terrify her. She would have to wait until daylight to see her way to the fishing village. However, if the water kept rising, she would have no choice but to feel her way up the steep rocky path in the dark to find higher ground.

She did not like the dark. Without the ability to see, her sense of reason gave way to fear. Her imagination conjured up monsters and poisonous crabs that conspired to do her harm. She squeezed her eyes shut in fierce concentration to drive away the fear and to conjure a resolution to her situation. She could crush the crabs with her father's leg. The water, although close, was not touching her yet. She repeated these affirmations to herself.

Finally, in the natural harbor of Isla Partida there appeared the running lights of a sailing vessel. She heard the anchor chain as it ran out of the *Volante* into the water, and the sound of the engine being thrown into reverse. Then she heard the sound of oars being pulled through the water as her parents returned for her.

She yelled out to them, "I'm here! I'm here!" jumping up and down and waving her arms.

Joe allowed just the bow of the dinghy to bump into what was left of the beach. Isabel tossed her mother her shoes and hopped into the dinghy with her father's leg under one arm.

He pulled it on and said, "Thanks."

"Good job, kiddo," her mom said.

While her mom cooked a can of soup, Isabel told her father that the crabs had scared her.

"What have you got to be scared about? You're a hundred times their size. Besides, you had a great adventure today."

"I know, dad, but it was scary."

"Don't be ridiculous, they are not even as big as your little fist," he said grabbing her hand and holding it up.

Isabel contemplated her feet.

"I am not ridiculous," she muttered under her breath.

From that day on, fear became renamed adventure. And that is how the word 'fear' exited Isabel's vocabulary; it was chased away by a hurricane, impending abandonment and two thousand fiddler crabs.

La Paz

The family had traveled up and down the Sea of Cortez. They had visited many seaside towns and met a variety of local people who shared with them a carefree nature and warm hearts. The family met only six other cruising vessels in this time. Ellen and Joe began to feel the strain of having to think so hard to speak a foreign language and wished for people to converse with in English.

Isabel on the other hand, was flourishing under the Spanish tongue. Much to their chagrin, she took to speaking to her parents only in Spanish as a sort of game. Isabel strained her parents in other ways too. Now eight years old, Isabel buzzed around the *Volante* like a hummingbird. She flitted to Joe for a question, barely stayed long enough for a response, and then she would zip over to her mother to ask for help with a brief art project. She would go fishing for an hour, then for a row, then for a swim, then shell collecting, then write in her journal. If they were near a town she would swim ashore and try to find other children with which to play.

Her parents just let her be free. They never scolded her when she announced where she was going rather than ask their permission. They did not have a set dinnertime and so she was never in trouble for missing a meal. She was smart enough to use the VHF radio to call her parents before dark and tell them where she located. As long as they felt she was safe, they left her to her own devices.

They headed the *Volante* for La Paz; a place they had passed on purpose at the beginning of their trip as they had heard La Paz was a port of call for every cruiser in Baja. Now, just for this reason they headed there in hopes of refueling their yen to escape people like themselves. They longed to speak English. They were greeted by a harbor teeming full of American and Canadian cruisers, as was evidenced by the American and Canadian flags that flapped from every boat's rigging. The flag of origin flew under the Mexican flag out of respect for the host country. This act of giving the Mexican flag the place of honor was one of the signs Ellen and Joe looked for when they decided whether or not to approach another yacht. They had found that people who flew their own flag at the top of the rigging, or who flew no Mexican flag at all, were arrogant people whose only reason for coming to Mexico was to make themselves feel better at the expense of a people whose greatest attribute was exactly the friendliness and greatness of heart that these arrogant foreigners trampled.

Joe and Ellen wanted no part of such ugly behavior.

***

In 1983, La Paz starred as a major trade port because there was no importation tax imposed upon electronics. Residents from the mainland would arrive in huge ferries whose bows opened like the jaws of a gigantic steel shark, and regurgitated passengers onto the shore to go into a buying frenzy. They dragged huge mafia suitcases after them in which to put their purchases. Many left the ferry at a sprint as if all the TV sets would be gone if they took too long getting from the ferry terminal into the town.

The ferry would arrive early in the morning after an overnight crossing from Puerto Vallarta or Mazatlán and then leave again that night. The travelers would run from shop to shop all day until the ferry blew the whistle announcing its departure. The passengers would return to the mainland pulling gigantic loads of televisions and radios in their suitcases big enough to hold several dead bodies and a cello. The people would try to tell the customs officials on the mainland that the suitcases only contained personal articles, like toothpaste and underwear. The joke was that the prettier passengers got away with the charade while the rest had their wares confiscated for lack of payment of the import tax.

The customs depot in Puerto Vallarta was full to the ceiling with electronics that the original buyers had been unable to pay the import tax on after having spent all of their money on such a huge haul. The officials would then sell the televisions at reduced rates after midnight from the back door of their office, which is probably why there was never an electronics shop in Puerto Vallarta until La Paz stopped being a free port. When it did close, La Paz lost half of its shops overnight and changed from a bustling town full of prosperity and ferries full of electronic miners to a sleepy town in Baja with a large gringo community.

The *Volante* arrived at the height of the electronics craze. Three times a week the town would be flooded with mainlanders and the cruisers all knew to stay aboard their vessels until six in the evening to avoid the crush of humanity that descended upon the town. There were a lot of cruising children for Isabel to pal around with, and soon Isabel was only home to sleep, and sometimes not even then.

Isabel was the youngest of the bunch. The cruising kids would take her fishing or on trips to the local hotel to swim because she could speak Spanish. She would politely ask the concierge for permission to use the pool, and then order Cokes and ceviche to keep all of the kids happy. They would swim, run around the pool like banshees and have water fights. They were never asked to leave. Isabel assumed this was because of Mexico's wonderful attitude that all children are lovable and need lots of attention and laughter.

Isabel's favorite activity at the hotel was to order the Fruit Plate Grande and a strawberry daiquiri, without alcohol. The fruit arrived on a large bright blue platter covered in the freshest fruit in the most marvelous colors. The smells of tree ripened papayas and nurtured pineapples filled her nose. She lounged in a chair poolside soaking up the warm breezes and wrapped in the happy contentment of a full belly, a happy mouth and a strong sense of belonging. She felt like one of those ladies in the movies who lounges around the pool, sitting in the lap of luxury and chatting with her friends. With happy eyes and full bellies pure

contentment emanated from all of the cruising
children.

The Mexican Popsicle

The fresh fruit popsicle was another of Isabel's favorite Mexican inventions. The Mexican popsicle outshone the American popsicle by far. Where American 'popsicles' were nothing but cheap, plastic, dyed, sugar water full of toxic artificial flavorings that left the mouth and teeth dyed atomic hues of a day-glow palette, the Mexican popsicle was a work of art, an ode to the beauty and lushness of Mexico itself.

The Mexican popsicle came in a rainbow of natural colors, each one representing a different fruit. Whole pieces of fresh fruit shone through the clear plastic wrapping as the salesperson handed it across the counter. A strawberry popsicle was nothing less than a mound of strawberries miraculously frozen onto a wooden stick. A cantaloupe popsicle was a slush of orange melon ground by itself and stuck, succulent and sweet in the freezer only to be plucked from the depths of the cold when eaten. A lime popsicle consisted of the freshest natural limeade possible, that would make the mouth pucker and bring tears of joy to the eyes because of its tartness.

The Mexican popsicle was a necessity for survival in the desert from June through October, when temperatures reached one hundred and twenty degrees and only cooled to one hundred and five degrees in the shade. A Mexican popsicle, poised in front of one's nose and pushed into and out of the mouth, the juices forming as it melted and sucked from its stick skeleton, could sustain a person for at least four blocks in the scorching heat of a desert summer.

And how smart! Right there, right as one finished the last bite of heaven, would be another popsicle shop, an oasis in the middle of the boiling street, where the ability to continue thriving in a hundred-and-twenty degree heat could be bought for fifteen cents and came in forty refreshing flavors that dripped off the tongue.

On the outskirts of town a man with a popsicle cart sold salvation from the desert heat in a tiny white cart with bells attached to the handlebars. He did not have to call for people to come to him. A jingle of the bells on the handlebars as the cart rolled along was sufficient to rouse the suffering from their sleep of sweaty despair and run to him with fists clenched full of pesos. The people drowning in their own sweatiness, threw their money at the savior as he hurried to grab popsicles of all concoctions from his tiny oasis on wheels.

Isabel thought the Mexican Popsicle Man should be a rich man. To her, the popsicle was as much a necessity as milk and bread and Isabel wondered that perhaps it, too, was regulated by the government to keep its price affordable to all.

Regulated or not, Isabel decided she would just appreciate its existence.

Crazy Johnny

There are many different kinds of cruisers, also known as 'yachties'. There are adventurers, retirees, the sick and insane, the arrogant, the purely stupid and the real seamen. Crazy Johnny was a real seaman.

He grew up a fisherman on the East Coast of the United States. He was a short, stocky man. His red hair and beard paired with his crazy tendencies to excess gave him the air of an irate Viking. However, he had a fondness for children. He calmed in their presence and became a teacher and confidante. He taught Isabel about all the knots fishermen use in their nets, and how to remove warts with dental floss. He taught her the names of all the shells he had collected, and told her the secret to clear the pressure from her ears when she dove. He taught her sea shanties that she sang as she rowed.

She loved Crazy Johnny and called him the Viking King.

Johnny, however, was not beloved by Ellen. To Ellen, Crazy Johnny was just a bad influence upon her husband's already heavy drinking. The men bonded over their mutual fishing pasts, their lives full of hard work and a mutual hatred of law enforcement. They one upped each other on their stories of arrests, being chased around the decks of the fishing boats by sea lions, and who could out drink the other.

Crazy Johnny confided to Joe that he had come to Mexico to escape a broken heart. The two of them would get together and think nothing of emptying a large bottle of rum and sing sea shanties until the night became morning and Joe would come home covered in vomit. Joe would not be himself for days afterward, and stumbled around the *Volante* in a daze of green sickness.

Ellen feared Isabel's association with Crazy Johnny, because she did not believe his intentions were pure. She could not reconcile in her mind the loud alcoholic who corrupted her husband with a teacher and mentor to her child. And no one could blame her. In her presence he was a complete nuisance who got her husband drunk on cane alcohol and filled her child's head with ideas and dreams that could never be attained.

On three occasions she had to calm a sobbing Isabel when she explained there was no such thing as mermaids, talking seahorses or trainable hermit crabs. On three occasions she had to extract her husband from random boats and bars where she had not been invited. Going out together was one thing, but leaving the wife at home, alone, to worry and fret as the hands of the clock progressed closer to dawn was no good for a happy marriage. Ellen wished there was some way to just make Crazy Johnny go away.

Moreover, she could not understand Crazy Johnny's girlfriend, Patty. Patty seemed a worldly woman who knew about art and literature. She cooked French cuisine, and made sushi delicacies. In the cruising world, where anything more than a bathing suit was considered dressed up, she was known as a lady of style who somehow managed to keep her silk blouses and pencil skirts unstained and ironed. She listened to Rachmaninoff and Chopin, for goodness sake, and it was not rare to hear Italian opera blaring from their portholes in the evenings. What was she doing with the crazy, alcoholic Viking? The entire cruising community wanted to know.

Then one early morning, there came a thunderous yell from their boat. A shattering of glass after glass ensued. Curse words and insults catapulted from bow to stern. Then came the sound of high heels on a deck, followed by the unmistakable sounds of a person jumping into a skiff and oars pulling through the water.

"Where the hell are you going?" a thunderous voice boomed. "Where the hell are you going, you damn bitch?!" They were the last words anyone heard from the *Kivi* that night.

By daylight it was clear that Patty had left Crazy Johnny. He sat alone, head down in his cockpit. No one was surprised at Patty's departure. No one knew what to do for Crazy Johnny. They just left him sitting there. He did not move for two days.

Finally, Joe rowed over a case of beer, set it in the cockpit in front of Crazy Johnny, opened a beer, and handed it to him. Johnny looked at Joe with a teensy lift of his head. As acknowledgment he took the beer from Joe's hand, but he did not drink the beer. The bottle just hung loose in his grasp as if it might slip out at any moment.

Joe went over every day to see Crazy Johnny. Crazy Johnny did not move much. He became sunburned and blistered, and his entire skin peeled like a snake's. After three more days, Joe brought over four slices of French toast covered in butter and syrup.

"Buddy," said Joe, "you look so bad that even Ellen feels sorry for you. She made you breakfast."

Joe set the plate down and cut the French toast into little bites with the side of a fork. Then he lifted up one of the pieces to Johnny's lips.

"Come on, it's really good."

Johnny gave Joe a look of depressed pity. Joe pushed the toast into Johnny's mouth. At first Johnny did not chew, but as the sugary syrup made its way to his senses Johnny realized that he felt a smidge better. Joe held up another bite, and this time Johnny opened his mouth. He took in the next bite of French toast and chewed and swallowed. Nothing had ever tasted so good. He took the fork from Joe. Over the next half hour he ate the rest of the French toast. When he finished he gave the plate and fork back to Joe.

"Tell Ellen thank you."

When Joe left Crazy Johnny, he returned to the *Volante* and relayed his message to Ellen.

"He may have thanked me, but I still think he's a lunatic," Ellen said.

***

At midnight on their thirtieth night in La Paz, an incidence of madness occurred that changed Ellen's mind about Crazy Johnny. The family slept below decks when a loud, panicked knocking on the *Volante's* hull awakened them.

"Joe! Joe! Are you in there?" Crazy Johnny yelled.

Ellen turned to her husband and even in the dark he could see the look on her face telling him to get rid of Crazy Johnny, The Destroyer of Domestic Bliss. Joe sighed and climbed out of their bunk and up to the cockpit in only his underwear.

Crazy Johnny was relieved to see Joe.

"Joe, man, Patty came back. She flew all the way down here from Seattle. She wants to marry me, man. What the hell am I going to do?"

Joe looked at Johnny for a minute. The love of Johnny's life had come for him. The idea that a sane woman would fly all the way back to La Paz for Johnny after he had chased her out of her home in the pitch dark in a foreign country and would want to marry him was incredible. She must be just as crazy as he. Two crazy people perfect for each other.

"I think it's a great idea," Joe said. "Go get married. She must truly love you if she came back."

"I know she loves me, man, and I love her. But what have I got to give? She is a classy woman, and I, well, I..." Johnny looked dejected.

Joe thought this over for a minute, but he was saved from having to give an honest response by a tired water rat looking to rest on his way to shore. It climbed aboard Crazy Johnny's inflatable raft and slid to the floor exhausted. Johnny tried to scare it away by waving his hands in the rat's face, but the rat did not budge.

From under the inflatable seat in the middle of the inflatable raft, Johnny pulled a machete. At the sight of the gigantic knife the rat's adrenaline kicked in. Crazy Johnny swung the machete in a Conan the Barbarian swing over his head and brought the blade crashing down. He missed the rat and sliced a sizable hole in the inflatable raft. The rat scurried around the raft in a panic as Johnny tried to chop off its head. Johnny made slice after mad slice until he reduced his inflatable raft to a pile of rubber ribbon that slowly sunk as the air left its tattered body.

The rat fled the sinking raft, swimming with all his might, and continued on his way to shore. Johnny looked around him as the water came up to his knees, defeated, machete still in hand. He sunk along with the raft, standing straight up in the middle of the lost vessel. He sunk without rebellion. Defeated by a water rat. Infinite defeat. He went down with the raft like fate had determined him to die at that exact moment, the machete still raised in one hand over his head.

Joe watched from the cockpit, confident that at any minute Johnny would put out his hand and grab the swim ladder that was no more than a foot away from him. The proud Viking King stood where he was planted, too proud to move. Joe leaned out from the *Volante* and grabbed Crazy Johnny by the shoulder. Johnny allowed himself to be pulled aboard, a defeated man. Joe looked at the despondent Johnny and shook his head.

Still in his underwear, he put Johnny into the family's dinghy and rowed Crazy Johnny back to his boat. Patty waited for them. She pulled Johnny out of the dinghy and hugged him to her. She hugged him so tight Joe could tell that she wanted to be a sugar cube to be melted in Johnny's mouth, eaten alive, disintegrated and put into his bloodstream to become a part of him; the nutrition for his soul. Any hate, and historical wrongdoings evaporated back to nothing and never existed; the true definition of forgiveness.

Ultimate forgiveness is so rare, and yet here was a stunning example. Johnny could feel it. He looked Patty deep in her eyes, probing her mind, making sure she saw all the ugliness he had to offer. He saw Patty walk past the ugliness and straight to his true self. He closed his eyes and melted into her. A grateful Patty nodded a thank you to Joe.

"I'll see you at the wedding tomorrow," Joe said and he went back to the *Volante*.

The next day a much improved Johnny greeted the family on the beach. He had a twinkle in his eye and a bounce to his step. Even his hair seemed redder. An adorable Patty glowed with joy. The Captain of the Port married them. Joe and the other cruisers in port all pitched in to give Jack a new inflatable boat as a wedding present because they did not want Patty to have to swim ashore.

"Honestly, who the hell keeps a machete in an inflatable boat?" was what everyone said when they heard the story of the rat attack.

"The Viking King," said Isabel.

Ellen liked Isabel's name for Johnny. She knew it was spoken in admiration. Thenceforth, Crazy Johnny was no longer 'Crazy Johnny of the Drunken Debauchery', but The Beloved Viking King. Through many a shared night of storytelling over beers and barbequed fish everyone came to know him as such, even Ellen, for there is nothing sexier and more endearing to a woman than a man who is deeply in love with his wife.

Isabel's Punishment

On occasion, Isabel's parents would hoist her to the top of the *Volante's* seventy-five foot mast for punishment or to shut her up when she would pester them, mostly because it was the best way to get her the furthest away from them when she was a pain in the ass. Attaching her to the main halyard and hauling her seventy-five feet up into the air was the best way to get her the farthest away from them possible. They would not let her down until she calmed down and yelled her apology to them from on high. Sometimes she stayed up the mast for the better part of the day.

On this occasion, however, Isabel had asked to be hoisted up on her own accord. She took in the view from her new height. She was the queen of the sky. Isabel surveyed her subjects below and shouted her happy majestic commands to the wind and the parrots that were her loyal knights and courtesans. She commanded the birds to fly, the wind to blow, the water to ripple. She munched on a peanut butter sandwich and pretended it was a chocolate bar, the most delicious and hard to find substance in the world, and therefore, only royalty such as herself were allowed to enjoy its taste. Out of the pocket of the boatswain's chair she pulled her journal and her pencil and she jotted down the contents of her kingdom.

On such fantastic meanderings of the mind Isabel would go to faraway lands and visit the Emperor of China for tea and discuss important matters of policy such as who was a better swimmer, Snoopy or Barbie, pet fish versus pet crab, boogie boarding versus surfing. Isabel might decide to take a trip to India and ascend her throne wrapped in a sheet to ask the Maharajah if she could ride an elephant when they went on a safari to draw pictures of all the wonderful animals in her country.

When her parents believed that she had been up the mast long enough they lowered her down, against her will. Isabel tried hard to impose her majesty upon them, but they still firmly believed they were her parents and not her subjects, so Isabel gave up until she could rise again.

José

While in La Paz, it was necessary to go back to the States to renew the family's tourist visas. There was a man named José one could pay to come around in his ponga to check on boats while cruisers were away. He would make sure the bilge did not fill up, and that the engine's batteries did not go dead. Joe and Ellen had heard good reviews about his boat sitting, so they hired him to look after the *Volante*.

José went over to the *Volante* two weeks before they left so that Joe could explain to him how to work the bilge pump, turn on the engine if he needed to move the *Volante*, and to give him the US phone number where the family could be reached in case the *Volante* sank.

José was a man in his mid-fifties with rheumy eyes and a big belly. He wore a cowboy hat, faded blue jeans and cowboy boots. It was incongruous to Isabel to see José in his land-based trappings powering through the harbor in his ponga. Something was not right about him.

José really seemed to like the family and offered to take them to the Conasupo, a government subsidized grocery store that was a lot cheaper than the regular grocery store. The store was far away from where they were anchored, even by bus. So, when José offered to give the family a ride to the store in his beat up truck, and get them through security, Joe and Ellen were thrilled. They could not say enough about José's kindness and generosity.

On the appointed day the family dressed up and went to meet José at the dock. It was a day so hot their lungs burned with every breath. They tried to dodge the scorching sun by ducking their heads, but the heat reflecting off the sidewalk burnt their faces when they looked down. The family was so relieved to be out of the heat when José arrived. They climbed into José's truck. There was no air-conditioning, and even with the windows rolled all the way down, going fifty miles and hour, there was no relief from the baking heat.

They rode for thirty minutes in his avocado green 1970's Chevy pickup truck to get to the Conasupo. There was a plastic cover across the truck's bench seat. When they arrived at the Conasupo José told Ellen and Joe to go ahead into the store and he would look after Isabel. Joe and Ellen asked him if he needed to go into the store with them. He said no. All they needed to do was to pay for the groceries.

The three men with M-16s guarding every door intimidated Ellen and Joe, not because the soldiers did anything, but because of the nervous anticipation of death one feels when surrounded by people holding M-16s. However, they were not stopped as they entered the store, and they relaxed.

Isabel really wanted to go inside with her parents, because she was sure it was air-conditioned in there. But Joe and Ellen were delirious with joy at the prospect of having a baby sitter, even if only for thirty minutes, and took off into the store without so much as a glance back at their daughter. The prospect of a half-hour of peace away from their only child was nirvana. Any parent can relate to the joy that even the prospect of a few minutes to oneself can bring.

Isabel tried not to act too disappointed. She did not want to hurt José's feelings. As her parents walked away she turned towards him and gave him a smile and a shrug. He looked at her for a moment and then his eyes followed Joe and Ellen into the Conasupo. As soon as they disappeared through the front doors he asked Isabel to give him a little kiss. In her experience thus far in Mexico she was accustomed to giving people kisses on the cheek all the time, so she did not think it an odd request. She leaned over to kiss him on the cheek. However, her sweat acted like glue and she found her legs stuck to the plastic seat cover of José's truck which prevented her from reaching him. She leaned away.

He asked for a kiss again. Isabel did not respond as she tried in vain to unstick her sweaty legs from the plastic seat cover. As she tried to think of how to say, "Stuck to the seat," in Spanish, José pulled her off the front seat with a rip comparable to a full leg band-aid being removed. She made a quick, harsh intake of breath. The backs of Isabel's legs burned. He shoved her onto his lap and forced his fat, slimy tongue into her mouth, prying her jaws apart with one hand. She could not breathe. She struggled, frantic to get away, but she was wedged between the steering wheel and his fat belly. His suctioned mouth was over hers and it would not let go. She pulled his hair. Her fists beat his shoulder. Her vision darkened. Then she heard and saw nothing.

"What happened?"

Isabel heard her father's voice.

"I don't know. It must be the heat. She just fainted."

She felt a hand under her head. The feel of plastic under her legs made her remember what happened. She tried to sit up too quickly and fell over. Joe steadied her and José leaned in to help.

Isabel saw José come towards her and slapped his hand away.

"Poor thing. She is tired from the heat." José said.

"I guess so, she is awfully hot. Let me get her mother," Joe said.

Isabel scrambled to go with him.

Her father pushed her back into the truck with a gentle hand.

"You wait right here. I'll be right back."

"No, I am coming with you. I want to go into the store." She started to cry and ran for the store's entrance. She did not care if the guards had had big guns. She ran straight towards them. The armed men did not even blink at her.

Joe lifted his hand to José as if to say, "I'm sorry for my daughter's behavior," and followed Isabel into the Conasupo. She grabbed his hand as he came up to her.

Ellen saw her daughter with her husband and was irritated. Their precious time to themselves had been ruined.

"She fainted from the heat," Joe told Ellen.

Ellen softened.

"Sweetheart. Come here." She gave Isabel a hug. She looked over Isabel at Joe.

"Did you find your wallet?"

"Shit. I forgot to look." Joe went back out to the Chevy.

The air conditioning was a pure hit of pleasure. The tortured hot, sticky feeling disappeared and was replaced by lightness. Isabel's feet lost their cement filled feeling and she was able to walk without shortness of breath. But even in the serene feel of the air conditioning Isabel clung to her mother's hand for dear life. Joe caught up to them and Ellen gave him a worried look about Isabel. Isabel looked too pathetic to try to cheer up, so they did not even try to offer her a package of cookies for a smile or a box of Chicle for a hug. They just walked the store in silence, filling their cart with necessities, until there were no more aisles to see.

As they checked out, Isabel could see José's Chevy through the glass window.

"Let's take a taxi home."

"Why would we take a taxi home? José is here with the truck."

Isabel watched the young boy pack their grocery bags and wished she could work in a Conasupo so she could stay in the air conditioning and not have to go back into the truck.

José hurried towards them with an exaggerated motion of helping the family unload their cart. As the groceries were piled into the truck bed Isabel said, "I can ride in the back with the groceries."

"No, you are sick and need to be where we can see you.'

Joe opened the door to let Isabel climb in first, which would have put her right next to José. Isabel refused.

"I feel nauseous. I might need the window," she said.

Her parents agreed.

The ride back to the dock was interminable for Isabel. She kept her face pointed out the side window for the entire ride. When they unloaded the truck with José's help Joe and Ellen thanked him.

"Say good-bye to José, honey," they coaxed her.

"No."

"Don't be rude," said her father.

Isabel looked her father right in the eye, clenched her jaw and walked away to the dinghy with a white plastic bag of groceries in her hand. Joe and Ellen were horrified by their daughter's rude behavior. They both apologized to José on her behalf.

They rowed back to the *Volante* in silence.

When the dinghy was unloaded Isabel's father grabbed her by the arm.

"What's your fucking problem, kid?"

"José shoved his tongue in my face. That's why I fainted. I couldn't breathe."

Joe and Ellen looked at each other.

"No, honey. You are confused. You fainted because of the heat."

"No, José stuck his big, slimy, tongue in my mouth," said Isabel, enunciating every syllable and pointing at her lips, in the angry hand gestures people do when they are really irritated that they are not being understood.

Joe and Ellen looked at each other over Isabel's head and exchanged raised eyebrows. Then they shrugged at each other in that 'what do you think, I dunno, what do you think' way. Their solution was to send Isabel to her bunk. They had no idea what to do, or what to believe.

The next day when Joe saw José's ponga go by he flagged him down to talk to him. Isabel saw her father motion to José.

This is it, she thought. *José is sure going to get it now.*

The image of her father, a fair Luchador, with cape billowing in the wind behind him, in a mask of white and silver, came to her. With chest thrust out and hand on hips he would face the evil José, just like she saw on the wrestling posters all around town. He would make him tell the truth. She would be vindicated. This would be her moment of justice.

José pulled his ponga alongside the *Volante*.

Joe studied José for a minute. He looked him square in the eye.

"Hey, my daughter tells me you tried to kiss her in your truck."

Without missing a beat, an indignant José replied, "What? Me? How can you even think I would do that to your daughter, señor?" José looked down at his feet.

"If you are going to accuse me of such lies, I cannot look after your boat. I cannot believe you would not trust me with your daughter," José said, his voice rising in intensity.

"José, I am not accusing you of anything," Joe said firmly. "I am asking you a question. You have told me no, and I believe you,"

"OK, then I'll take care of your boat. I'll protect her real good, señor."

José and Joe exchanged a solid Mexican handshake.

José fired up the outboard engine on his ponga and off he went.

A flood of conflicted images overpowered Isabel's brain. Why had her father asked if José had kissed her? José had kissed her. Brutally. She had told her father this. There was no need for corroborative statements. And how did he believe José and not her?

The white cape and mask flew off. Just a man stood in place of the Luchador.

Isabel could tell her mother was in the galley listening through the porthole. Ellen cast a glance at Isabel, that look that said yet again Isabel had gone too far.

"Isabel," her mother chided. "You cannot make up such stories about people. You know better. No dessert for the next two weeks."

Isabel felt as though the wind had been knocked out of her. She was awestruck that her parents did not believe her. How could her parents not believe her? She had told them the truth. She had done what they always told her to do and she had done it flawlessly. The betrayal was immediate, the rejection intense. Her brain space, which had once been filled with images of love, warmth, and play, became instead a bright white that could not be looked into without being blinded. She realized in that moment that she could only ever trust herself.

She picked up her journal. Instead of writing, she just made circle over circle on a single page until her pencil ran out of lead.

A week later the day came for the family to make the trip to the States. José came by to pick up the key to the *Volante's* engine. He asked Joe if he had any extra rope he could buy from him. While Ellen and Joe worked together to pull the rope from the aft lockers, José asked Isabel for a kiss.

She moved off the deck and into the cockpit to get away from him. "My parents are right there," she said in a tone of utter disdain, flinging her arm towards her parents as she moved away from José.

"Just a little kiss," persisted José.

She backed down the companionway, retreating to the safety of the *Volante's* interior. Two and two did not make four in this instance. She shook her head back and forth, "No, no. no, no, no. This does not make sense," she muttered to herself.

She opened up her journal, now full of page after page of paper covered in thick graphite, and began to swirl the pencil in the right handed circle that comforted her, and did not stop until the page was full.

A Border Crossing Trip

Time was running out. Ellen and Isabel's tourist cards expired in twenty-four hours. The family stood in a long line at the bus depot. They reached the bus doors only to find there were no tickets were to be had. They walked from the bus depot in despair.

A man and his son who had seen the family stand in line ran after them and pulled them around the corner. Ellen struggled to free herself from the man's grasp. But the man held firm and pointed with one hand to another bus. When the bus came gliding to a stop, the man pushed Ellen aboard. His son did the same for Isabel. Joe was the last to jump aboard. The bus pulled away from the curb. They paid the driver the fare, which he pocketed for himself. The bus was filled from floor to ceiling with humanity and its accoutrements. This was not the first-class bus the family had hoped to board, but it was a bus on its way to the U.S. and Mexico border in Tijuana.

Isabel sat on her backpack in the middle of the aisle. She shared the aisle with an odd assortment of cardboard boxes and a few other children. People of all sizes climbed over her with stunning agility when the bus came to rest stops. She was afraid to give up her seat on the floor for fear that she would lose it in the mass shift and settling that happened every time someone disembarked. She fell asleep against the knee of a man in blue jeans, and awoke with the seam pressed into her cheek like a scar.

The passengers became a bunch of chocolate chips that melted into one another during the heat of the summer night. As morning light came it was impossible to distinguish where one person began and another left off. People were surprised that the legs stretched across their laps were not their own and tripped as they tried to stand. When vendors came up to the windows to sell fresh fruit, all the passengers felt refreshed after the first bite.

When they finally reached the border twenty-four hours later, the conglomeration of humanity left the bus like layers of a bandage being removed. As the circulation returned to their bodies they waddled to the border crossing and handed the guards their passports and green cards. The guards did not even look at the pictures; they just welcomed them all into the United States with a weary wave of the hand.

While in the States, San Diego, the family went to the dentist, to the doctor, and then lastly a visit to the Bol Weevil where Joe consumed three one-pound hamburgers in a single sitting.

He picked up a hamburger and judged it from every angle on aesthetic appeal. He noted the redness of the tomato, the sting the onion brought to his eye, as well as the verdant green of the crisp Romaine lettuce.

He anticipated the first, juicy bite of perfection, the saliva gathering in his mouth. He inhaled through his nose and closed his eyes in pleasure at the hamburger's aroma. The excitement of a grain fed piece of beef entering his mouth without the fear of a staple having fallen into the ground meat, or the horror of the meat ruined by improper aging or feed, titillated him. He took slow bite after slow bite. He chewed without haste, savoring each and every atom of pure beef delight.

The waitress brought him another, and he ate it with equal detail oriented zeal. When he asked for the third hamburger she hesitated.

"Don't you think that you might have had enough, sir?"

Her eye glanced at the Budweiser clock on the wall and noted it was fifteen minutes to last call.

"No. I need another," Joe assured her. "I'll be fine."

Isabel was asleep across two chairs, and Ellen waited with her patience intact as her husband ate his last hamburger. She could see the iron and protein flood his veins as his face flushed a rosy red. He washed down each bite with a sip of beer. Joe's eating of the hamburgers was a deliberate and delectable ritual. The last burger arrived five minutes before closing and Joe sat there and relished every last drop of heaven without worrying about the staff mopping the floors around them.

Once satisfied, he wiped his mouth and pulled out his wallet, a motion Ellen took as the sign they were ready to go. He pulled out a hundred dollar bill and left it on the table. He walked past his wife who looked longingly at the bill, but she let the door close behind her instead.

They made it to the bus station just in time to make the six AM first class, Tres Estrellas de Oro, to return them to La Paz. They were given new tourist cards with their bus tickets. They rode home in the comparable modern luxury of the first class bus. Clear aisles, a clean bathroom, and even air conditioning welcomed them aboard.

When they reached La Paz, again, Isabel begged her parents to leave right away.

"We get it kiddo, there are more adventures to be had and more places to see," her mother told her.

Fine, thought Isabel. *Think whatever you want to think as long as it gets me out of here.*

Joe pulled up the anchor and off they set for Puerto Escondido, the best hurricane hole in the Sea of Cortez.

Puerto Escondido

Though constructed in the time of the Conquistadors to hide part of the Spanish armada, Puerto Escondido was a natural looking anchorage, The name was perfect because it meant 'hidden port'. Hills surrounded the anchorage on all sides, which kept kept the Spanish ships hidden. One of the hills was a man-made four hundred foot stretch of gray, pink and white rock piled thirty feet above sea level. However, it looked so natural that in the 1600's no one ever expected that behind that tall mound of rocks lay enough gun powder, horses and mercenaries to take over an entire country.

It was a small anchorage, perhaps a quarter of a mile long, with only one entrance, which was about twenty-five feet wide and a hundred and fifty feet long. To look at the entrance to the harbor one saw a perfect optical illusion. It appeared to be impassible.

Water rushed through and was thrown up in several areas, like water rushing over and around rocks in a river's rapids. The currents ran maniacally through the straight, twisting the bows of boats and pushing them towards the waiting jaws of hungry rocks that lay on either side of the entrance.

Not a single cruiser entered Puerto Escondido without a heavy sweat rising to his brow. The first mate always sat poised with the radio in hand to call for help, and the skipper always stood gunning the engine to wrestle his vessel out of the grasp of the water fiends that used his boat for their devilish sport. Rock maws spit foam and froth, snapping at the hull of any would be invader.

Once through the opening's devilish rapids, however, the water turned to glass inside Puerto Escondido. No matter which direction the wind blew the anchorage remained shielded. There was not enough room for waves to gather much speed or force inside the rock bowl of the harbor. Joshua trees dotted the hillside and stood sentry over the waters below them. It was the perfect place to sit out the summer's hurricane season.

Aside from a marina under construction at one end of the harbor, the only other business in Puerto Escondido was a little corrugated zinc shack that sold beer, sodas and ice. The kids in the harbor referred to it as the Coke Shack and the name stuck. The Coke Shack also had a covert poker game that was held at all times of day and night behind a tattered canvas curtain that was meant to shield the children's eyes from the depravity of gambling. The patrons played on a tiny wobbly table in chairs with uneven legs.

The owner always had a lit cigar in his mouth and a kind word for all of his patrons. He waved to the children and gave them packs of Chicle. However, Isabel and most of the other cruising children in Puerto Escondido that summer, were not allowed to go into the Coke Shack for fear that the shopkeeper's corruption might go beyond some minor gambling. Because the closest town of Lore to was twenty miles away, everyone patronized the Coke Shack no matter how afraid of depravity they might be.

While in Puerto Escondido Joe had to leave to return to the States to see the doctors about his leg. The ulcers in his skin had turned a putrid green and the leg was so swollen that he could press his finger into his flesh far enough for it to disappear.

He hobbled his way across the decks of the *Volante* in painful bursts of movement. He would sit in the shade under the large, bright blue awning and drink beer and eat the highly addictive painkiller Darvon until the pain was a figment of his imagination.

Most of the time Joe could function in this numbed state, but mix Darvon with a few extra beers and a shot or two of hard alcohol, and he reached a point of drugged drunkenness where he became invisible to his family as a husband and father. He became a numb spot that did not answer when spoken to and that did not participate in life. He would lose himself for days this way. Ellen hoped the doctors in the States could ease his suffering so that he would return as the vibrant man whose face lit up like a lantern when he smiled, and made those around him bask in the glow of happiness.

Ellen tired of being the sensible one. Joe's fade into numbness left her with a lot of responsibility. She made sure there was food to eat, fresh water to drink, plenty of diesel in the fuel tanks. She followed Joe's direction to the letter when he told her how to sand and varnish the rails on the *Volante*. She revised their budget. She planned and re-organized their schedule with an obsession and interest in minutiae normally seen only in accountants.

Her efforts were a waste in the cruising culture, where the mañana attitude reigned. Most came to Mexico to escape the constant critique and stress inherent in schedule and finance. Not only did her husband take her efforts for granted, but he was hypercritical of her work when she did what he told her to do. She was never able to sand well enough or varnish well enough to suit him. There was constant bickering, sniping and an occasional all out blow up aboard the *Volante*. Such explosions turned Ellen inside herself, and Joe turned back to the bottle.

Isabel would flee the scene. She would go for long walks along the beach and look for crabs and seashells. She might try to find a playmate if there were other children in port, but most of the time she just was left to lose herself in a fantasy world where everyone was happy, no one yelled, and a band of crustacean people ruled by Glinda the Good Witch populated the shores. These people ate seaweed and their main commerce was in sand. They had great cities made of driftwood and salt, with seashell columns and sea fan doors. She had found an outlet for the fear she felt when her parents fought.

Ellen and Joe had a knockdown, drag out argument the night before he was to leave for the States to see his orthopedist. Joe called Ellen every name in the book, and cut her down about her maritime abilities. Ellen yelled at Joe about his mismanagement of money and how he never took care of himself, that he was leading the family down a black hole from which they could never return. It was after dark and Isabel could not leave the boat. She sat in a corner and tried to read her book.

Joe gave Ellen a shove and she fell right onto Isabel. Isabel used both hands and both feet to get her mother off of her and pushed her onto the floor. Ellen looked at Isabel for a second. The pure hate in Isabel's face stunned her.

"You're leaving, too. Tomorrow the both of you are gone," Ellen told Joe and Isabel.

Joe was taken aback by his daughter's reaction to her mother falling onto her. He picked Isabel up by the ears and held her up to his eye height.

"You stay out of this," he hissed.

"You stopped fighting, didn't you?" said Isabel, looking Joe square in the eye.

It took all the self-control he could muster to keep Joe from hurtling his only child as hard as he could into a bulkhead.

"Go to bed. Now. You are grounded."

He then reached down and picked Ellen up with a delicate tenderness and led her to her bunk where they apologized to each other. Isabel's bad behavior of late was the one point about which they could agree. They came to the conclusion that their child was a spoiled brat and decided to ground her for a month. Which is funny, because the next thing they did was send her a two-thousand mile bus trip.

The Second Border Crossing

Joe and Isabel waited at the Loreto bus depot at six o'clock in the morning.

"It's gonna be good to get back the States for a bit, right? See some family?"

When there was no response from Isabel, Joe tried again. "You want the window seat?"

By way of response, Isabel climbed aboard the bus that had just squeaked and hissed its way to a halt in front of them, and took a window seat.

The first class bus of the Tres Estrellas de Oro proceeded towards the U.S. border at a speed of no less than eighty miles an hour. Joe looked out the front window and Isabel out the side. Neither spoke, not even when they realized that the relief driver was asleep on top of their bags down in the luggage compartment, which would have been a great starter to their 'Only in Mexico' stories.

Joe wore a shirt that read "Yucca" across his chest. Joe did not know that Yucca, aside from being a plant, is also what one calls a pimp in Mexico. As old ladies entered the bus at various stops, they saw a man in his pimp t-shirt, who had a leer in his grin as he smiled at them to welcome them aboard the bus. They hurried past him and then pointed at him behind his back and discussed his dirty shirt.

Trying to sleep sitting up on a bus is near impossible. By the time Joe and Isabel reached the border twenty-four hours later they were both exhausted. Isabel whined for food. Joe promised her McDonald's after they got across the border. His leg throbbed. The shooting pain he felt with every step shortened his already tight temper.

He hobbled up to the customs desk and showed their passports. The guard waved Isabel through and she kept walking. However, the border guard took one look at Joe and knew he was trouble. He recognized the arrogant set of his shoulders, the long, brown, down-turned mustache from the seventies, the utter disregard for eye contact. He knew he had a drug smuggler on his hands.

The guard flooded with adrenaline. He could not wait to bring this guy to down. He pulled Joe aside. Isabel, who finally realized her father was detained, waited for her father at the end of the long counter. The guard asked to see Joe's papers. Joe handed them over.

"Oh, I get it. I'm the lucky hundredth guy who randomly gets checked," Joe growled to the guard through clenched teeth while he smiled reassurance at Isabel.

The guard ignored Joe's attempt at a joke.

"Open your bag, sir," the guard said without looking up from Joe's passport.

"No problem," said Joe.

Joe opened his bag. The guard set Joe's papers out of reach behind him and rummaged through Joe's belongings. Not finding what he wanted, he pulled every item out of Joe's bag and tossed it into a pile on the counter. Joe seethed with rage to see his neatly folded clothes reduced to a crumpled pile of laundry. His toiletries were opened and sniffed by the guard.

The guard, disappointed that he had not found anything, just tossed Joe's documents at him, hitting him square in the chest with is passport, his tourist card falling to the floor. As Joe stuffed his belongings back into his bag he held his tongue for his daughter's sake, but his emotions took him for a ride. Joe shook with rage. His hands moved in a blur as the tried to shove all of his paperwork back into his wallet. The guard saw Joe's hands shake and he took it as a sign of guilt. He pushed the panic button and within three seconds six guards came running from every direction. Joe was spun around and pushed against a wall.

"Clasp your hands together on top of your head."

"What the hell's going on?"

"Silence! We're asking the questions here."

One guard proceeded to pat Joe down. When he got to Joe's artificial leg he jumped back and pulled his gun.

"He's got a device!!" the guard yelled.

The guards whipped out their guns.

"Slow and easy, remove the device."

"I don't know what device you're talking about, I have no devices!" Joe yelled.

"Cut the crap. I know you have a device!"

"You mean my leg? You want me to take off my leg?" said Joe incredulous.

"Whatever you want to call it, buddy, just take it off nice and slow."

All of Joe's anger and adrenaline ran through him. Joe sat on the floor and pulled up his pant leg to reveal what looked to the guards like a leg with a sock on it. Joe ripped his phony leg off in one fell swoop and threw it at the guard's feet. All of the guards followed the leg's trajectory with their guns. One guard approached it with caution, whispering nervous commands to his squad.

"Everyone stand back. I'm going to pick up the device."

Isabel stood clenching the corner of the counter. She had watched as the guards threw her father against the wall. She had seen her father rip off his prosthesis and throw it on at the guard's feet. She knew her father was defenseless, and unable to move without assistance. She trembled. She bit her lip hard to distract her from the reality in front of her. The guard moved in slow and nudged the leg with the tip of his shoe. Then he picked it up and looked inside. It had not occurred to any of the guards to look and see if Joe indeed had a stump where the artificial leg had been attached. They inspected the artificial limb visually, and then they put it through their baggage x-ray scanner, while Joe remained on the floor.

When they were convinced it was an artificial limb, they shoved it into Joe's lap without a word of apology. He had to scoop up his tourist card from the floor, as well as his bag, which had fallen off the counter when he was flung around.

A crowd had formed around Joe and it did not disperse until he had Isabel by the hand and had pushed his way through them to leave the border crossing. Isabel stumbled along next to her father who dragged her by the hand to the taxi stand where they took a cab to the San Diego Airport. Her hand was bruised by morning.

Meanwhile, back in Puerto Escondido

Meanwhile, back in Puerto Escondido, Ellen sat in the cockpit reading a book. She felt taken for granted. She bemoaned her fate and the fate of the millions of women everywhere whose worth was never seen. A boat called *The Mana* pulled into the harbor. She was perturbed when she looked over and saw a group of young, voluptuous, blonde girls frolicking on the foredeck with beers in their hands, and a tall man with dark hair and a beer in his hand behind the wheel. She rolled her eyes in disgust at the obvious male chauvinist pig.

To her further chagrin *The Mana* decided to drop anchor right next to the *Volante*. Ellen took her book and went below decks. She heard the sounds of *The Mana's* inflatable row boat being thrown over the side and the incessant giggling of the blonde women as they were driven to shore. To a graying woman in her forties who is ticked off at her husband, there is nothing more aggravating than a man making four gorgeous young women giggle. Nothing at all.

She stood fixing herself some quesadillas for dinner later, when she heard a knock on the hull of the *Volante*. She went above decks and there was the tall, dark haired man from *The Mana*. It took every ounce of her classy upbringing to not just turn her back on him in disgust and return down below.

The man introduced himself as Mike from Seattle. He was a massage therapist who had started a sailing tour business in Mexico. He had seen Ellen go below when *The Mana* had set anchor and he came by to apologize for any disturbance they might have caused. Ellen was caught off guard by the apology. She looked him up and down. The last time she had heard one of those it was from her daughter Isabel when she was three and had spilled her drink and said, "Oopsy." She looked at Mike and decided that maybe he was not as swine-like as she had imagined.

She invited him aboard and offered him one of Joe's beers. Mike declined and asked for water instead. Ellen knew she was going to like him. They chatted about the anchorage and Mike's boat charter business. He took groups of up to eight people sailing in the Sea of Cortez. He said he was relieved that his last ditzy group had left and that he had a week to himself until the next group arrived. Ellen told Mike she thought her husband could benefit from his massage talents as Joe had been in a massive car accident and had crushed several vertebrae. Mike was interested, and offered to give Ellen a demonstration of his abilities. Ellen was thrilled to get a massage. She turned her back to Mike and offered up her t-shirt clad shoulders.

"Well, to do a good job, you are going to have to down below and disrobe, and I'm going to have to go over to *The Mana* and get some sheets and my oils."

Ellen was taken aback by the thought of taking her clothes off. But, she rationalized, removal of one's clothing for the purpose of receiving a professional massage was a legitimate reason to get naked in front of a stranger. Therefore, after an initial hesitation she turned to Mike and told him to go and get his gear.

She nipped below decks and hurried to clear the clutter. He came back with his oils and sheets, and Ellen went into the head to undress. She came out wrapped in a towel to find the settee covered in white sheets. Mike stood warming oils between his hands. She lay down and he covered her with a sheet and pulled out the towel. She groaned in pleasure as he hit the hard knots and slicked them away with a gentle knead. He tackled her stress zones with a manual diplomacy so keen the knots would only have dared return if Ellen suffered a multiple whiplash injury.

For what seemed like too short a time, Mike erased all of her uptight posture. He molded her like a piece of clay into the real person she was beneath all of the tension and fear that had contorted her body with daily attacks or nerves and dread. When he was finished, he turned his back while Ellen returned to the head to get dressed. She was embarrassed to ask how much to pay him as the experience was so intimate that she felt money would sully the moment. Mike shrugged, and just said that the first one was free.

He thanked her for a lovely afternoon and went back to *The Mana*. Ellen knew right then and there that she was an amazing person who was not to be taken for granted, or yelled at, or pushed. Through one man's afternoon of kindness Ellen took control of herself again.

The Baja Bomber

Joe had his surgery, and Isabel played with her grandparents while he healed. Three weeks later they left San Francisco and hit San Diego. First stop, the Bol Weevil.

As Joe and Isabel left the Bol Weevil, two hamburgers heavier apiece, Joe stopped. There in front of him, like a ghost was a gunmetal blue, nineteen sixty-nine Cadillac Coupe de Ville, looking every inch like the one they had left behind in Sausalito. Neatly placed in the rear window was a For Sale sign. As they stood there admiring the car the owner of the car came out of the Bol Weevil.

"Saw you stop in your tracks there. You interested?" the stranger said, nodding his head towards the car.

Joe shrugged. "She's a beaut for sure. Bet she rides like a dream. But we are on the way down Baja, and we don't have much for money," and he turned to go, pulling Isabel along behind him.

"Don't want but five hundred for her," the stranger called after them.

Joe stopped. He looked at Isabel struggling under the weight of her backpack and the cardboard box of supplies he had given her to carry across the border.

Joe turned to face the stranger. "Done."

***

They drove into the Puerto Escondido anchorage parking lot in the gunmetal blue nineteen sixty-nine Cadillac Coupe de Ville with gigantic red tail fins. Ellen awaited them at the foot of the dock. Their arrival had been foretold by the smoke signals belching out of the tailpipe and the VHF radio users that lined their path. Anyone with a VHF radio within range was already atwitter with speculation as to who belonged to the gunmetal blue, Baja Bomber. Yes, the VHF radio, the nautical person's party line. Everyone listened in on everyone else's conversations.

On the way to the *Volante*, Joe rationalized the purchase of the Bomber. No longer would they have to hitch hike into towns to buy groceries. No longer would Ellen have to battle seasickness on travels to most ports. No longer was the family confined to explore only the coastal regions. Now the family would have even more freedom to explore than before. That was the original idea anyway.

Ellen understood that the car was meant as an act of attrition towards her, but she cast a skeptical glance at its polluting tail pipe before being convinced to go for a ride. The Baja Bomber was a smooth ride, just the way a Cadillac is supposed to be. Ellen could get used to such comfort. She was touched by Joe's thoughtfulness.

"You drive, and I will sail. No more seasickness for you, honey," he said smiling at her.

He seemed more lucid than when he had left and his eyes had returned to their natural human state rather than the fake glass doll eyes he had when he was lost to her in his inebriation. She was relieved that some part of her husband had returned from the trip to the States. She hoped that more of him would follow as he healed. Joe and Isabel had been gone for three weeks. In that time Joe had undergone two operations. The first involved moving a muscle from his abdomen to his leg to increase blood supply to the ankle. The second was a skin graft to cover the site of the first operation. He came back to the *Volante* with his leg wrapped in glowing white bandages. He hobbled along worse than before, but the whole family hoped that when that gauzy vessel of deliverance was removed, a miracle of healing would be underneath.

Joe had instant competition with the car. Truman from the *Mariner* took an instant interest in the Baja Bomber. He looked her over, walked around the Cadillac's perimeter, and then took Joe into the back of the Coke Shack where the children were not allowed to go. The kids did, however, sneak around the outside and eavesdrop to the sounds of beers being poured, more bottle caps being removed, and the slurred discussion on the merits of Cadillacs.

The next day, Truman left Puerto Escondido without telling his wife or son. He returned four days later, exhausted, behind the wheel of a gold-colored nineteen sixty-nine Cadillac Coupe de Ville. Truman, his eyes bloodshot from lack of sleep, his clothes full of crumbs and cigarette ashes, refused to return to his boat until Joe took a ride with him in his new car. He called Joe from the VHF radio in the Coke Shack.

Joe accepted the rumpled man's invitation and together they tore off into the infinite expanse of the Baja desert, dirt and smoke spewing out behind them.

"She's like riding on a cloud, isn't she?" Truman looked over to Joe for approval.

"Yeah, man, she's a real dream," Joe said appreciatively.

"I just had to have one. A man is a man in a car like this," Truman said, leaning back in the driver's seat.

Joe was not too sure if a car made a man. He had a car so his family could see more of the country. But, he could see his new friend had strong feelings about the car and so he did not disagree.

"There's some beer in the back seat. Grab me one, will you?" Truman asked.

Joe reached into the back seat and found three cases of Corona beer. He grabbed two, one for himself, and one for the driver, and cracked them open. They tore down the one-lane highway doing ninety miles an hour, drinking their beers.

Joe looked out the passenger window and admired the silhouettes of cacti in the evening desert. He loved how he could see all of the stars so clearly. He looked over to Truman to point out the star Betelgeuse and realized the man had fallen asleep at the wheel.

"Whoa, shit!" Joe yelled in panic as he dropped his beer and took hold of the steering wheel. He kicked Truman's foot off the accelerator and eased the car over to the side of the road. When the car came to a halt Truman's head fell forward and hit the steering wheel.

"Ow, man, you OK?" asked Joe.

There was no response from Truman.

Joe gently pulled Truman's head off of the steering wheel. His forehead revealed a gash three inches wide. Truman needed stitches. Joe tried to stop the bleeding by wrapping his t-shirt around Truman's head. He shoved Truman over and drove them back to the anchorage.

Truman's wife already knew that something was wrong with him; female intuition. She sat waiting in their dinghy at the dock with a first aid kit and a large towel to dress any wounds or clean up any messes. She thanked Joe when he handed her husband back to her. Joe dubbed the gold Cadillac the Golden Goose because it had laid a real goose egg on Truman's head.

The cruiser doctor is always a person who has the highest regard for everyone's health but his own. They drink a lot. They smoke. They never engage in any of the water sports available, but choose to lounge without sunscreen on their decks and let the breezes tickle their skins so that their bellies can grow ever larger. The cruiser doctor is also willing and able to make boat calls at any time, in any weather.

This cruiser doctor, a man ten years out of practice who went by the name Curly Joe because that was the name of his boat, ventured over to the man in need, Truman. Without any ceremony he cleaned out the wound. He applied lidocaine into the wound to numb it, which made Truman howl. Five minutes later, when he was sure the tissues were good and anesthetized, the doctor took a large surgical stapler out of his back pocket and placed ten staples in a jagged line that followed the gash's travel across Truman's forehead. The doctor then took a bottle of tequila and a pack of cigarettes as payment and went on his way.

One may think that falling asleep at the wheel and waking up with gash in one's head might dissuade a man from further automobile related activities, but that never seems to be the case. True to human nature, Truman and Joe started their second childhoods. They spent long hours working on their cars. Every inch was polished. Trips were made twenty minutes south to Loreto's machine shop to have customized pieces of metal made and then covered in chrome.

Three weeks later the cars glistened in the sun with all their chrome in place and paint jobs redone. Not much work must have been done on the engines, however, for although the cars shone like pieces of new jewelry, the engines still kicked out massive quantities of black smoke.

Joe and Truman started to wear their hair slicked back and spoke the English of their youth, throwing phrases like 'nifty' and 'far out' around. They walked with the youthful swagger of absolute confidence. When Truman started to roll his cigarette packs up in the sleeve of his t-shirt there was no turning back.

At the end of the month the entire anchorage was invited to an exhibition race between the Golden Goose and the Baja Bomber. The race was to be held on a stretch of desert highway between Puerto Escondido and Loreto. The blue Baja Bomber and the Golden Goose would race head-to-head for the first time. The entire anchorage was jazzed with excitement. Cruisers wore blue or light brown shirts to symbolize who they thought would win.

On the appointed day Ellen and Truman's wife put on their makeup and did their hair in fifties style ponytails with handkerchiefs. They giggled like schoolgirls as they watched their men put the final polish on their cars. Ellen held a homemade flag with a blue airplane on a white background she had made out of a pillowcase, a pair of cutoffs and a piece of driftwood. Truman's wife held a similar flag with a gigantic egg glued to it made out of aluminum foil that had been spray-painted gold. The cruisers rallied under the flags. Picnics were laid out, and a pile of wood for a bonfire was collected by the children. There was no way to get closer to a carnival atmosphere in the cruising world than this.

The men lined up side by side on the one lane highway. The idea was for the two men to go a mile up the road and then flip a u-turn and come back for the finish. They revved their engines and showed each other their teeth. They hid their eyes behind dark sunglasses. Ellen handed her flag to Isabel, and walked between the two cars. She pulled the baby-blue scarf from her hair and held it up as the starting signal. Little dirt devils spun across their path in foreboding. The wind flipped the scarf around in Ellen's hand. The men hunched over their steering wheels, both with steely-eyed focus on the road ahead.

The scarf came down.

Squealing wheels and clouds of smoke choked the crowd's senses. The two Cadillacs tore past Ellen and away from the group of spectators who strained their eyes to see them through the fog of exhaust. They were off!

The group heard a low diesel rumble behind them followed by the angry honking of a horn. People scattered to different sides of the road, flinging themselves off the pavement to avoid being squashed by the Tres Estrellas de Oro bus as it came barreling straight down the middle of the one lane highway.

The spectators watched as the bus screamed after the Baja Bomber and the Golden Goose as they raced neck and neck to their turning point. The two Cadillacs reached their halfway destination and spun around, flinging dust and rocks in the air, with the twenty-ton Tres Estrellas bus headed right for them.

The no-nonsense steel bus, complete with bathrooms, reclinable seats, luggage racks and huge luggage compartments below, came barreling towards them. The sleep deprivation and machismo of its driver made it a road-hog mercenary, and a couple of Cadillacs in its path would make no difference.

As the bus continued on its despotic course, the two men had about three seconds to comprehend that they were going to have to give way in this game of chicken, or die. They looked at each other. Neither man wanted to lose this race. But death is so final.

"Dammit!" Joe cursed as he took his foot off the accelerator and let his car slide off the edge of the road. The sand brought him to a halt in front of a gigantic saguaro cactus that leaned over the hood of the Baja Bomber as if trying to peer in the windshield.

"Fuck!" he yelled at the cactus as he smacked his hand down hard on the steering wheel.

Truman tried to overcome the pull of the desert's sand on the Golden Goose's wheels. He kept his foot on the accelerator, and crashed through four cacti. Sand blasted out from the wheel wells. Prickles from the cacti sailed through the air and rained down, some with such force that they pierced the car's metal. He came to an unheroic halt when the Golden Goose met head on with behemoth boulder that seemed to have been placed by God to stop the destruction being made in His desert. Truman was left slumped over the steering wheel, the closed cut in his forehead brought back to bloody life.

The spectators ran for the two cars. The Baja Bomber was intact. With a few gentle spins of the wheels and the careful placement of rocks behind the tires she was extricated from the stare of the cactus and the grip of the sand.

The Golden Goose was not so lucky. She looked like she had gone to war with a porcupine. Little cactus quills stood out from her body at odd angles, leaving holes behind when they were pulled out. The front end wrapped around God's boulder, where it stayed. The engine would not start, and the Golden Goose had to be towed back to the anchorage by the Baja Bomber with the boulder still in the grill. Truman had to visit the doctor for another injection of lidocaine and was stapled closed again.

The cruisers celebrated the day's excitement with beer, cane alcohol mixed with limeade, cookies and Coca-Cola.

Over beers, the two men slapped each other on the back.

"Man, you should have seen your face when that bus rode up your tail."

"Yeah, this critique coming from a man who drives like a drunk old-lady."

They laughed and teased each other until the early hours of the morning.

They went to bed that night jovial, but conquered. They would leave the highway bravado to the Tres Estrellas de Oro. In the future they decided they would just use the cars for transportation, not testosterone tolerance testing.

Christmas in the Cruising Community

Christmas was a community holiday among cruisers. Gifts were bought for family members and opened in the morning. The rest of the day was spent with the extended cruising family at a potluck party. The Christmas in Puerto Escondido was an especially large affair that lasted for two days. The first day was spent at the beach protecting the pans full of fresh cooked food from red ants the size of quarters, while a pile of driftwood was constructed in the middle of the seawall of stones.

When the food was uncovered for human consumption at four o'clock in the afternoon, it revealed an international variety of cuisine. There was Jamaican jerked chicken, enchiladas, Chinese chicken salad, ceviche, apple pie, blintzes, sushi, barbecued clams and crab, and a baked ham. The cruisers climbed up the mountains of rice, beans, and tortillas, using their forks and spoons to dig in and grab hold. They ate until they had decimated the gourmet landscape. The tiny crumbs that remained were carried off by the large, red ants that had watched and waited for the humans to fall asleep and not notice them.

As the cruisers sat digesting their dinner, large sparks flew from the fire like mini rockets. The adults made their terrible concoction of rubbing alcohol, lime juice and water and became very drunk. As soon as the children found out that the adult's precious drink was flammable, they had a wonderful time dipping the ends of sticks that they used to roast their marshmallows into the bottles of alcohol and creating torches. The children ran waving their flaming sticks around the bonfire and the drunken, passed out adults.

The children shrieked with joy and the adults let out raucous laughter. A perfect atmosphere of Bacchanalian chaos reigned on the beach creating an amazing high for all involved. The sparks from the bonfire floated up off the beach and became a spinning fireball that slowed down as people fell asleep and forgot to put wood on the fire. The bonfire's flames settled to a small pile of glowing embers. They fell asleep on the rocks and did not care that red ants feasted on the exposed parts of their unconscious bodies.

The next day the party started back up at five o'clock in the evening, which was just enough time for the vestiges of the previous night's hangover to dissipate. This time the party took over the docks of the new marina. The marina held just over thirty boats, and the dock space just barely accommodated all the members of the cruising community. Ice cream swirled in a hand-cranked ice-cream maker, a rare treat in the refrigeration-deprived world of most cruisers. A tall cactus served as a Christmas tree at the foot of the docks, strung with Christmas lights. The children made paper decorations and pierced them on the cactus's quills to hold them in place.

The docks were an unbalanced place to have a party. The fingers that made up the docks tipped and swayed as the revelers walked across them. The vast majority of people made an effort to sit down and have what they wanted passed to them so they would not suffer the embarrassment of trying to walk holding a plate of food and a drink while being flung off balance by the ill constructed docks. So many people loaded down the docks that some of them detached from the pilings that were supposed to hold them in place. They floated into the harbor, little parade floats of revelry sent into the midst of the harbor. Several dinghies gave chase and the fingers full of people were towed back to the party.

Joe had an industrial strength cable winch, which he used to strap the two main docks together. It was late in the evening and he had drunk a fair amount of beer and cane alcohol, as had the rest of the adult congregation, with the exception of Ellen who was still recovering from the night before. Joe had to untie a dinghy and move it so that he could place the come-along between the two docks. As he untied the little boat a drunken man came staggering up to him.

"That's my fuckin' boat you're fuckin' with, asshole!"

"I'm just moving it over, man. No harm, no foul."

"Fuck you, man!" the other man yelled at Joe. He stared at Joe who had already turned away and gone back to fixing the docks. The man felt he was not someone to be ignored. He lunged at Joe and knocked the both of them into the water. They came up sputtering for air.

"What's your problem, man?" Joe yelled at the man.

The other man swam for the dock. "I'm gonna kill you, you son of a bitch! I'm getting' my gun!" He hauled himself out of the water, fell to the side and then staggered to his feet and stumbled his way to his boat.

Meanwhile, the party had gone silent at the sound of the large splash the men made as they fell into the water. Truman ran to pull Joe out of the water.

"You better get out of here man," he told Joe, "that guy is bad news."

Joe's attacker was known in the cruising community for his bad temper. In general he was avoided for his foul temper and propensity to start a fist fight over any perceived slight. He was tolerated in the present company for one reason alone; the large supply of marijuana on his boat that he gave away for free. Even when he was stoned he was mean and picked fights wherever he could. His boat was appropriately named *El Macho*, which was how he acted; arrogant, full of testosterone, and too eager to prove his manliness through violence. It's also what everyone called him. (His real name was George, but that name did not live up to his crappy demeanor, so El Macho he became).

Joe did not want such a jerk to get away with tackling him in front of the entire Puerto Escondido cruising community, so despite Truman's warning Joe tried to follow El Macho. However, as soon as Joe saw El Macho fall off his boat onto the dock with a gun in his hand, Joe decided he should retreat.

He backed his way down the tipping docks, looking around, desperate to find something to hide behind. El Macho came at him like a tank, knocking people out of his way, kicking food containers and shoving whatever stood in his path to one side. He left a trail of chaos in his wake.

Out of nowhere stepped a newcomer, Marina. A gorgeous blonde with long tanned legs and big breasts, Marina boldly stepped into El Macho's path. .

Lucky for Joe those breasts were right at El Macho's eye height. He stopped chasing Joe just long enough to get lost in those mounds of flesh and forget where he was going. Marina made cooing noises to the drunken psychopath while she shooed Joe behind her back.

Joe, however, seeing a moment of weakness in El Macho, bristled for a fight. He stomped towards the gun-laden man ready to rip him from his mammary eye-delight. But Truman pulled Joe off course and pushed him to Ellen.

"He's not worth it," Truman hissed into his ear.

Ellen piled Joe and Isabel into the dinghy and rowed them back to the *Volante*. Joe passed out in the dinghy on the way. Ellen did not try to rouse him. She tied the dinghy up to the back of the *Volante* and let Joe trail after them attached only by a thin piece of rope. She turned on the engine. She used the windlass to pull up the anchor and she guided the *Volante* out of Puerto Escondido in darkness. She did not care if they violated maritime code and did not sign out with the Captain of the Port and Immigration. She knew if they did not leave immediately that her husband would end up dead.

***

When Joe finally awoke he could not figure out where he was. He pulled the dinghy up to the *Volante*. As soon as he placed his hand on the *Volante's* stern Ellen turned towards him.

"If you are still drunk when you try to come aboard I will cut you loose in the middle of the Sea of Cortez," Ellen said coolly.

Joe looked at her and thought for a moment of cutting himself loose and rowing back to Escondido to finish off El Macho, but then he realized the Ellen had removed the oars from the dinghy. He sat in the stern of the dinghy and folded his arms over his chest, defiant.

"Fine. Where the hell are you taking us?"

"Bahía de los Puercos. The Bay of the Pigs. It seems fitting."

Joe considered arguing. He considered just powering his way past her. But then he took a sincere look at her and he knew her attitude towards him had changed. He was no longer the omnipotent authority of the sea and the treasure of her heart. He was a drink-crazed maniac who had put himself and her family at risk. She had mutinied. There remained no shred of trust between them today.

"Come on Ellen, that guy was an asshole!"

"Frankly, I am surprised you even remember anything!"

"Look, I need to come aboard. I am burning," he said, one arm up to shield his eyes from the sun.

"Fine, get some sunscreen," she said without looking at him.

Ellen kept her back to him as he climbed aboard. After he slathered on the sunscreen, Joe looked to Ellen. He tried a smile, hoping she would smile back.

"Ellen, I am sorry."

Nothing.

"Shit! What about the car?"Joe asked. He looked hard into her face and then shrunk back.

One look at Ellen and he knew there was no reason to even think about the car. The car had been left in Puerto Escondido and they would not be going back for it.

The family traveled in silence. Isabel buried herself into one of her books, hopeful that by the time she finished her book this disagreement would have blown over.

They dropped anchor in Bahía de Los Puercos without a single word exchanged among any of them.

Joe whipped up tuna fish sandwiches for dinner, and tidied up around the boat. He tried to tiptoe around Ellen, which is a feat in a living space where the floor is only eighteen inches wide. When he bumped into her he said, "Sorry." She did not respond, and remained overly immersed in her book. He looked up and saw Isabel on the cabin top with her book turned toward the skylight because it had grown dark. He sighed. Then he plunked himself down at the chart table and plotted their course to the mainland.

He spent the night in the cockpit.

At first light, Joe started the coffee water boiling and pulled up the anchor. Ellen came up the companionway and sat in the cockpit, looking only dead ahead. Joe shook his head. This was going to be a long crossing.

Phosphorescence

The fierce sun did nothing to break the icy quiet between Ellen and Joe. Isabel went about her day ignoring them. When the sun set, Isabel dragged the end of the jib sheet in the water to conjure up phosphorescence from the water. These microscopic creatures would lie unseen on the water's surface in large masses. With just a little physical excitement they glowed.

Upon the sea, Isabel watched the large ripples of phosphorescence the *Volante* made as she pushed her way through the water and headed for the mainland. In the warm, gentle breeze Isabel was happy to watch the light show for hours. She sipped her favorite soda, grapefruit Fanta, and ate crispy chicharrónes as she gazed out on the calm, dark waters. She sighed with contentment.

Suddenly, out of the gorgeous calm of the evening there appeared a barrage of torpedoes aimed straight at the *Volante* from all sides. Great tubes of phosphorescence targeted the *Volante*. Isabel screamed and braced for impact.

When there was not a loud "BOOM!" she unscrewed her eyes and looked towards the bow where large explosions of phosphorescence popped up all around. She ran to the cockpit.

"Dad! Look!" She pointed to the bow scared to death.

Joe laughed at Isabel.

"Kid, it's just dolphins!"

Isabel could see their shape now. The dolphins' shiny bodies glistened and glowed against the dark water background. As they jumped from the water some of the phosphorescence stuck to their skins and they seemed to be dolphin spirits guiding the family through the night.

Isabel jumped out of the cockpit and ran back to the bow where she tried to communicate with the dolphins by whistling and knocking on the hull. Isabel woke up her mother with all the noise she made. Ellen came up on deck and she was delighted to see the dolphins leap and dance in their merry ballet.

Joe clicked on the spreader lights so they could see the dolphins better. After about a minute, hundreds of tiny streaks of light came swift for the *Volante*. Some of the small bolts of light leapt up and sailed through the air. As a mass, the sea creatures made amazing patterns and a light-littered chaos around the *Volante*.

The family watched the aquatic fireworks display with rapt attention. New patterns formed all around them, interconnected and shot away. One tiny light bulb jumped up out of the water and smacked Isabel right in the cheek. She threw herself backwards away from it in shock. She looked down and saw that what had hit her was a small squid.

"How rude!"

The streaks came upon the *Volante* faster and faster. If the dolphins were torpedoes, then the squid were the artillery who received back up from the flying fish that chased the squid. An all out offensive was launched upon the *Volante*. Some creatures plummeted head first into the *Volante's* hull, while others did suicide missions by diving into the cockpit. They created an amazing display as their glowing bodies flew through the air like bullets ricocheting off of each other in a wild array of patterns and speeds. Like moths to a light bulb, so were the sea animals attracted to the spreader lights.

Isabel ducked for cover behind the cockpit combing while Joe ran to turn off the spreader lights. The attack stopped. The family scrambled to throw as many creatures as they could back into the sea before they suffocated.

With the last flying fish and the final squid thrown back to the sea, Joe sat down in the cockpit and laughed a hearty belly laugh. Soon all of them were laughing until tears ran down their cheeks.

Finally, the cold snap had broken.

Isla Isabela

By the third day at sea, both Joe and Ellen could not see straight from exhaustion. They put in to Isla Isabela to get some rest. A lone, inactive volcano in the middle of the Sea of Cortez, Isla Isabela was about a mile long and made of gray and black volcanic rock. A millennia of currents polished and broke off parts of the island, sending them into the sea. A fishing village sat upon the beach of lee shore of the island. Joe set anchor right in front of the fishing village and collapsed in his bunk.

After the family slept, they took to exploring the island. The men in the fishing village did not look up from the nets they mended when the family walked past, nor did they try to barter for any beer or cigarettes. They seemed to tolerate the intrusion upon their island by pretending the family was not there.

They lived in mud and thatch huts set above the high-tide mark on the beach and drove the classic Mexican fiberglass pongas. Joe and Ellen smiled at the men in greeting, but no eyes looked up from the fishing nets.

"Must not like tourists," said Joe with a shrug.

The crater of the volcano teemed with life. Blue-footed booby birds walked away from their nests and took cover under light-green scrub brush as the family approached. Frigate birds circled the crater like modern pterodactyls as they stalked the pelicans, waiting for a moment of weakness when they could steal their fish. Sea gulls and terns sat on the sidelines and watched the aerial warfare. Green iguanas no shorter than six feet in length lay on boulders of petrified lava as high as Ellen's waist absorbing the sun's warmth, while crabs from hermit to land crab marched along the rocky paths in search of protection and food.

For all the birds Isabel expected to see lots of green, leafy trees, but what dotted the crater's slope were spiky plants that looked like Joshua trees. The vegetation consisted of sparse bushes and a few scraggly tufts of grass placed at intermittent points around the island. The family stood on the rim of the volcano and looked down into a crater filled with dark green water.

An edge of the volcano had worn away and allowed seawater to enter the crater. Large fish chased smaller ones and ate them up in one bloody bite. Isabel had the distinct impression that she was in an episode of the TV show, The Land of the Lost. She expected at any moment for a dinosaur to swim out of the volcano crater and chase them back to the *Volante*, or for there to be a low rumble and a swoosh of steam as the long dormant volcano hissed back to life. She walked with cautious steps around the blue-footed booby bird nests in an effort to not awaken the imagined creature in the depths of the crater.

As they were about to get into the dinghy, Isabel caught a hermit crab and put it in her pocket to bring back to the *Volante*, unbeknownst to her parents. Every kid should have a pet she had been told, so here was hers.

Once aboard the *Volante*, Isabel set the hermit crab up in a Tupperware bowl with paper towel bedding, a jar lid of seawater and a few canned peas for food. She hid the Tupperware in her bunk, under her teddy bear.

The family had dinner and went to bed early. Isabel snuck a look in the Tupperware container and could already tell that the hermit crab did not look good. She snuck up to the cockpit to let the hermit crab have some fresh air. She dipped her hand over the side of the boat and brought a handful of fresh water to the tupperware for him. She sat the hermit crab on the deck next to her. She looked towards the top of the island and watched the mass of frigate birds and pelicans start their dinner battle above the volcano crater.

The frigates glided on the air with obvious ease, and waited in mid-flight for the pelicans to do the hard work of diving head first into the sea after their prey. Once the fish was caught, the frigate bird would swoop in and attempt to steal the fish before the pelican could swallow his thrashing victim in one gulp.

Isabel yelled at the frigates, enraged that they would lead a life of thievery and steal from the hardworking pelicans.

Her mother heard her yells and explained frigate birds to Isabel. The frigates, for all their dependence upon the sea for fish, could not swim due to physiological reasons. Contrary to Darwinian logic, the frigate was not a waterproof sea bird. The water would not run off his back like a duck's and instead, he would become waterlogged and sink should he pursue a more honorable method of catching his dinner.

Once she understood the frigate's need to steal to be able to eat, Isabel cheered for the frigate birds when they did grab a fish. Just to be fair, though, she still cheered for the pelicans when they were successful in keeping their prey.

At three o'clock the next morning the family awoke to a great bouncing up and down as the waves shook them around inside the *Volante*. A storm had kicked up. There was nowhere for them to go for protection from the waves. The swells rolled in one after another, without any sign of letting up.

As the *Volante* bounced she came down hard upon the earth with her great, leaden keel. All fifteen tons of the *Volante* shuddered with each thud. The impact jarred their teeth. Joe jumped into action, started the engine and pulled up the anchor. They left the prehistoric nature preserve behind them.

A Force of Nature

By early dawn the waves had subsided, but a dead calm came upon the sea. They could no longer see Isla Isabela. They were surrounded by the Sea of Cortez. The sun never seemed to actually rise; the sky merely became a little brighter as the morning came. The gruesome gray sea was an absolute reflection of the grim gray sky.

As the *Volante* moved across the mirror surface her wake folded in upon itself and left no trace that she had ever been there. The air was so still it felt as though they were inside a vacuum.

Joe, at the helm, looked out upon the horizon and froze. Off the bow, in the distance he could see a great column of water lift up from the sea and disappear into the sky; a magnificent tornado of water.

The waterspout danced a precarious, drunken waltz across the sea's reflective surface towards the *Volante*. There was no way to call for help. They were too far from shore and their radio was out of range. Joe imagined the waterspout picking the *Volante* up and batting her about, only to be thrown down with the impunity of a spoiled child discarding a broken toy. Ellen saw it too. She sat tight-jawed and pale across from Joe, frozen in place. The immensity of their situation was crystal clear to her.

Isabel sat on the bow and Joe called her to the cockpit. As she walked to the stern Isabel saw another great column of water, its herky-jerky movements mimicking the first waterspout, off the *Volante's* stern. The two seemed to call to each other in a dance of enticement and courtship. Isabel pointed and Joe whirled around.

"Shit!"

The waterspouts seemed intent only upon each other. Joe turned up the engine and took a sharp turn to starboard, hoping to get out of their path undiscovered. "Come on, girl, come on," he pleaded to the *Volante*.

Even though the engine let out a deafening roar of sound, the family all held its breath and watched in awe as the waterspouts closed in upon each other, with the *Volante* stuck right between them. As the waterspouts came closer, Ellen saw Joe's knuckles turn white upon the tiller. Eight knots is not fast enough to get out of the way of a tornado.

The family wanted to be like the mice that slunk out the door while their adversaries entertained one another. The *Volante* continued out of the waterspouts' path at a relative snail's pace. The air thinned as it was pulled from sea level and sucked up into the atmosphere.

Just as quickly as the waterspouts had churned up from nothing, a mild breeze blew and the water fell to back into the sea with a thunderous crash. The massive churning winds sucked up into the sky and disappeared. Joe and Ellen looked at each other is disbelief.

"Can it be?" asked Ellen.

"Shh," Joe whispered, straining to listen for an errant gust of wind or a thunderclap.

They waited in a strained, shocked silence, scanning the skies and the horizon for any evidence of the water spouts. Finally, the entire family let out a collective sigh of relief. Ellen's face slackened. Joe stood stoic at the tiller.

Isabel returned to the bow with her stow away hermit crab in her pocket. She took the little creature out of her pocket only to realize he was dead. She felt so ashamed. She had killed a little creature that had done nothing to her. She had just wanted to be his friend, but she had been selfish and taken him from his home. She held her hand over the side and returned him to the sea.

Making it to Puerto Vallarta

The *Volante* traveled through the night on a course straight for the harbor at Puerto Vallarta. The family could not see the lights of the town yet, but they knew they were getting close.

It was four-thirty in the morning. They had favorable conditions; under sail a good wind blew them right where they wanted to go and the waves worked to push them closer to their destination. They relished the smooth sailing and kicked back in the cockpit enjoying the ride.

And then, from somewhere around the *Volante*, they started to hear the sounds of a cocktail party; laughter and the clinking of glasses, a few shouts thrown in for substance. At first Ellen thought they had caught a radio wave in the rigging - a strange and rare occurrence when the rigging on a sailboat acts as an antenna in the middle of the ocean and bring the radio waves into one's mouth where metal fillings act as the receiver.

The cocktail party, however, grew louder, and was accompanied by the sound of splashing. Joe yelled for Ellen to get on the radio and try to hail the approaching vessel. Ellen tried all the hailing frequencies. No response.

Joe turned on the engine for better maneuverability, but the noise of the engine drowned out any sound of the oncoming vessel, which had been the only evidence he had that another vessel existed.

All three strained their eyes into the dark of the too early morning looking for any sign of an approaching vessel when out of the blackness came a huge tuna boat.

Jolly sailors floated two stories over the *Volante's* decks drinking beers and falling down with inebriated joy. The tuna boat lumbered past the *Volante* no more than twenty feet away. The splash from her bow sent spray over the *Volante's* decks. Not a single person aboard the tuna boat saw the *Volante*, not even the man who leaned over the rail and nearly pelted them with his vomit. The stunned family watched in relief as the tuna boat disappeared into the blackness behind them. They settled back to their seats in the cockpit.

Just as the family caught their breath, it came, the sound of water crashing against a hard surface in large quantities. The crash was loud enough to be heard over the roar of the diesel engine. In the blackness ahead of them the family saw huge clouds of phosphorescence being thrown up in their path.

"What is that?" Isabel asked.

"I don't know..." Joe's voice trailed off and his eyes widened as he came to a horrible realization.

"Get the engine on and back it hard, Ellen!" Joe yelled. He ran to the mast and dropped the sails to prevent further momentum. The sails fell in a huge billow of canvas onto the deck.

The engine roared as Ellen powered it up to stop the *Volante's* forward motion. The *Volante* came to a halt fifty feet before a tiny beach of pebbles topped by large pinnacles of rock. The waves crashed onto the beach and threw phosphorescence everywhere, like dim fireworks. The *Volante* stood a boat length from doom that came in the form of a tiny isolated land mass about two miles out from Puerto Vallarta. Aside from being deadly, it was really rather beautiful.

Joe cursed the chart makers in a litany of colorful language that is not appropriate for the land lover's ear, but had everything to do with their unscrupulous characters and the dubious methods they used when they surveyed the coastal regions of Mexico. Again Joe pulled out his chart and wrote 'ROCKS' in big red letters with a felt tip pen, his hand shaking with rage.

Puerto Vallarta

When they steered around the 'ROCKS,' the lights of Puerto Vallarta shone in the distance. Joe still seethed with rage. His family has been endangered once again because of faulty charts and sloppy guidebooks. He muttered obscenities under his breath. He went below to grab a beer and punched the cabinside with his fist. With more foul language falling from his mouth he returned above decks.

He made his way around the decks of the *Volante* in angry, frustrated movements. Although none of his words were directed at her, Ellen took each word as a personal insult. The more he ranted, the madder she got. By the time the harbor's mouth opened before them he no longer existed to her. The closing of the emotional gap that happened as they braved the waterspouts, opened wide as Ellen took in her husband's harsh words and pulled further away from him. There is nowhere to escape to vent, nor is there a place to hide from another's temper out on the ocean. These issues intensify in limited living space, and aboard the *Volante*, a small emotional bomb waited to go off. They set anchor in Puerto Vallarta in the dark.

The next morning Isabel opened the hatch and took in the absolute green of the trees that covered every hill around the harbor and beyond. She had never seen so much vegetation before. And after the desert of Baja, this was about as much green as a person could see and still maintain their sanity. Where Baja had been a super hot, dry, heat, the mainland proved to be muggy and damp. The sweat sat on her brow and did nothing to cool her because it was too damp of a climate for the sweat to evaporate. Instead, the moisture clung around her like a sauna. *We're going to need a lot of popsicles here too*, she thought.

After breakfast they made their way to check in with the Captain of the Port and Immigration. The family walked down cobblestone streets to catch a bus into town. These were elaborate busses with wooden floorboards and bright red fringe curtains and an altar to the Virgin Mary on the dashboard. Not only were the busses decorated with elaborate jewel-toned fringe and small yarn pom-pom ball curtains, Bible verses and words of encouragement were written on the walls such as *'Do unto others as you would have others do unto you'* or *'Don't forget to smile'*.

Half way into town, a frail looking older man entered the bus dressed in a white guayabera and white linen pants. He asked the driver's permission to sing and sing he did. At the top of his lungs he belted out several traditional Mexican corridos in the voice of a raspy crow. Afterwards, he walked through the bus with his hand out to accept any coins the passengers wished to give him. As the family would find out after many trips into town, not all of the musicians were good, but even the bad ones proved entertaining.

The family disembarked from the bus downtown and walked to the open-air market where they bartered for fruits and vegetables from high-energy men and women in brightly colored clothes. The produce hung as colorful decorations in the stalls, enticing Ellen to buy them. Merchant after merchant proffered row after row of fresh fruits, half of which they had never seen before. Guayabas, huge plantains still on the stalk, papayas, pineapples, all at the peak of ripeness stood ready for inspection. Their fabulous array of jewel-tone colors and delicious smells of peaceful sweetness overtook their senses.

They marveled at the beautiful silver jewelry, and the colorful blankets that lay in great stacks in every stall. Women with gorgeous copper skin in bright dresses strolled past with buckets of live crabs balanced on their heads. Men leaned out of the stalls with everything from leather goods to large fish, trying to entice them to buy. So much color and beauty of design exploded their imaginations, and barraged their eyes with a Technicolor overload.

One woman seductively held up two cantaloupes for Joe to squeeze and he became a little short of breath, but Ellen intervened on his behalf and they did not buy any cantaloupes at all.

Piñatas in all kinds of colorful shapes and sizes hung over Isabel's head; huge stars and fish, cartoon characters, animals, tacos. She reached up to try to touch them in vain. Then somehow the big orange fish swam down from the eaves and ended up in her arms. She looked over to see a lovely older lady, the long rod with a nail in it still in her hand, smiling at her. Isabel persuaded her parents to buy her the bright orange fish piñata that would end up living at the foot of her bunk for a month before he was broken open.

***

At immigration an official greeted them and their bags of produce and large orange fish piñata with gracious hospitality, and proclaimed the family 'the first of the season', which accounted for the currently empty harbor in which the *Volante* anchored. He offered them coffee and pastries and gave them a brief history of the town.

He was delighted to hear that Joe and Ellen had been to Vallarta in 1969 when there had only been one motorcar, an old WWII army Jeep, that belonged to the only American in town at the time. He had the Jeep shipped to him in pieces which he assembled it in his front yard. Gasoline was brought to him in big, red, jugs that sloshes along on the top of the bus that traveled up and down the coast. The bus swayed and bumped so much on the unpaved roads that the jugs arrived half empty and the bus was turned into a gasoline soaked firetrap.

After such a nice meeting the family hated to leave, but the sun slipped ever lower in the sky. They bounced through the cobblestone streets on the crowded bus back to the *Volante*. Isabel stood holding a post in the bus. She had a great time bouncing into the air when the bus traveled over the larger bumps. Someone grabbed her by the waist and pulled her onto their lap as they went through a particularly sharp turn. Terrified, Isabel turned to see her captor; two teenage girls who ran their fingers through her hair and pressed their fingers into her skin.

Isabel said, "Hola."

They raised their eyebrows in surprise.

"¿Hablas español?"

"Sí, hablo español."

Isabel carried on a conversation with the girls until it was time to get off the bus.

After riding the busses for a while, Isabel became proud of the courtesy shown to each other by the people of her adopted country. Men gave up their seats for women, the young yielded to the old, and when it was too crowded to give up one's seat, babies and children were taken from their parents onto stranger's laps so the parents could hold onto the railings with both hands. Aside from the initial pushing and shoving to get on the bus, riding a bus in Mexico was the politest place Isabel had ever been.

Joe hoped to ignite memories of love in Ellen's favorite port of call. Puerto Vallarta was full of romance that oozed from the fruit on the trees and left blatant scents of love in the air. Green and blue parrots flew through azure skies, crossing a yellow sun and returned to their perches in green and orange date palms or coconut trees.

Ellen was not dissuaded from her change of heart right away. Instead of melting in the luscious jungle setting under the spell of languor that wafted to her with every breeze, Ellen bought metal and canvas to make a dodger to protect them from the waves they would meet on their way back up the coast to the United States.

Joe, however, persisted.

1969 in Puerto Vallarta

Joe and Ellen had first been to Puerto Vallarta in 1969 before they were married. They traveled as part of the Doctors Without Borders program. They drove to Mexico in a Volkswagen microbus full of medical equipment.

For seven days Joe had done all of the driving. At dusk on the eighth day he finally let Ellen relieve him behind the wheel when he was sure they were only an hour from their hotel.

In the fading sunlight, silhouettes of palm trees filled the landscape. Venus took up its dusk position next to the moon. Joe and Ellen held hands as they drove. Joe gazed with adoring eyes at Ellen the Beautiful. The up and down dips of the desert road's arroyos further lulled them into a sense of peace and calm. They were just two lovers on a romantic drive through the Mexican jungle.

Just as they crested yet another dip, something large blocked the road. With no time to react, the car collided with the massive object. ... *WHAM!*

The front of the microbus instantly shortened by four feet and left Joe and Ellen pinned inside.

They watched as the sleeping cow they struck got up and walked away.

The Angels of Mercy, who travel the lonely highways of Mexico in their blue trucks of mechanical redemption, cut them out with tin snips. The Angels arrived just in time, too, for a hurricane was brewing. As they pulled Joe from the wreckage, the sky opened up and soaked them in a torrential downpour. On the drive to the hospital the winds blew, and pieces of houses flew past.

Joe and Ellen were taken to the nearest hospital, which was three hours away in Puerto Vallarta. The winds pushed the large truck side to side. Palm trees bent at forty-five degree angles under the force of the wind. As the winds grew louder, the driver kept turning up the music so he could sing along with his corridos. Ellen and Joe thanked the Angels of Mercy again for saving them and hobbled inside the hospital.

The hospital swarmed with people. Some held towels to their heads, others held crying children, all while people in white coats and scrubs ran up and down the hallway.

Ellen and Joe checked in and sat in the waiting room for hours waiting for treatment while the hurricane wreaked havoc outside. People huddled under the eaves outside waiting to be seen.

Eight hours later a young woman in a white lab coat called Joe and Ellen into an exam room where they waited for yet another hour.

Ellen really had to pee, and asked for directions to the bathroom in her broken Spanish. In her sign language she grabbed her lower abdomen as a sign she had to pee. The nurse hurried Ellen away.

When Ellen did not return in a few minutes from her bathroom break, Joe became concerned. In trying to locate his wife, he asked a security guard where to find the women's bathroom. The guard did not understand Joe's pidgeon Spanish. Joe tried to show the guard what he meant by making the universal sign of a man urinating. The guard promptly escorted Joe out of the hospital for "vulgar behavior". The security guard kept his eye on Joe through the window, annoyed that he had to deal with a pervert on such busy night.

Joe slipped around the side of the building and snuck back inside through the cafeteria, holding his injured hand to his chest with his good hand.

Finally, Joe found Ellen.

"Where have you been?" he demanded.

"Trying to escape an emergency gynecological exam!" Ellen exclaimed.

"What?" he said, shocked.

"Where the hell have *you* been?" she demanded.

"Getting kicked out of here trying to find you," he retorted.

The looked at each other, and out of nowhere they started to laugh. Slow at first, then shaking with laughter, tears in their eyes.

"Apparently, our Spanish is not as good as we thought," Joe said as he wiped away a tear.

Finally, the harried, but kind, doctor found them. With the tenderest of touches he palpated Joe's hand and arm. He called a nurse to place a temporary splint. Joe needed his right thumb pinned; it had shattered upon impact with the cow. A nurse gave him a preoperative sedative right then and there, before either he or Ellen had a chance to say no.

When Joe was feeling good and drowsy they rolled him on a gurney to the stairs and asked him to walk down them to the operating room. He looked at the orderly, and then he looked at the stairs, pointing from himself to the stairs and then back to himself. He could barely stand. The sedative was working perfectly.

"You serious?" Joe slurred.

The orderly nodded his head. In his sedated state, Joe was confused and out of place. He could not make sense of why they would give him drugs on one floor and then do the surgery on another floor. He refused to go down the stairs. In angry tones he told the attendants he did not understand why he had to go down the stairs.

"I'm supposed to have surgery! Why are you making me leave?" he yelled at the orderly.

The attendants, obviously used to their patients becoming dysphoric, prodded him in gentle Spanish that it was OK to go down the stairs.

"Come on, amigo. It's OK. Surgery is good for you." The attendant smiled at Joe, trying to look kind, but Joe just saw rows of large white teeth in his face.

Joe felt dizzy and nauseous and he tried to sit down on the top step. He miscalculated the distance and missed. The orderly grabbed for Joe in vain. Joe somersaulted down the stairs with his broken hand and arm, crashing into the stairs and walls as he fell all the way to the first floor. The orderly ran after him. He checked Joe over for any new cuts and scrapes, picked him up and put him on a gurney and wheeled him into the surgical suite. Joe had made quicker work of getting down the stairs than most of the patients before him.

The surgeon worked with deft skill and speed. Within thirty minutes, Joe's thumb was prepped and pinned and put into a white plaster cast. He awoke with Ellen holding his good hand, slumped in a chair next to his bed, half asleep. She had not received any injuries other than major bruising down her whole front in the shape of the seat-belt.

It hurt for her to button her jeans. She wished she had her suitcase so she could put on her comfortable sheath dress. But there, in the misery of the hospital room, with the lights flickering on and off, unable to hear each other over the incredible roar of the hurricane raging outside, Joe and Ellen united in pain and love.

Modern Vallarta

Ellen rowed herself to the cruise ship dock. She tied up the dinghy and looked toward the *Volante* with a sneer. She knew she would be leaving her husband and daughter stranded for a while without the dinghy and the thought gave her immense satisfaction.

Ungrateful, unappreciative jerks, she thought.

She marched to the bus stop and joined the mob of humanity that shoved its way onto the already packed bus. The jolt and lurch of the bus across the uneven streets shook a little of Ellen's bad humor off of her bones. It was hard not to chuckle as she watched the red fringe windshield decor and altar sway back and forth as the bus careened down the cobblestone streets. Adrenaline can make even the most serious things funny. Besides, such things as pom-pom fringed bus shrines and cobblestone streets just did not happen in the United States. She rode the bus to the end of the line and then strolled, looking for an uncluttered place to think. She took the path less traveled and left the main street.

She strolled down to the Old Bridge, and walked next to the riverbank in the shade provided by old date palm, coconut and mango trees. Next to the river the air became heavy and even more humid, and the smell of raw sewage was masked by the polite smell of jungle fruits that hung heavy off the branches. The occasional squawk of a wild parrot and the swoosh of wings, the clanking of decrepit busses along the cobblestone streets and the sound of slow moving water as it wafted its way down the river to the sea soothed Ellen's tightened being. She exhaled.

There, lost in calming thought, wandering down a beautiful path amongst the green trees, she ran into a man who sold Huichol yarn paintings. He had twenty colorful depictions leaned up against the gray cement of the bridge's buttress. An assortment of beaded bowls and gourds flowed out of a large canvas bag onto a sarape for passersby to see. Vibrant greens, blues and reds, a pop of yellow, an explosion of orange met her eye. Images of deer, rabbits, peyote, cactus, and grass were pressed into the beeswax with yarn or beads to make gorgeous pieces of art. The yarn paintings each had the artist's rendition of a dream in color as the artwork, and on the back, usually written in pencil, was the story of the picture written out, and the artist's signature.

"You are an American, aren't you?" he asked. His broad grin and effusive handshake knocked the rest of Ellen's funk right out of her.

His name was Pedro and he was from New Jersey. In the early seventies he had traveled to the Sierras and become lost. Starving and delirious, he was taken in and cared for by the Huichol Indians, one of the last native tribe left intact after the conquest. When he made a full recovery in their care, he became a champion for the Huicholes out of gratitude and admiration for their culture. He was taken by how the spirit world governed their lives and their relationship with nature. They used native plant extracts to dye the yarn in their intricate embroidery work. They were an agricultural community that subsisted on corn, their main crop. But, they also harvested peyote, the cactus fruit known for its hallucinogenic effects. They used the peyote to gain their ritual visions that they transferred to their yarn paintings and gourds.

Ellen and Pedro struck up a conversation about the Huichol community's healthcare needs. They were low on medicine and technology in part because they were an isolated mountain community accessible only by burro or airplane. The Huicholes also seemed to be marginalized by the majority population in Mexico and treated as second-class citizens. In addition, no one seemed to take Pedro seriously when he asked for help, which may have been due to his long hair, cowboy boots and straw hat. Ellen, however, saw the cause and not the man. She offered assistance by way of making contacts for him in the medical community in the States.

Pedro was beside himself with gratitude. After selling Huichol art on the streets for years, Ellen was one of the few people to actually offer to help him in his quest. He spoke to her with enthusiasm about his mission to improve healthcare for the Huicholes and he listened in rapt attention as Ellen made suggestions of generic antibiotics, as well as more ways for Pedro to be able to raise more money for his cause. She promised to get in touch with the fundraising groups at her church and at the hospital. Ellen and Pedro spent the rest of the afternoon drawing up lists and plans.

Pedro listened to every word she said with rapt attention. He looked deep into her eyes as they talked and watched her hands as she wrote herself notes. He was amazed that they had found each other; two Americans miles away from their native country, one by land the other by sea, and yet Providence had brought them together in this mission to help the Huicholes. He gave her the address of the house he was staying at in Vallarta and invited Ellen and her family to lunch the next day. They shook hands and parted ways.

She returned to the *Volante* invigorated that she had met a person who saw her amazing abilities of goodness right away. She felt wonderful to be trusted. She laughed at everything and hugged her family.

The next day the family left for Pedro's house. This time, the family traveled by taxi. The only address was the name of the house. No street name, no number.

"A La Casa Azul, por favor."

The taxi bumped along the usual cobblestone streets until the edge of town. There the driver took a sharp left and headed inland. They came to a point where the taxi had to stop because ahead of them was a sort of cliff-face with houses inserted into it. The only way to get to the houses was on foot. Narrow, dirt paths lead from the main street below to the maze of beautiful houses above.

"Allí está La Casa Azul," the taxi driver said as he pointed upwards at a bright blue house.

Out of breath from their climb, the family walked through large iron gates, past a garden of hibiscus and coconut palms, their trunks covered in yellow honeysuckles, to an enormous whitewashed palace with large white tiles throughout. Pedro was house sitting for a friend.

Pedro's wife, Monica, was out by the pool caring for their two children and washing Huichol clothes by hand in vinegar and salt to make sure that the colors from the woolen embroidery thread would not run. Monica's English was not very good, and Joe and Ellen's Spanish was rather poor, but they managed to convey a sense of camaraderie to each other with a lot of smiles and hugs. The friendship between the families was immediate. Joe made his contribution by building shipping crates to send the Huichol artifacts to the States, and Isabel helped by babysitting Pedro's two young sons. She loved to make them laugh.

The family spent enough time with Pedro and Monica to see their younger child learn to walk, to learn one son was deaf, and to learn that Pedro's mother, who lived with them, was unhappy with Pedro's choice of wife.

Isabel watched Pedro's wife work without end for his cause, love his children with more love and tenderness than she had ever seen a mother care for her children. Monica would cook, clean, smile and nod without complaint. His mother criticized Monica's cooking, scolded her over her care of the children, and chided her for not putting the margarine in the refrigerator.

"What is the matter with that old lady?" Isabel asked her parents.

"Nothing that a good swift kick in the ass would not help," said Joe.

Isabel could not understand why the pale old woman, who sat in a chair and breathed rattling breaths, had such resentment for Pedro's wonderful and devoted wife.

Pedro's sister was also at the white palace to recover after plastic surgery. She sat by the side of the pool in a broad brimmed hat and large sunglasses and did not move. She gave Isabel a wan smile of acknowledgment, but she did not speak. She was a TV star in a major soap opera. The family might have cared more if they had a TV, but as they did not care, they left her alone to sit by the pool and walked past her like she was a nice piece of statuary.

Pedro's sister preferred being ignored; it freed her from the responsibilities and energy it took to be nice to family for extended periods of time as well as people she did not know. She did not speak because her face was chiseled with pain. Bandages and plasters covered every inch of facial skin. However, she helped her sister-in-law and played with her nephews in a quiet way. Monica relaxed in her presence.

The only time Pedro's sister left the house was to go to the airport to return to the States under cover of deep night. When she left, Isabel only noticed she was gone when she walked past the place she had sat by the pool and noticed something beautiful was missing.

During the time at the whitewashed palace, Ellen and Pedro put together an introduction to the Huichol culture and history, as well as examples of their art and sent them as a package to Ellen's church, asking if the church would participate in a fundraiser by way of a fashion show. The idea was to draw attention to the Huichol plight, as well as to educate people on the other half of the continent, hoping a few kind souls would make donations to help the Huicholes.

Ellen and Pedro waited in vain for a reply. They would not get a response until after the *Volante* was docked back at the Corinthian Yacht Club in Tiburon, California. That is fodder for another story.

Guadalajara

One day, Pedro approached Ellen.

"My father-in-law has throat cancer, and his voice box was removed. I bought him this little device to help him talk, but he does not know how to use it." He smiled a little sheepishly. "It did not come with any directions."

"Oh, yes, I used one of those at a demo back in the States." Ellen recalled.

"Well, I remember you telling me that," Pedro confessed, glancing down at his hands. "And I wondered if you might help show him how to use it?"

"Sure. I am not an expert, but I might be able to help."

"Great!" he exclaimed, then paused. "The thing is, though, he lives in Guadalajara."

"Perfect," she laughed. "Now we will see more of the country."

As the family traveled to Guadalajara, they witnessed the shift of the inland landscape. Sandy beaches gave way to mountains. Vital, green trees pooched out of the cement where they would not let themselves be confined by urban encroachment. All through the city trees flourished as thick, untamed, asymmetrical odes to nature. The trees pushed aside the urban crud of cement and rebar, and made piles of rubble out of sidewalks and foundations.

The house of Pedro's father-in-law was a large, adobe house with eight rooms. It was very dark inside, as if the walls had soaked up all the light from the one light bulb that hung, unprotected, in the center of every room. In the living room, the short, elderly man had lost all his wrinkles to the darkness, leaving behind only his enthusiastic personality. He ignored Joe and lavished his attention upon Ellen and Isabel.

As soon as Ellen showed him how to press the machine to his throat and make large mouthed words by making big movements with his lips and tongue, he talked to everyone.

Tears came to his eyes. He grabbed Ellen's hands.

"Gracias, gracias."

The old man turned to his wife and said, "Te amo, mi reina."

He turned to one son and told him how proud he was of him. He turned to another son and told him if he did not marry his girlfriend, he would disinherit him. The sons gave their father a huge hug. It was a great night. The father-in-law had a lot stored up that he wanted to say, that they had to replace the batteries twice in the little machine.

Isabel was surprised when she found herself alone in the living room with him that he was able to speak just fine in a whisper. In the darkness Isabel could not see his lips move and his whisper was so quiet that Isabel had the marvelous sensation that he was speaking to her via telepathy. She felt so special to be a part of the supernatural. She would not have been at all surprised if the old man had been able to fly or move tables with his mind. In fact, she expected it and watched him without rest for their entire stay, suspicious that he hid his other powers from her.

The next morning the elderly man took Ellen and Isabel to his shop where he sold Huichol articles. They entered the shop and he handed Isabel pieces of Huichol clothing. Isabel put on a tunic embroidered around the neck and hem with brown deer and green bushes. Next came a dress with a six inch high piece of embroidery around the bottom of lizards and bunnies and green balls of peyote on a red background. Then there was a red and white piece of fabric that one could wear as a shawl or pull back over one's hair like a giant scarf. There was a long, green, wool belt with pink flowers down its entire length that he wrapped several times around her waist and tied in a square knot in the front. And last, he put a large straw hat with acacia thorns hanging down from the brim and red fabric stretched across the top on her head.

The acacia thorns symbolized a pilgrimage to the ocean, and the peyote symbolized the Huicholes ritual use of peyote to have visions. These visions were then translated into artwork on clothes, the yarn paintings they had seen, beaded masks, gourds and jewelry. Ellen took many pictures of her daughter in full Huichol regalia and knew that the elderly man was thanking her for teaching him to use his voice maker.

The *Volante* family left Guadalajara without seeing any of the tourist sites. They drove away from the beautiful city set into the lush greenery of the mountains and returned to their seaside utopia of palm fronds and sand, certain for the first time they had done some good in the world.

The Return to Puerto Vallarta

Upon return to Puerto Vallarta, Ellen teemed with the vibrance that the confidence and knowledge of a good deed done brings to a person, but as they pulled into the harbor, something blocked their view. The *Pacific Princess* took up the entire cruise ship dock.

"Oh, my God! It's The Love Boat!" Isabel cried.

She turned to her parents. "Please, please, please, let's go aboard!" she begged.

Her parents exchanged looks, certain getting aboard the *Pacific Princess* was an impossibility. The Love Boat had been one of Isabel's favorite TV shows back in the the States and the *Pacific Princess* was the ship upon which the show was based. Isabel was sure that she would meet Vicky and Captain Stubing, a TV father and daughter to whom she could relate with her seafaring father and lifestyle.

Ellen was just as thrilled as her daughter to go aboard The Love Boat. They walked timidly up to the purser, the person responsible for the ship's administration, and asked if they might take a tour of the ship. As the man radioed up to the bridge to get permission to let them aboard, Ellen gave her daughter a quick speech about how "The Love Boat" was a TV show and that they were not going to see any movie stars. Isabel did not believe her.

Joe looked the ship up and down and saw no merit in her massive steel hull or her gigantic radio and radar display. Such immensity was a bourgeois waste to Joe's utilitarian disposition. He went along with this frivolity of touring The Love Boat only to please his wife and daughter.

The purser got the OK from the Captain. As he let the family aboard he smiled and said, "Make sure your hair is looking good ladies, we're filming today and we need extras."

"Yeah!" yelled Isabel.

Ellen and Isabel exchanged looks of pure delight. Joe rolled his eyes.

A member of the TV crew ushered the family into a set of deckchairs. Isabel sat in her deck chair and took in the pleasure of being a real live extra. She looked over at her mother and was pleased to see her mom as beautiful as any movie star, holding a club soda in one hand and soaking up the sun. Her father sat on the other side of her with a club soda in his hand, and after a few minutes of fidgeting and looking bored, he layed back and enjoyed the opportunity to be famous by taking a nap.

They were allowed to stroll the deck as part of their work as extras. Isabel marveled at how small the actual swimming pool was. It looked like a medium sized hot tub filled with cold water for people to step into if they got too hot. Joe explained to her that with the rolling and pitching the ship could do in heavy seas that a small pool was practical as it would prevent too much spillage. They walked past Vicki and Captain Stubing as they did a scene on the pool deck.

By the end of the day Ellen and Isabel felt they were firmly ensconced in the Hollywood world, and were old acting pros as they disembarked. They watched the *Pacific Princess* pull away from the dock at eight o'clock that evening into an amazing sunset of reds and yellows.

They were sad to think their TV careers had been so short, but they were content to have spent the day rubbing elbows with the rich and famous. One day they hoped to see themselves on a rerun.

Timeshares

When the *Volante* arrived in Puerto Vallarta there was only one timeshare condominium. The notion of a timeshare was novel. Joe and Ellen went to the sales pitch in the hopes that if they had a place for their family to stay that they would come and visit.

They wanted to show their families that they had achieved their dream, and they also wanted them to enjoy the paradise they had found. Maria, a nice woman who was originally from Guadalajara gave the sales pitch.

She seemed to sense that the *Volante* family was not like the usual tourists who came to her city and expected to drink and party all night long. They actually were interested in the culture, architecture, history and art.

She liked the family very much, and introduced the *Volante* family to her husband, daughter and son. Her husband, Luís, was originally from Boston and he was a timeshare salesman, too.

The brother and sister took Isabel into their home on the beach. There was a tall concrete wall that surrounded the property. The top of the whitewashed wall was covered in broken bottles and glass, a deterrent to burglars. The garden was filled with sand and driftwood that had been placed in an artistic manner. The upper floor of the house had three large rooms filled with sunlight and gorgeous nature oil paintings by the mother.

Maria and Ellen made a wonderful connection. They were able to discuss art; Ellen was an amateur pencil artist and the wife was an avid painter. She took Ellen to her painting teacher's studio. The teacher was enraptured by Ellen's tale of travel on a sailboat. The painter had never been outside his home state. When Ellen complimented him on a painting of Gringo Gulch in Puerto Vallarta and the gorgeous pink clouds he had put in the sky, he told her, "You must take this painting with you and let it travel as I will never be able to."

Ellen looked at the artist with her mouth open. "Thank you, that is very generous, but I could not accept such a gift," she finally managed to say.

The artist pulled out the painting, and without wrapping it up he gave it to her.

"No, thank *you*," he said.

As the two women left the artist's studio, Maria turned to Ellen. "He has been given three months to live," she said. "He has lung cancer."

Ellen stopped and looked back at the studio.

"You have made him very happy," Maria continued. "He has found a way to make a dream come true, and you are now a part of that dream of flight."

Ellen thought of her and Joe's dream of flight. *There are so many ways to be in the act of flight, Ellen thought to herself. So many ways people dream of letting go of the mundane.*

She smiled a sad smile to her self and hugged the painting to her chest.

While the mothers were seeing the artist's studio, the children were left to their own devices in the pool back at the timeshare complex. Isabel was happy to play with children her age. They swam in the pool at the condo complex and ate lunch in the palapa bar that leaned out halfway over the pool. They took their boogie boards to the beach right outside the gates to the complex and surfed. No adults chased after them. The kids were free to just enjoy being kids.

That evening, Isabel stayed over at their house on the beach and ate tart tamarinds and sweet rice pudding. The son, Little Luís, had a train set to play with and the daughter, little Maria, had a wonderful set of Barbie Dolls. Isabel felt she was in heaven. Furthermore, she was allowed to speak English because the salesmen wanted their children to be bilingual, so no one laughed at her mispronunciation.

Crossing the courtyard on the way back to the main house, Isabel stopped and pointed.

"What on earth is that?" she exclaimed.

There, in the middle of the courtyard was an animal that looked like a cross between and raccoon and a weasel staked out on a chain leash. He scampered out of the children's way.

"That's a coatimundi!" Little Luís told her, in a tone that clearly meant that only an idiot would not know such an animal. He watched Isabel take a few steps back.

"Don't worry, he is friendly," said Little Luís.

Isabel looked at the long pointy claws, the sharp teeth dripping with spit and the weird tuft of hair on the coatimundi's nose, and decided that no matter how friendly that animal might be, there was no way she was going to touch it. She kept walking.

"What's its name?" she asked, hoping to keep the focus off of herself and keep it on the coatimundi.

"Baby," said Little Luís, and tossed the coatimundi a whole mango, which the animal proceeded to tear to shreds in three seconds flat.

"Oh."

***

During this time, Mexico faced a massive devaluation of the peso. The peso went from twenty-five pesos to the dollar to a hundred pesos to the dollar over night. The following week the peso dove again to a hundred and fifty pesos to the dollar. Stores closed several times to re-price their merchandise. People's savings devalued by six hundred percent in just a matter of days. There was no devaluation insurance. The whole country took a major hit. In just a few short days the entire population plunged into poverty or heavy debt. Only landowners, holders of American dollars or gold, had anything left of true value. As seems to be the case in all such situations, the poor were left even poorer.

The exchange rate remained very unstable. Bank to bank the rates differed as they fought to buy the lion's share of dollars from tourists. A bank that offered a hundred and sixty pesos to the dollar in the morning offered a hundred and eighty pesos by afternoon. Private businesses set themselves up as money exchange places to be able to guarantee themselves the safer dollar and keep their doors open.

Lucky for the family, Joe and Ellen kept most of their money in traveler's checks and only cashed them as needed. However, as they sat and pored over their finances, Joe's leg throbbed, the familiar pain of a major infection. Joe cringed. He knew his health was about to cause a major devaluation of the family's bank account. The old frustration and weightiness of his reality fell on him like a ton of bricks.

He went to the local pharmacy and came home with all the antibiotics he usually took during these crises of infection, but the infection wouldn't clear up. The ulcer in his leg doubled in size every day. When it became the size of a saucer he made his travel plans. He anchored the *Volante* right in front of the Mexican navy base near Puerto Vallarta, and set an anchor from the bow and tied a line to a substantial looking tree trunk on the shore.

Joe had absolute confidence that the Armada would take good care of the *Volante*. He had seen the young men swim out to the *Volante* and use her as a swim dock when the family was ashore. He preferred to have a military force to back up his family. Joe told Luís he was leaving, and asked if Ellen could come to him if she needed anything.

"Sure, no problem," Luís said. His eyes lit up as he leaned into Joe a bit. "You mind exchanging a few dollars for me at the border?"

Joe, always ready to help out a friend said, "Sure, why not?"

Luís had found that one could buy pesos in Tijuana for two hundred and fifty pesos per dollar. The exchange rate in Vallarta averaged one-hundred and eighty. Joe agreed, wanting to help his new friend. Luís went into his bedroom and came out with a large white envelope.

Joe took Luís's money and headed to the *Volante* to pack. When he opened the envelope he found five thousand dollars in hundred-dollar bills. Joe held up the wad of cash and flipped through it.

Damn, thought Joe. *If I get caught with this much money on me they will put me in prison and throw away the key.* He shook his head. *Well, I promised a friend, so I have to do it.*

Ellen walked in on Joe admiring the stack of money. "Oh, my God, they are going to think you are a drug dealer and throw you in prison," she screeched. "What are you thinking?!"

Joe understood her fear; he had a hard enough time getting back into his own country with his olive complexion, bulging arm muscles, and scowl-enhancing mustache. Plus, he oozed a loathing of authority that policemen could sense a mile away, and made them come sniffing after him.

"Honey, it is going to be fine," he said, slipping an arm around her waist.

"Right," she said, defiantly, pushing his arm away from her.

"Fine," she said. Any married man knows that form of 'fine' means big trouble in the matrimonial bliss department.

Joe got a haircut, trimmed his mustache and bought a button down shirt, the first he had even owned. He stuffed as much money as he could into his phony leg and the rest he crammed into ten money belts he strapped at tightly to his body as possible. He did not sleep the entire twenty-four hour trip to the border.

He brought a thick sweater to wear over the top of all the concealed money bags. He looked himself over in the restroom mirror at the Tijuana bus station, and took a deep breath. He walked with as calm a gait as possible towards the border crossing. He held up his passport and tourist card and flashed it to the guards.

They waved him across.

Joe worked hard not to look surprised, took a deep breath and got into a cab, the sweat pouring off his brow.

***

Joe's doctor took one look at his leg and hospitalized him on the spot. He had a culture taken of his leg that grew four different kinds of bacteria. Each bacterium required a different antibiotic. He ordered up massive quantities of cefazolin, penicillin, ciprofloxacin and clindamycin to be pumped into Joe for the next five days. The doctor told him that if he had waited another seventy-two hours for treatment, he would have amputated the leg.

"You need to be careful in the tropics, Joe," his doctor warned."All that warmth and humidity are great for bacteria."

"Yeah, I can see that," said Joe who looked mournfully down at his leg. The swelling was so bad that when he pressed his thumb into his own flesh it disappeared. When he pulled his thumb out it left a dent that took about ten minutes to fill back up.

The nurse wrapped Joe's leg in a gooey bandage that was supposed to suck all the exudates from the infected ulcer. Instead, the bandage could not keep up with all the discharge and became a dripping cesspool of bacteria and pus. They had to attach a suction pump to a drain in his leg and pull off the exudate mechanically.

When the infection cleared, they harvested skin off his left butt cheek and used it to cover the hole in his leg. At this rate, if Joe needed another skin graft, there was only one other spot on his body to harvest his own skin; his right armpit. With each set back Joe cringed. He hated the hospital and did not want to be there any longer than necessary. He had spent enough of his days there. Finally, after two weeks, he found himself discharged with four large bottles of antibiotics to protect the skin graft, a huge bottle of pain pills and a duffle bag full of bandaging materials to take with him back to Mexico.

Freedom.

While Joe Was in the States

Isabel had the stomach flu.

Waves of nausea rolled over her ad infinitum, and her muscles ached from the exertions of vomiting. Ellen sat by Isabel's side like an angel, soothing and comforting her, reading her stories and wiping her face with a cool washcloth.

By the second day Isabel felt better and could stand. She walked from her bunk to the galley, a distance of no more than five feet, and it exhausted her.

Out of nowhere there came a terrible grinding sound. The *Volante* gave a lurch and Isabel fell down.

Ellen bounded out of her bunk, right past Isabel and up onto the deck. The *Volante* lurched again.

Isabel followed her mother above decks. Isabel saw her mother looking up in horror at a thousand foot long cruise ship that was at a right angle to the *Volante* and no more than twenty feet from the *Volante's* bow.

The ship had torn loose from the cruise ship dock. The captain of the ship was trying to push his way back to the dock by using his thrusters. Every time the thrusters engaged, the water in the harbor became a dangerous vat of turbulent water that pushed and and flung the boats about as if they were little toy tops.

The entire harbor roiled in turmoil. In the past three days at least forty-five boats had arrived to spend the hurricane season holed up in Puerto Vallarta. They all anchored close together in the cramped anchorage area.

As the ship used its thrusters, tons of water gushed towards the innocent cruising vessels. Their anchors uprooted in the violent thrust of water, and the boats swung like spinning tops into each other. Some boats were pushed over sideways and their rigging became entangled in their neighbor's rigging.

Everyone scrambled to put out their fenders to cushion the collisions. The calm waters turned into a hellish mixture of mud and angry waves. The boats lay trapped between the beach behind them and the huge cruise ship looming upon them.

Ellen and Isabel looked up and saw the captain of the ship looking down at them; a terrible took of distress upon his face. The wind pushed the ship ever closer. Isabel and Ellen couldn't even get into their dinghy to get to the beach just forty feet behind them because the waters were too rough and the boats tossed into each other with crashes and clamors; without a doubt they would be crushed.

Men from the Armada base came out to watch the impending tragedy. There was nothing they could do without putting themselves in definite danger. One cadet walked over and tightened the *Volante's* stern line from shore. Having this stern line running to the shore is the only thing that kept the *Volante* from spinning around like all of the other boats.

Ellen thanked God Joe had thought of it before he left. In the midst of the flailing vessels the *Volante* sat relatively unperturbed, suffering only minor jolts and shudders. Still, she remained in the cockpit ready to kick on the engine.

The cruise ship crept closer, stalking the cruising vessels, wearing them out in a battle of nerves. Isabel could see into the cabins whose portholes were at her eye height. Belongings lay strewn across one bunk. Another was made up neatly enough to pass a naval inspection.

Isabel thought the *Volante's* bow would go straight into the messy bunk. She envisioned the shattering glass. Then she heard a metallic 'thunk' to her left. The cruise ship bumped into the *Yelapa Princess*, a large, rusting, steel tour boat that was anchored right next to the *Volante*. The *Yelapa*

Princess was hard aground, and the pressure of the cruise ship had no bearing upon her.

The *Yelapa Princess'* steel bow prevented the cruise ship's further advances upon the *Volante*. Finally the cruise ship lowered down lifeboats filled with bow and stern lines and took the ropes to the opposite shore, about six hundred feet away. The ropes were secured to gigantic cleats on the cruise ship dock and the ship winched herself away from the cruisers without causing further chaos.

As the ship pulled away, a collective cheer rang through the harbor. People hugged each other and broke open bottles of alcohol saved for special occasions. The cruisers began the ritual clean up after a disaster.

The yachtie community came together to untangle the rigging of the boats that had been stuck together. Spare rigging and tackle were given to them for free. Cruisers with diving equipment retrieved lost anchors and chains in return for beer. Putty patches were placed and ribs made to strengthen breaks in hulls.

By the end of the afternoon a feeling of intense camaraderie and festival had overtaken the harbor. The rigging welder's sparks were heralded as a testament to the collective cruiser courage and strength under fire. Three days later, the cruisers held a collective picnic on the beach in front of the Armada to celebrate their group survival with the soldiers.

"You know," Ellen said to Isabel, "I always thought the *Yelapa Princess* was kind of an eyesore. Now I think she is the prettiest boat around."

Isabel nodded in agreement.

Joe Returns

Joe returned to Puerto Vallarta by plane where he did his best to look like just another tourist looking for a season of fun and sun. Complete with Hawaiian shirt, tourist guidebook, and huge aviator sunglasses. The immigration officials waved him through and never searched his bag.

He went straight to his new friend's real estate office to deliver the money. That's when Luís offered Joe a deal; to run money back and forth between Vallarta and Tijuana. Luís had set up a money exchange place in his real state office and had ready access to tourist's American dollars.

As a man in the timeshare business, Luís saw a lot of Americans, and would exchange the tourist's money for a better rate than the banks in town, but not as good as the rates in Tijuana. He wanted someone to go and make the exchanges in Tijuana so he could stay in Vallarta and rake in even more dollars.

Luís offered Joe thirty percent plus expenses. Joe accepted the offer without consulting his wife. Running the exchange rate racket was a good, legal deal. He knew Ellen would be happy for the extra income. He returned to the *Volante* full of good cheer and a bag full of presents.

Ellen looked at the bag of gifts with a sneer. After all, they were on a budget. Joe smiled and explained the money-exchange plan. He was excited to have a lucrative and legal means to care for his family.

"Fuck, no, Joe," she said with a ferocity that frightened him.

He realized that his honest wife was much more interested in truth than legality.

"I am afraid, Joe," she yelled. "If some bandido gets wind of all that money under your shirt you are a dead man! Isabel and I will be stuck here by ourselves! I can't get the boat home by myself!"

Joe stared at his wife.

"And another thing, Joe," she continued in that condescending tone caused by frustration and disregard, "all you do is spend that precious money on crap! Crap!" she yelled flinging her hand across in front of her indicating the little Barbie dress Joe had bought for Isabel. Isabel, who had the Barbie dress in question half on her doll, hid the doll behind her and looked from her mother to her father not sure if she was in trouble.

Joe knew, as Ellen further lectured him on fiscal responsibility, that she would not accept the deal he had made with the real estate salesman. Joe took a deep breath and sighed.

"Look, Ellen, I know you are not happy about it, but I have to go back to the States next week for more procedures. We need the money. We really, really need this money," Joe said, raising his hand to put it on her shoulder. Ellen shrugged his hand off her shoulder before he even had a chance to place it on her.

"Damn it all to hell, Joe!" Ellen swore.

While it was true that there was no law against exchanging money in Tijuana, it was not the legality of the situation that bothered Ellen. Ellen did not like the idea of her husband trafficking in money. It was Joe's dark complexion, his seventies mafia mustache and terrible temper that kept her on edge. Even back home she was used to the traffic stops and the lingering looks from policemen as Joe walked down the street. There had always been something about Joe that was far too interesting for law enforcement.

"Damn it, Joe," she yelled. "If the police don't arrest you just for being you, then some thug is going to kill you for that damn money!"

Joe shook his head, weary from arguing.

"I need to think," he said.

"There is nothing to think about, Joe. Fucking nothing."

Ellen spat her words at him as he climbed into the dinghy and rowed to shore.

***

Joe came home at nine o'clock that night.

"I am doing it, Ellen."

"I cannot believe you would degrade yourself and our family in this way. I can't fucking believe it!"

Joe looked at her, incredulous.

"What are you talking about, Ellen? It is legal! I am breaking no laws. I am able to give us an opportunity to continue our dream to travel the world. We have barely even scratched the surface here in Mexico. There is still so much more to discover."

Ellen shot him the death glare.

They did not speak that night.

The next morning, Joe left for the border again. When he returned three weeks later Ellen did not speak to him, but he did not care. He knew he was doing something good for his family. He took Isabel for ice cream and to the swimming pool. He popped more of his pain relievers into his mouth and waited for the worry to dissolve.

In total, Joe made eight trips to Tijuana. If the government had not stepped in and made exchange rates uniform, Joe was sure that he could have made enough money to pay for Isabel's college education. But with each trip, despite the influx to their savings account, Ellen became more sure that she needed to return home.

The Britannia

Ellen longed for intellectual stimulation. There had been far too many nights of drinking and debauchery for her. Mexico, as a country full of history, dance, art and music, had only revealed itself to her in brief intervals. She had a glimpse of the baile folklórico, a traditional Mexican dance, as the family passed by the open doors of a dance school. She had seen a gorgeous mariachi walking his dancing horse to cool him off after a show, but a full-blown display of Mexico she had not seen.

Aside from the Huicholes, the beach towns the family encountered were small and seemed to lack anything other than the day-to-day necessities for existence. Beer was the main culture she saw; beer, popsicles and tacos. This is not to say that she was disappointed in what she had seen. To the contrary, she was impressed. But the tiny tastes of culture she did see were so fabulous as to make her starve for more. She wanted a moment of luxuriant culture and she yearned for such an experience to come to her.

Then, one morning, as she looked out the porthole while washing the breakfast dishes, she saw the English Royal Yacht *Britannia* drop anchor just outside the harbor. It would be difficult to get any deeper into a culture than seeing what Puerto Vallarta would pull out for the Queen of England.

The celebration for the Queen was to start with a magnificent concert at the nicest hotel in town. Placed airily above the sea, the hotel's opulence was seen in its hardwood stairs and delicate engravings in gold and silver in the walls. Huge panes of glass peered like many gaping eyes towards the horizon, while in the background a velvet green curtain of palm fronds and flowered vines hung in lazy repose. When Ellen found out that there would be a free dress rehearsal the night before the Queen's performance, Ellen made sure she, Joe and Isabel attended.

En route to the small concert hall in the hotel, the family strolled through the lush courtyard garden thick with tropical flowers in brilliant colors and all shapes and sizes whose syrupy floral aromas wafted to them one after the other.

They sat on large sofas made from dark wood in the distinct nineteenth century Spanish style and nibbled on canapés of ceviche and smoked oysters. Beautiful rainbow platters of fresh fruit and massive jungle centerpieces made from palm fronds and banana leaves covered in hibiscus and bougainvillea blossoms filled the tables that lined the hall.

The free concert was the dress rehearsal for the royal performance that was to be given the following day. While they listened to the heroic tunes of a new Mexican composer, the red carpet rolled out for the arrivals of the President of Mexico and the Queen of England. Isabel felt amazing just to think that she was in the very same hotel where royalty would be the next day. She could not sleep that night for all of the visions of princesses and knights in shining armor that ran through her head.

Early the next morning Isabel's parents woke her, put her in her only dress and brushed her hair. Joe even put on slacks and his button down shirt while Ellen put on a nice blouse and skirt and put her hair up in a French twist. Joe rowed them out of the harbor and there she was, the *Britannia*, an amazing navy blue ship with brass polished so bright it looked like gold.

Joe rowed within a respectful distance; he did not want to make any of the Queen's guards nervous. The crew was busy on deck preparing the Queen's launch for departure, polishing this and tightening that.

The Queen made her appearance on deck and walked with a regal air to her launch without a touch of haughtiness. She was so secure in her own composure she seemed to move as a solid piece of the ship. There were only two men with her—her husband and the pilot of the launch. Isabel thought she was so brave to be traveling without bodyguards, just like a private citizen.

The Queen spotted the family as the launch left for shore and she gave them the royal wave. They did not have to share the wave with another soul. They were the only people out in the large bay watching her depart her ship.

"I saw the Queen of England!" cried Isabel happily.

The Queen made her way to the cruise ship dock where she disembarked to mariachi music played by a band of thirty men in bright blue caballero suits and gigantic straw hats with hat bands embroidered in shiny, navy-blue thread. Ten white dancing horses moved to the music for the Queen's pleasure. Beautiful girls with colorful flowers woven into their hair escorted the Queen to her car. Isabel watched until she could not see the car any longer.

"Wow, a real queen!" Isabel shook with delight.

The Queen must have returned to the *Britannia* late at night, for although the family kept a diligent eye pointed in the blue ship's direction, they never saw her again. Nor did they see her leave her ship again, but they knew she must have, because for the first time the family bought the local newspaper just to be able to keep up with her activities. They knew she bought silver jewelry as souvenirs from a local artisan who made one of a kind pieces, and that she had met with the President of Mexico for a day and discussed politics and art. They read that she had seen a special exhibition of baile folklórico where professional troupes had combined to put on a show of one hundred people to showcase the dances indigenous to the state of Jalisco, and that she had been particularly impressed by a group of young men who made their horses dance in her honor.

In honor of Queen Elizabeth's departure, the Armada turned out in its entire splendor to send the *Britannia* on her way. They brought in the tallest war ship Isabel had ever seen and tied it up to the cruise ship dock. There were scores of young navy men in their dress uniforms with their hair slicked back. They looked handsome as they saluted their president and the Queen. An even bigger mariachi band, this time dressed in jet black suits with silver buttons that ran up the pant legs and jacket sleeves, played several songs for her, and a man played traditional corridos in a voice that reached for the soul. They were a far cry from the hoarse crows on the bus.

Three men who had performed on their dancing horses showed up unannounced on their gleaming white horses and did an impromptu routine to the music. The baile folklórico spun and swirled its way across the dock in a general flurry of bright colored ribbons and told stories of love thrown away and recaptured that, somehow, was even more amazing than their first performance.

Then the Queen was off in her royal blue yacht, headed for an unknown destination.

****

The Mexican Armada ship remained tied to the cruise ship dock overnight. That night a lightning storm erupted. The rain came down in torrents and all of the cruisers ran to attach jumper cables to their shrouds—the rigging that holds the mast up on either side—and let the ends of the jumper cables hang in the water. This funny act helped to prevent electrical fires and the sizzling of electronics aboard the cruising vessels by grounding the boat if a bolt of lightning was to hit the mast. Otherwise, the electricity from the lightning traveled down the radio wires and into the boat where it melted wiring and destroyed boats with electrical fires.

The drawback was that the lightning's energy could also travel from the water up the jumper cables. Joe experienced this first hand when he reached over to turn the VHF radio off and was shocked hard enough by a bolt of lightning that had struck the water next to the *Volante* that he was thrown backwards. When he recovered his breath he had a good laugh when he looked in the mirror and saw that his curly hair had straightened.

Isabel watched the navy ship through the porthole. The ship was as tall as a five-story building. Being the biggest metal object in the harbor, the lightning strikes aimed straight for the navy ship. The lightning would hit the top of the ship and the electricity would travel down the side of the ship like a swarm of gigantic white and blue static spiders until it hit the water.

Joe wondered what the ship's electronic equipment must look like after such a storm. Isabel just hoped that all of the soldiers wore rubber-soled shoes so they would not be electrocuted every time the lightning struck.

Ellen listened to the rampage of the weather and marveled at how much she enjoyed the unbridled emotions of Mexico. The people were warm, and showed affection for one another at every occasion. She relished the huge 'BANG' and 'BOOM' as the thunder rumbled and lightning cracked over the harbor in an unleashed, unchoreographed outpouring of primordial emotion. Mexico had finally revealed itself to Ellen in all its splendor.

May Fiesta

The beginning of the rainy season marked the end of the tourist season. As the last full flight of tourists left Puerto Vallarta, the local inhabitants geared up for a fiesta, the likes of which can only be compared with a celebration when a population has rid itself of a major parasitic infestation.

The plaza filled with vendors. Artists awoke at dusk and set up portraiture stands along the sea wall. They exhaled in relief as they were finally able to paint the amazing seascape of Bahía Banderas without tourists blocking their view.

Mexican delicacies of mango with chili powder, birria, and mole filled the air with their lofty aromas. Couples walked hand in hand, pressed into each other. Children flocked to the men and women who sold colorful plastic toys that hung from long wooden sticks they carried over their shoulders. The elderly took up position on the numerous benches in the plaza and along the malecón, the stone embankment along the waterfront, to watch the younger inhabitants walk through the glory of a warm tropical evening at sunset.

The bandstand filled with musicians in the plaza. Across the street on the beach a stage filled with local singers, comedians and children's dancing schools. Children played games of lotería. The children not playing Mexican bingo all seemed to have fistfuls of sparklers.

The population, who walked with sparklers in hand to light their way through the darkening evening, lit up the streets. The adults, dressed in all their finery, danced by the hundreds in the plaza. Great masses of humanity swirled and twirled their way in the romance of the warm evening. Men's cologne and women's perfume mingled into one scent of ardor. There was not an unhappy face to be seen.

Isabel noted with pleasure that they were the only non-Mexican people in the plaza, and the way people ignored her she felt she must truly blend in with everyone. Oh, to belong!

In the middle of the malecón there was a large pole perhaps thirty feet high. Attached to the pole at all sorts of angles hung bundles of fireworks which increased in size as they went up the pole. A few pinwheels hung off the sides and something resembling rockets jutted out in all directions.

Joe took one look at the pyrotechnic pole and knew he had to see it set ablaze. As soon as the sun went down he made sure they were always in sight of the display. But the pole was never lit. Finally, in asking a passerby, he was told that the pole would not be lit until the last day of the fiesta, which would be in a week. Sure enough, every day for seven days, the people of Vallarta gathered and mingled every night until Sunday.

Finally, on Sunday night, the malecón and all the balconies around the pole filled with people packed close to each other. A man, dressed unceremoniously in a t-shirt and cotton pants, struck a match and lit the long fuse that ran to the first bundle of fireworks.

At first, there was only the quiet sizzle of the fuse. But then there was a little 'pop' and the first bundle of fireworks went off. A few bottle rockets soared through the air with a high-pitched scream. Then another bundle caught fire and a full-fledged red firework shot straight up into the air and exploded into a gigantic spray of red sparks high over the crowd and a massive cheer was let out.

Faster, the bundles began catching fire. Faster, the explosions came and pinwheels began to spin and throw sparks into the crowd.

Fantastic bursts of red, yellow and green consumed the sky. And as the fuse sped up to the very top of the pole there was a brief moment of delay. The crowd went silent.

BAM!

The huge bundle on top exploded and fireworks hurled into the air, bottle rockets careened into the crowd, pinwheels flew off the top of the pole and the sky turned into a fireworks filled oblivion of explosions, color and smoke.

Fiesta week was officially over.

La Cruz

Just before the May Fiesta, the harbor in Puerto Vallarta had also become overcrowded because it was now hurricane season. Puerto Vallarta was a decent hurricane hole, although not as good as Puerto Escondido. Therefore, in the summer months Puerto Vallarta would fill to the brim with boats in all shapes and sizes seeking refuge from impending high seas and even higher winds.

The harbor became cramped and the people became cranky. Tensions grew. They burst one night when a couple chatted as they rowed past a drunken man's powerboat. He pulled out a flare gun and shot it at the happy pair because he thought they were being too loud. Joe watched from the far side of the harbor as the flare hit the side of the rowboat. He decided they had to leave Puerto Vallarta.

A few miles to the North of Puerto Vallarta was the town of La Cruz de Huanacaxtle. La Cruz was also a hurricane safe spot as it was still in the Banderas Bay.

The family fled from the frenetic life in Vallarta to enjoy the sleepiness of a small fishing village. There was one school and two restaurants. Those who did not work at the school or the restaurants, fished.

The family liked La Cruz for its cozy ambiance. In the tiny harbor the *Volante* was the only foreign vessel amongst thirty pongas.

Their second day in La Cruz the family had lunch at the restaurant that was one block up from the beach. It was ran by a family of eight. One of the waitresses was only about three years older than Isabel. Her name was Luisa and she became Isabel's friend as soon as they smiled at each other. Luisa and Isabel went all over the town together, watched TV, and played with Luisa's group of friends.

She took Isabel to the sewing store to buy a cloth tortilla holder for her to embroider. Isabel found out later that Luisa's brother, Jorge, had actually bought the tortilla holder for her. Isabel had no idea at the age of nine, that when a boy of twelve buys a girl a tortilla holder to embroider it was a sign that he liked her.

When the sun went down the whole family went out in Luisa's family's fishing skiff to catch barracuda, which were good for eating. Joe and Ellen were wary of their little daughter trying to catch a fish that was known to be of a man-eating variety, but quickly gave up their reservations when they saw the entire town show up at sunset, babies too, to catch these fish with their mouths full of razor sharp teeth.

The single women of the village who were of marriageable age grouped themselves into several boats,dressed in party dresses, high heels and full make up for the occasion. Isabel could not take her eyes off of one such woman who stood at the bow of her boat in red stilettos and a red cotton dress with spaghetti straps. She wore large, gold earrings in the shape of the sun. They glinted as the young men turned their flashlights on her.

She seemed to not notice them. She merely jiggled the fishing line she had dropped in the water and would wind or unwind the fishing line from around the small Clorox bottle that served as the most common fishing reel in Mexico.

When she caught a barracuda she yanked it out of the water in one large pull and it landed on the deck of the boat and immediately began to gasp for air.

Isabel fully expected for the young woman to rip off a stiletto and use it to put the fish out of its misery, but as soon as the young men heard the splash of water as the barracuda was yanked to certain death, they rowed as fast as they could to be the first to put the fish out of its misery for the dark haired beauty in the red dress.

Beauty In A Red Dress thanked the young man who assisted her, then turned her back on him as she dropped her line into the water again. The young man and his crew pulled away with sad strokes of their oars. They knew better than to try to make conversation, but hoped that their moment of help would give them an opportunity to speak to her when they were back on land.

After a couple of hours of fishing everyone retired to the beach where a fire blazed. The men took the fish and cleaned them, saving the guts for the next day to help attract more fish. The older people of the village wandered down to the beach with blankets and tortillas. Everyone took turns skewering the fish on sticks and turning them over the flames. Potato pieces and butter were wrapped in foil and placed on the coals and within fifteen minutes the crowd had mouthwatering spuds to go with their fish.

The small beach was covered in blankets of all shapes and sizes. Upon them babies slept, the elderly dozed, and the married couples held hands and looked at the stars. A little further down the beach the younger people flirted and joked and boys played a lazy game of soccer.

The young man who had come to the aid of the Beauty in a Red Dress approached her. He felt emboldened by his full stomach and the cover of darkness.

"Would you like to go for a walk?" he asked her. He could feel his face get hot and was glad she could not see it.

However, when she said, "Yes," she raised her hand to push the hair out of his eyes and the tips of her fingers grazed his forehead. He knew she could feel the electricity that flooded him at her touch. She revealed nothing and took the hand he offered.

They walked back and forth on the short beach in full view of the village's entire population. At eleven o'clock, the blankets were folded and the fire put out. The new couple was the last to leave the beach. They were pulled apart by their mothers as they reached the street. They walked arm and arm with their respective mothers all the way home.

***

One day Luisa took Isabel to school with her. The school was comprised of three small concrete buildings spread around a dirt yard. The inside of the rooms looked like typical schoolrooms; neat lines of desks faced a blackboard and the teacher's desk. There were two trees in the yard and a picnic table stood under each tree.

The children lined up to gain entrance to the schoolroom and there was some sort of routine of touching the shoulder of the person in front of you and marching in line that Isabel did not know. She knew she was in for it.

Isabel had a difficult time keeping up with the class. They were learning the parts of the brain in Spanish that she didn't even know in English yet.

Next was the math section. Isabel had always been terrible in math, but sighed in relief when fractions was the subject for the day. Those she understood really well.

She was asked to do a reading out of a history book. Isabel thanked God Spanish was phonetic, because the only thing she had ever read in Spanish were comic books. However, upon trying to pronounce the word *cajón* —which is Spanish for 'drawer'—she slipped and pronounced it *cojone* which is the word for testicle. Her classmates burst out in laughter and Isabel's face turned red for half an hour. She sat down in her seat and stared at the cover of her journal. She did not dare look up.

Recess was particularly interesting because Isabel had to learn all of the Mexican games that girls played. There was the traditional hopscotch and jump rope, with which Isabel was familiar, but the rules to these games were not international and Isabel was called out for many a mistake she did not know she had made.

It was also at recess that Isabel figured out that Luisa's brother, Jorge, liked her. Every recess he would find their group and sit with his friends and watch the girl group play. After a week, he asked Isabel to the movies. She realized that Jorge was asking her on a date and at nine years old, Isabel was unprepared for dating.

As luck would have it Luisa stepped in and said she would be the chaperone. A chaperone was a great invention if one was unprepared for the dating scene. All Isabel worried about was to get her parent's permission to go to the movies. Isabel did not mention Luisa's brother. Thrilled that their daughter blended into the native life so well, Isabel's parents gave her money and their permission to go to the movies.

At the appointed time on the appointed day, Luisa came to the *Volante* in her family's dinghy and picked up Isabel. As they rowed ashore they giggled and laughed about the boys in school. They walked up the hill to the movie theatre arm in arm. They started to pass by a tiny traveling carnival, comprised of one teacup ride and the man who operated them. No one else was around. The solitude of the man and the amusement park ride astonished Isabel. She asked her friend if they could go for a spin and Luisa agreed. For three minutes they spun in fast, little circles and laughed until their faces hurt. Dizzy, they stumbled their way towards the movie theatre like two drunks on a bus.

Isabel bought them popcorn and Luisa told her they had to buy a box of hard candies that were wrapped in pieces of white paper. Luisa found them seats, and Isabel saw Luisa's brother there, but he sat in the row ahead of them.

The movie started and the mayhem began. Isabel soon learned that the popcorn was not for eating. It was used to pepper the crowd, especially people one liked. Notes were written on the candy wrapper and used to pelt boys they thought were cute.

As the lights came up for intermission it was obvious that there were no adults in the entire theater. The whole experience was unlike the movies of her home country where adults flicked the back of a child's head if she so much as fidgeted in her seat. Isabel filled with the euphoria at the bedlam they were allowed to cause. She scribbled and chucked notes with abandon. She had no idea what movie was being shown.

Luisa and Isabel got up to stretch and it was only then they made contact with Luisa's brother. He took the two girls to the concession stand and bought them both more soda and popcorn. Then they watched the second movie with equal popcorn flinging gusto and Luisa took Isabel home. Dating was much less stress, and much more fun than Isabel had suspected and she decided she liked this dating thing.

It was not meant to be, however. Isabel got dumped the next day. They were at school and one of the girls asked Isabel her birth date so she could look it up in the fashion magazine horoscope and see if she was compatible with Luisa's brother. It was then they realized Isabel was only nine years old.

Although the other students were impressed that she kept up with them in classes, and they did not shun her as a friend, Luisa's brother did not ask Isabel to any more movies.

Isabel did not care and continued to go to the movies with Luisa any way. Isabel decided that breaking up with someone was not really that hard to do.

The Wildlife Restaurant

The second restaurant in La Cruz would never be allowed in the U.S. because of health code laws. The laws would not be broken because of rotting food or cockroaches; they would be broken because there were animals running loose all over the restaurant.

A large, green parrot hopped from table to table stealing tortillas. A dog, tall enough to reach his nose directly into one's plate, ambled about and the patrons soon learned to hunch over their food to protect it. The cat swatted at one's heels until one dropped a piece of fish. There was a raccoon and an armadillo, as well as a ferocious coatimundi, which roamed the restaurant's floor.

The coatimundi snuffled along the floor and looked for scraps like everything else in the menagerie. He had an easier time of it than the other animals, however, because customers saw him coming and threw food to him to keep him and his razor sharp claws at bay.

The restaurant served a variety of odd meats such as ostrich, goat, and snake, all of which were raised in pens in the backyard of the restaurant. Isabel thought that the owner of such a restaurant must have been an old safari hunter and that he tried to keep his images of wild adventures alive by watching the patrons writhe in fear at the sight of wild animals trying to steal the food they had just bought.

Another exciting part of La Cruz was that the power supply to the town was from a generator. The electricity shut off at ten o'clock as it did in most generator dependent communities in Mexico. The proprietors of the restaurants knew this and kept Coleman lanterns on hand to prevent total blackouts.

The owner of the local palapa bar, however, never turned his lamps on until five minutes after the lights went out. Scorpions and tarantulas would drop from the thatched ceiling and his son would paralyze them in a flashlight beam. He would then pick them up and place them in a jar full of alcohol de caña to kill them; pest control at its finest.

Every night, a few moments before the lights went out, everyone in the bar would pick up his drink and go outside. The patrons would continue their conversations and eat until the owner lit the Coleman lanterns and the owner's son came outside with his gruesome jar full of nocturnal beasts held up for all to see. The patrons would yell, " ¡Bravo!"

and go back into the bar to finish their fare. No one told the new gringo about the nightly ritual.

Joe, unaware that spiders and scorpions would hurl themselves out of the palapa's rafters, stayed put when the regulars filed outside. He sat at the bar sipping his Dos Equis in the dark. He was sure that at any minute the old Coleman lanterns would be lit. He felt the soft plop of something landing on his right shoulder. As he turned to look he felt another plop on the top of his head. The sensation of many delicate legs moving through his hair made him stand up. His beer crashed to the floor.

With a slow, deliberate movement, Joe reached to the top of his head and felt the large, fury rump of a tarantula still there.

"Holy shit!" he yelled, as he frantically swatted his head.

A jolly shout of raucous laughter erupted outside from the regulars. Joe took no notice.

In the meantime, the scorpion on his shoulder decided to seek out higher ground and started the climb up his neck. With the first tickle of critter-feet across his skin, Joe flipped his right hand to his neck while his left hand swatted at the top of his head in mad, slashing motions. To the amusement of the patrons when they returned to the bar, they found Joe in the middle of the bar doing the heebie-jeebies dance in a puddle of beer and crushed glass.

The bar owner laughed at Joe's plight. Joe had flung the tarantula and the scorpion and they ran for cover back in the thatch. The bar owner approached a jittery Joe with a new Dos Equis. He pushed Joe towards a bar stool, and was the first to give Joe a congratulatory shoulder grab. The gringo had braved the dark, the tarantulas and the scorpions. Joe had embarrassed himself with great bravado. Every man clapped Joe on the back and laughed at him in a good-natured way. Several men bought him beers. By one o'clock in the morning Joe was singing corridos at the top of his lungs with his new friends.

The next afternoon, two of his new buddies, Jesús and José, pulled up in their ponga. Filling the ponga was a gigantic hammerhead shark. Joe was impressed. He had no idea how those two had landed that shark without sinking their ponga. He clapped to two men on the back.

Isabel pointed to the shark's teeth. Jesús cut out one of the teeth and handed it over to Isabel. She looked at the razor sharp tooth in her hand with a mixture of fear and awe. Jesús saw her staring at the tooth, and immediately he started to cut out the entire jaw of the shark.

"No, no por favor, no," cried Joe. He held up a finger.

"One tooth is enough," he tried to tell them.

Jesús stopped cutting.

He and Joe exchanged smiles.

When they left to finish cleaning the shark, Isabel was already below working on her shark tooth necklace.

Church

In La Cruz there was a diminutive man of perhaps fifty who sold herbs from a small wooden cart. Gregorio would wheel his cart back and forth across the three blocks of the La Cruz malecón, the wide walkway that bordered the water. Families and couples would stroll along the malecón in the evenings sampling food from improvised stands if any were open.

Gregorio spoke to Isabel out of the blue one day and asked about her mother. Before she could answer he handed her a sprig of chamomile and told her how to make a tea out of it so that her mother would get well.

Isabel was taken aback. In truth, her mother was aboard the *Volante,* sick in her bunk, with a stomach bug.

Isabel took the chamomile to her mother and told her what Gregorio had said. Ellen did not make the chamomile into a tea, but rather used some chamomile tea bags that she already had. The next day, Ellen felt much better.

When the family went ashore to stretch their legs for the day, Ellen decided to thank Gregorio for his recommendation. As it was Sunday, he was not at the malecón with his cart. He was there, however, with his entire family in his Sunday best.

He asked the *Volante* family to go to church with them. Joe and Ellen looked at each other and thought, "Why not?"

So, off to church they went.

One of Gregorio's daughters had a child out of wedlock, Gaby. This was the day that she was to be confirmed. They all went into the La Cruz church and their group took up an entire row of pews. Many young children were there to be confirmed or baptized that day.

La Cruz was too small to have its own priest, so a traveling priest came to town to do services, weddings, baptisms and confirmations four times a year. Many people in La Cruz would endure the hour long bus ride into the city to go to the magnificent church in the center of Puerto Vallarta for Sunday services. They preferred the large metal crown and gorgeous jewel tones stained glass windows to the white washed out building turned church in La Cruz.

Stuffed into the pew in La Cruz, Joe and Ellen politely tried to make heads or tails out of what the priest said in Latin. As a Protestant she was not used to church services in Latin. The priest went amongst the congregation and confirmed the children as they were held in their parent's arms. When the priest came to the family's row the mother handed Gaby to Ellen and told the priest that Ellen was to be the godmother.

Ellen held the child in shock and nodded consent to the priest. Thus, Ellen came to be the godmother of a child in La Cruz completely by surprise.

After the confirmation, the family went to Gregorio's house for a celebration. He lived in a two-room house with all of his progeny and all of his progeny's progeny.

The first room held a small kitchen and a table for four with three chairs. The floor was of packed dirt that was swept clean. The second room was much larger and filled with beds. There were six beds of all different sizes. In one of the beds was a pair of children who coughed, and Ellen held Isabel back from visiting so that she would not become infected. Isabel was sent outside to play with the older children.

Isabel watched as some of the children pulled eggs out from under chickens that made their nests in the crooks of trees in the yard and threw them on the ground to watch them splatter. Some of the eggs contained partial embryos. The children poked and pulled the undeveloped chicks apart. Isabel did not understand the waste and she was horrified they killed the unborn chicks. There were eighteen people living in the tiny house and she was sure any one of them would have been happy to have an extra chicken for the dinner table.

But even more horrific to Isabel was the mutilation. She held down her vomit as one little girl pulled an embryo apart by its two, slimy, underdeveloped legs and ripped it in two, holding up both halves to show Isabel. The egg white dripped off the tiny corpse and ran down the little girl's fingers.

One of the older girls dropped her underwear and peed in the middle of the yard while a flock of chickens walked past, unperturbed by the violent death of some of their offspring. Isabel did not know what to do.

She went back inside where Gregorio was telling her parents about an outboard motor that he wanted for his ponga.

"It's a good engine, amigo," he said, slapping a picture he had placed on the table in front of Joe. "I can get to the fish faster than the other guys! Make a better life for my family," Gregorio said as he swept his hand in front of him indicating all the mouths he had to feed.

Outboard engines, especially the seventy-five horsepower kind that the little man wanted, cost a lot of money—far more than Ellen and Joe would be willing to spend on a present. They did not have an outboard engine of any kind for their own dinghy. Furthermore, they just did not have that kind of money.

That's when it clicked in Joe's head why Ellen had been asked to be the godmother; so they would feel compelled to buy Gregorio an outboard engine. Joe stood up, pulling his wife and daughter with him as he said a hurried, but cordial, good-bye and hurried out the door.

Immediately, Joe raised anchor and they returned to the busy harbor at Puerto Vallarta where they would be under the watchful eye of the Armada who only wanted from them the use of the *Volante* as a diving board when they were not home.

Yelapa

Just ten miles south of Puerto Vallarta slept the town of Yelapa. It was a tiny village tucked into the jungle, visible from the sea only by the occasional thatched roof that protruded under a thick veil of palm trees and gigantic ferns. On the beach were kitchens covered in palm fronds. Tables were set up out front to serve food to tourists that would arrive by boat.

Women wandered the beach with several different kinds of pie piled on top of their heads calling, "Pie, de limón, de coco, de nuez." The best flavor was the lemon pie whose filling was the consistency of good custard and whose real lemon bite could be felt for hours after eating. Isabel was in awe of the pie sellers. Why hadn't anyone in the States come up with a pie concession? They had ice cream, nuts, popcorn, hot dogs, but no pie.

The Yelapans, Isabel thought, *are geniuses.*

The beach was separated from the town proper by a small cliff in a manner that required tourists to hire a horse and/or a guide to show them the way to the town. The actual path to the town was not really a path, but a labyrinth of twists and turns through people's front yards that required climbing over fallen palm trees and up steep steps cut deep into the cliff.

Isabel wondered if the owner's of the yards they climbed through received any sort of compensation for random people traipsing across their property. Later, she found out that the shortcut into the town lay behind a clothesline that was always full of king sized sheets, and a large dog that was staked to a rope in the corner of the yard.

Isabel thought, *How smart to hide the trail and make the unsuspecting tourists pay to invade one's town for the day.* She chuckled to herself as she walked behind the clothesline. She beamed to be one of the people able to fit in enough to figure out the secret path to town.

There was no way to get to Yelapa by car, so there were no cars in the town. The mode of transportation was either by foot, by horse or burro. Two tiny children passed the family riding a burro covered in plastic bags full of groceries being chased along the path by a woman equally covered in plastic bags full of groceries yelling at the burro to be careful with her children and to not drop the eggs. The burro tipped his ears back in her direction, listened and continued on his way, a resigned look on his face.

Finally, this was the Mexico that Joe and Ellen had wanted to see. The undisturbed Mexico. A place of simplicity and function. A mecca where the only act was of survival, not the interminable procurement of more, just for the sake to have more. The kindness in all of the inhabitants pervaded even the dirt paths of the small town. Men and women asked after the family's health without knowing them. Offers of assistance that weren't needed were made. Smiles and nods of friendship greeted the family wherever they went. There was no sizing them up. No attempt was made to get what they had. Just the purity of the people themselves was offered.

Isabel loved the people. For a long time she had wanted to change the color of her skin, make it brown, and darken her eyes and make them black so that no longer would she hear the whispered, "La gringita viene," as she approached.

"I am not a gringa," she would retort. "I am a North American just like you."

Oh, to have those black, sparkling, laughing eyes full of kindness. Nothing could be more beautiful. To be seen as different, or other, gnawed at Isabel. An only child upon the vast sea wants to belong, perhaps, even more than any other child looking for their place in this world. To have her otherness so obvious that from a distance that people called her the 'little white girl' as if that was her name did not hurt Isabel's feelings. What bothered her was that people made assumptions about her, and what made her tick, even before she said hello, just based on the color of her skin.

Every time this happened, Isabel would distinctly remember from the States a TV clip of Martin Luther King's I Have a Dream speech. The clip showed the magnificent Dr. King giving his speech in Washington. The line Isabel remembered was : "I have a dream that my four little children will one day live in a nation where they will not be judged by the color of their skin, but by the content of their character." As a small child watching this black and white clip on their color TV, she took it for granted that this notion of treating a person a certain way because of the color of their skin was a thing of the past, a historical artifact about which one needed to be reminded to not let it happen again. She never knew that people who even talked about skin color actually existed anymore until she realized that her name in this new place was "The Little White Girl."

***

Ellen made a friend in Yelapa. The locals called her Juana La Gringa. Her name was really Joanna, but phonetically speaking Juana was the closest translation. Ellen and Juana hit it off immediately despite Juana's life of romantic love stories, marijuana and her nomadic nature. Juana's house sat right on the water. Just a little breakwater separated her living room from the waves.

Every part of her house was thatched; the ceiling, walls, and the shower stall in the bathroom. Two hammocks swung in her living room, as well as a bed elevated off the floor by tiny ropes and topped off by a canopy. There were enough big bugs and scorpions in Yelapa that no one slept on the floor. Nor did anyone have a bed without a canopy to catch the bugs that flung themselves out of the thatch when the lights went out.

Sleeping in a swinging bed was like sleeping on the boat; they both swayed and hypnotized one to sleep.

Juana's house was always full of people drinking wine and smoking while they discussed philosophy and religion. Isabel did not realize that she had just met her first true Bohemian.

Everyone loved Juana for her generous nature and her earthy tones, how she turned pain into comedy with a mere flip of verbiage. Isabel loved how Juana spoke to her as an equal instead of relegating her to the shallows of baby talk. She gave Isabel her first copy of the *I Ching*. Juana felt everyone should have her own copy. Isabel sat and read the entire volume in two days, and then Juana discussed it with Isabel as if they were two professors. Isabel felt for the first time that she was going to like being an adult.

Juana was an art dealer who specialized in Huichol art. Ellen was so excited to hear of this amazing connection and knew she would be able to use it to help Pedro and his cause.

Ellen loved the artwork for its fantasy and novelty, but as a person from the medical community, she saw an opportunity to help an entire people by embracing their artwork. In addition, she liked the idea that she was helping an indigenous culture to survive by participating as a translator between Juana and the Huicholes. Juana, despite owning a house in Yelapa and having spent the majority of the last fifteen years in Mexico spoke a poor Spanish. Ellen's confidence soared and she was happy to have broken the mold on the types of people she let into her life.

Juana was thrilled to have help with her art business. She was intrigued that a person like Ellen would want to hang around her. Usually people like

Ellen shunned her as a pariah because she went against conventions held sacred by the uptight and unworldly.

Juana's competitor for artwork in Yelapa was an American English professor who lived in a house way up in a tree. One arrived to the professor's house by walking up a very steep hill. There was a point when the tree and the hill were the same height, and that was where the professor's front door stood. The tree house had a marvelous front door painted with a bright green bird with long purple tail feathers on a background of cobalt blue. The knocker was a large brass conch shell which one rapped three times in order for the door to be opened.

When the family met the professor she was kind enough to take them on an outing. They went by ponga to the small, rocky islands just outside of Yelapa. They all snorkeled and the professor and the ponga driver caught fish and barbequed them. They were the most delicious fish the family had eaten.

They explored the island and found a small party of teenage school children with their teacher on the far side of the island. He had brought his mathematics students to the island as an end of the year present because they had all done well on their exams. Isabel was again impressed by a country where a teacher would take his classroom on an outing that he had to pay for to celebrate his class' accomplishment on their exams.

The generosity in Mexico astounded Isabel. At home generosity was measured and doled out only if one person deemed another to be deserving. In Mexico, it seemed everyone deserved generosity. Smiles abounded, kind words outnumbered the cruel by a ratio of a thousand to one. She let go of her guard and it floated into the depths of the Pacific where it would never be resurrected as a sane, and coherent piece of life's equipment for her.

The competition between the English professor and Juana was fierce enough that Juana did not go on the island outing. When the family returned to the tree house, there were three Huicholes in full traditional dress – broad brimmed straw hats with a band woven of bright colors and acacia thorns hanging from the edge that symbolized a pilgrimage to the sea; white tunic shirt with slits running all the way from the wrists to the waist—as if they had been forgotten to be sewn up —but held closed by a long wool belt covered in an intricate design. The belt kept the kidneys warm up in the mountains. The pants were long and white with a drawstring waist of the same simple linen as the shirt, the cuffs covered in fabulous colored designs in wool thread. In a historic sense the pants were to keep the Catholics happy when the Huicholes descended from the mountains into the Church run towns and cities, but now the pants were a matter of course.

The men wore shawls in red or white also trimmed in fabulous embroidered designs. The trio had walked down from the mountains, taken a bus to Puerto Vallarta, and then taken a ponga to Yelapa carrying all of the artwork they had to sell. Some of the yarn paintings were six feet long and five feet high and each man carried at least three that size plus smaller yarn paintings and various ceremonial masks, beaded bracelets, bowls, woven belts, and clothing pieces.

The yarn paintings were made upon thick pieces of plywood that had been covered in beeswax. The yarn was pressed into the beeswax and stuck there in the design desired by the artist. On the backs of the paintings the artist wrote his interpretation of the dream or vision he had had that inspired him to make such a painting. Most of the depictions of the dreams scared Isabel. They were of bright green snakes and vermilion blood, big fiery suns and silver moons, squiggles of yellow lightning and green balls of peyote.

Joe and Ellen thought they were beautiful. In fact, Joe insisted on getting a four-foot by three foot yarn painting covered in hummingbirds, an apparent deer-phoenix creature, candles, deer and people. The yarn painting was too big to fit down the hatch and ended up being wrapped in enough plastic to make it resemble a cocoon, and living lashed to the cabin top. Somehow the yarn painting would survive the elements and emerge mostly intact.

Rabies

Aside from all of the creepy crawly critters that lived in the thatched roofs of the palapas in Yelapa, the family heard of a further terror they had to protect themselves against. Another cruiser, Jane, had been to Yelapa about five years earlier with her family and had a scary story to divulge to Joe and Ellen.

Jane's family traveled to Yelapa and enjoyed all of the delights, the pie, the waterfall, and horseback riding. They returned to the boat late in the afternoon only to find that the seas had kicked up. Their boat pitched and rolled with such force that the she became very seasick. Jane decided to go ashore and spend the night in the tiny palapa hotel on the beach. No other member of her family wanted to leave their familiar bunks. Jane was too sick to care.

Yelapa was remote enough that although there was a constant supply of running water the power was provided via generator. At ten o'clock every night the electricity shut off, just as it did in La Cruz. Utter blackness would consume the town, with the exception of a few dots of candle light that shown bravely into the darkness. Jane did not worry about electricity. She was too sick and so grateful to be in a still bed, that she flopped onto the covers and fell asleep.

At two o'clock in the morning, however, she was awakened by a searing pain in her forehead. She yelled out, and in a frantic, tripping, scramble, she searched for the light switch to no avail. She screamed for help. The hotel manager came running with a flashlight.

"¿Qué pasa?" the manager asked, shining his flashlight in her room.

She squinted and pointed to her forehead. The hotel manager lifted his flashlight to her face and an extreme look of worry came over his face.

"Vampiro," he said.

"¿Vampiro?" she repeated.

He made the sign of wings flapping and big fangs with his pointer fingers and then pointed to her forehead.

"Vampiro," he said again.

Then he said three other words that she understood, "Ponga, Vallarta, hospital."

Jane grabbed her bag, and by the time she had the bag's strap on her shoulder, the manager was leading her by the elbow down to the dock where he loaded the stunned woman into a ponga.

He then gave a list of instructions in Spanish to the driver. He repeated the word 'rápido' many times.

The driver stopped first at Jane's boat. He dashed aboard leaving Jane in the ponga. He went below and dragged Jane's husband, Frank, out of bed. The ponga driver, in doing his best to save a stranger's life, received a punch to the jaw and was thrown onto the deck where the driver pointed to Jane in the ponga. She told Frank about the vampire bat. Now it was Frank's turn to dash below decks and pull his two teenage children from their bunks. They all set off to Vallarta in the ponga at top speed. No one spoke during the trip.

At the pier in Vallarta the ponga driver went ashore with them and hailed a cab. He told the driver where to go and to get there fast. He pointed to the mother's head and repeated the dreaded 'vampiro' word again. Frank embraced the ponga driver and apologized, still thanking him thru the window as the taxi pulled away.

The taxi driver floored it and ran the one stoplight in town. He honked his horn at an elderly man who led his burro weighted down with sacks of beach sand. At the hospital the taxi driver went into the building with the family and explained to a nurse that his fare had been bitten in the head by a vampire bat. The nurse ran for a doctor. A second later the doctor appeared. He took Jane into an exam room and came back out in less than five minutes. He looked at the husband.

"Your wife needs to fly to Los Angeles," he said in perfect English. "Here I can only give your wife the rabies shots in the stomach. It will be very painful, and she will need many injections. At UCLA they have developed a vaccine that you can take after you have been bitten and it is only a series of three shots in the arm."

"I'm going to LA," said Jane, and went to the curb to hail a taxi without waiting for her husband to respond.

The doctor yelled after them, "I'll tell them you're coming!"

With that the family went to the airport where the mother was put on an eight AM flight to LA. They did not have enough money for the whole family to go. Jane spent a depressed and worry ridden three hours on the plane.

When she landed, she planned to grab a cab and head for the hospital. To her surprise, as she disembarked she was greeted by a man with disheveled gray hair holding a cardboard sign that said 'UCLA - RABIES' in big red letters. The doctor in Vallarta had forgotten her name in the hurry to get Jane to the airport.

The man with the sign sat her in a wheelchair and handed her the sign. No one stood in the way of the madman running with a woman in a wheelchair holding a 'Rabies' sign.

He drove them to UCLA into the Experimental Animal Testing Division. Jane saw the sign and gave the driver a funny look, but when she opened the car door and heard dogs barking, Jane froze.

"Wait a minute. Aren't I supposed to go to the hospital to get these shots?"

"Well, these shots are so new that the hospitals don't carry them yet. We keep them in the dog lab."

"The dog lab? You're kidding me, right?"

"Well, you are going to be the first human being to receive this vaccine. The doctor from Puerto Vallarta said you were quite willing to become the first human test subject."

Without warning, Jane vomited right then and there; the events of the last 24 hours were more than Jane could stomach. However, it was just enough for her to realize that jumping back on the plane to Mexico to have her stomach pumped full of painful injections in a country where she could barely ask for a glass of water was out of the question. So, on shaking legs, into the dog lab she went.

Word traveled fast of her arrival to the lab. The entire staff turned out to watch her receive her first shot. She was monitored for anaphylactic shock for twenty-four hours. Then she was released onto the streets of LA until her next shot the following week. She had strict orders to call them if she felt dizzy, nauseous, had blurred vision, insomnia, diarrhea or in any other way felt strange. She stayed in her motel room waiting for signs of any neurological imbalance. She would bring a glass of water to her lips and ask herself, "Does this make you afraid?"

Jane did not leave her room until Rob, the man from the lab, came to pick her up.

"Rob," she said the moment she opened the door to let him in, "do I look OK?"

He seemed a little puzzled. "Yeah, you look OK. Why?"

"I don't look a little rabid to you?" she asked, barely looking at him, afraid he would say yes.

"No, you look like a plain Jane, Jane," he responded, holding out his hand to lead her to the car. "Now come on, the vets are waiting."

***

After the second shot, she took herself to Disneyland, because you only live once.

After her last shot, the staff of the Experimental Section gave her one of the official dog bone tags that proved she had been vaccinated against rabies.

"Here you go, Jane, shots are done, and you are fully vaccinated."

She held up the little dog bone shaped tag and let it spin on its chain. One side had the expiration date of her vaccine and the other side read, *To Jane With Love, The Dog Vets.*

She smiled and put the necklace on.

"Thanks, guys. May I never see you again," she said with a grin.

***

Jane returned to her family in Puerto Vallarta and vowed never to stay on land again. The rabies tag never leaves her neck.

Having heard the harrowing tale of the rabies vaccination, Joe and Ellen hung mosquito netting around their bunk and Isabel's to protect them from the vampire bats. As they worked together on this project of mutual protection, Ellen, her self-confidence boosted by Pedro and Juana, forgot her misgivings about her husband. Instead she remembered why she fell in love with him. She remembered that they were a team as she held the Velcro to the mosquito netting and he ran it through the hand crank sewing machine. She smiled in pleasant contentment at Isabel who turned the handle on the sewing machine. The domestic bliss hypnotized her. Her bad memories hid behind the happy ones, and she lightened.

For his part, Joe was better able to keep his calm on his new pain medication, but he noticed that if he missed a dose the pain returned worse than before. He would break out in a sweat and have to run for a pill. Ellen did not notice this new habit as she was caught up in the happy fact that, for the time being, he was drinking less alcohol. What she did not realize is that he was taking so many antibiotics that a few extra pain pills thrown into the mix went unnoticed.

There was no one definable moment when Joe knew he was an addict, but he knew it was an addict that he had become. If he was being truthful, he realized he had been one for many years, since his burn unit days. But now, he realized that there were layers to his addiction, that addictions could pile one on top of another, some stronger than others, and some working together to strengthen themselves.

Pills and alcohol. My friends, my demons, he thought.

He rattled the bottle in his pocket as he did every so often to comfort himself that pain relief was always close at hand, and went about the business of hanging the mosquito netting.

That night the huge waves Jane had told them about rolled into Yelapa.

"I am not going ashore," said Ellen emphatically as she puked into a bowl, too seasick to stand.

"Nope. Me either," said Joe.

He hoisted the anchor and off they went to San Blas.

San Blas

San Blas was famous because the world record for the longest ride on a wave by a surfer had been set there. As soon as Joe saw the shape of the bay he knew how the record had been won.

The waves broke far away from the beach and then swung along the entire length of the crescent moon shape of the bay. They never hit shore until they ran into the breakwater at the far end of the bay, a distance of no less than three miles.

A massive rock formation jutted out from the beach where the waves first rolled in. Several fishermen sat on the rocks and cast about for fish in the surf. Low lying mangroves spread across the backbone of the beach, leaving a long beige stripe of sand paralleling it down the entire crescent moon of the bay.

They arrived in the late afternoon, which was a good time for surfing as was evidenced by all the surfers in the water and on shore who watched the waves rise and rhythm.

The surfers lined up on the beach like a primitive tribe with their surfboard shields surveying the battlefield. Then, one at a time, the aquatic warriors left the safety of the sand and leapt into the sea. From where the family stood as casual observers on the *Volante*, the waves looked like they were running ten to twelve feet, which was not uncommon in hurricane season. The waves created from a hurricane can travel farther than the hurricane itself, which is lucky for surfers because they can enjoy the waves without the wrath of the storm.

The waves broke so far from shore that the *Volante* had to anchor a mile from the beach to avoid the breakzone. While they ate an early dinner, the *Volante* family watched as one-by-one the warriors tried to conquer the front of the breaking waves so far from shore.

The warriors were repelled by the shear force of water that knocked them off their boards and pushed their entire bodies swirling and spinning under the water until they turned blue. The sea would relent, allowing them a brief gasp of air before flinging surfer and board back under its watery headlock and send them back to shore covered in sand and deprived of oxygen.

Finally, a few surfers made it out past the breakpoint. They sat on their boards, exhausted after such a struggle, and waited for their strength to return. The water was warm, at least, and the surfers did not look haggard, stiff and pale as they so often do in the States. Loose and warm, they sat astride their surfboards and waited. They regarded the waves as friends now that they were on the other side of them.

One man made his departure for shore. He paddled, caught his wave, rode it for about ten seconds and was catapulted off its crest to be pummeled by the waves. Another man left to catch his ride back to the beach and glided along a bit further than the first, but he must have made a derogatory remark to the water god for he was flung off his surfboard and sent flying through the air. He landed in the angry water with a *pop*! before he was dragged beneath the waves for the usual punishment.

A third man watched and waited. Ellen thought they might have to invite him to stay for the night as the sun started to set. He sat casually on his board and did not seem to be looking for the perfect wave. He sat on his board bobbing in the water like bobbing was what he had showed up to do that day.

A quiet hum in the distance could be heard. Just a soft, low-pitched hum. Without turning around, the man lay down on his board and began to paddle. With bronzed, muscular arms he paddled in loose strokes. As the humming wave came underneath him, he gave one last push and came to his feet. He did not ride all crouched and straining like his compatriots. He seemed merely to lean a little this way or that to achieve his changes in direction. The wave carried him the length of the bay and then dropped him with a careful deceleration right in front of the breakwater. His friends on the beach watched him through binoculars. A cheer went up for him. The war party jumped into their cars and went to pick up the victorious warrior. The most peaceful warrior had conquered the sea through diplomacy.

"I want to learn how to surf!" exclaimed Isabel.

"Honey, where are we going to put a surfboard?" asked Ellen.

Isabel looked up and down the narrow decks.

"OK, maybe boogie board."

"OK, maybe boogie board," Ellen agreed.

***

The next morning the family arose early. They did not see any waves. They took their dinghy ashore and set out to find a grocery store. It was the Fourth of July and the only thing the family had to celebrate with was a can of Vienna sausages. Joe held up the can.

"The USA will not stand being celebrated with these. We need meat!"

They were able to hitch a ride into town with a young couple that was trying to get back to town in time for work.

They told the family about a jungle ride through the mangrove swamp where mosquitoes the size of one's hand sucked their blood, water snakes in vibrant orange and black stripes that tried to jump into the boat, and enormous spider webs dropped out of the mangrove trees that would be big enough to catch a little girl like Isabel.

Joe thought the Jungle Ride sounded terrific. After they went grocery shopping he was going to take the family to try it out. Isabel was terrified. What little kid wanted to be chased into a gigantic spider web by snakes to have her blood sucked by gigantic mosquitoes?

They finished the grocery shopping and hired a taxi to take them back to the beach. Joe made a deal with the driver to come back for them the next day so they could go on the Jungle Ride. Isabel hoped that the driver would forget.

The family got out of the taxi and walked over the small sand dunes that separated the road from the beach. They stopped in their tracks. The waves ran ten to twelve feet high. They dropped their grocery bags next to the dinghy and waited while Joe gazed out into the waves and tried to calculate their force and timing. Ellen and Isabel sat in silence, hoping that the decision would be to hitch a ride back to town and spend the night in a motel. Joe loaded the groceries into the dinghy and Ellen and Isabel looked at each other in silent protest.

"You sure about this, Joe?"

"We got this, Ellen," Joe said with a wolfish smile.

Isabel knew that smile. The hairs on the back of her neck stood up.

Joe dragged the dinghy to the water and pointed her bow into the incoming waves. Joe took his place at the oars. Ellen stood outside the dinghy and ran to push them off the beach. She was able to run for quite a ways in the shallow water. With a final mighty shove she threw herself into the dinghy face first and then righted herself into her seat in the stern.

Joe rowed as fast as he could. Isabel turned to face the waves and knelt down on the floor of the dinghy. She had a hand on each gunwale for support. They rowed right into a series of three big waves.

Isabel yelled to her father, "Dad! We're not going to make it!"

Joe looked over his shoulder at the oncoming waves. He rowed even faster, desperate to make it past the break point, where the waves stopped being large, rolling masses of water that one could bob over, to toppling skyscrapers of water that crushed and killed people. The first wave came and they rowed up the steep side of it. They slipped backwards for a moment, but Joe dug deep within himself and they climbed the wave as it tried to break over them.

The second wave came in quick succession. It attacked them hard, filling the dinghy with water and made their newly bought groceries float. The dinghy rode dangerously low in the water.

The third wave did not relent. It came after them on the scent of blood. The water crashed over them. Through the swirling mass of water and foam Isabel turned her head and saw her father still rowing with all of his might and her mother clutching the dinghy with one hand while the other clutched a loaf of bread to her chest. Her ponytail swirled out behind her like a possessed piece of seaweed. The seawater tried to be inviting, tried to whirl its way around their bodies, warm and comforting, enticing them not to struggle.

Please let us up, Isabel thought. *Please, we're just trying to get home.*

Isabel's lungs burned. Suddenly, the water ceased to be upon them and Isabel was coughing out saltwater and sucking in fresh air. The dinghy was so loaded with water that the top of it was even with the water's surface. All three of them sat dazed for an instant and then they leapt to action to bail. Somehow they were just past the break point. They were waterlogged, but safe.

Joe, his humor unfazed by their near death experience turned to Isabel. "Makes Cabo look like a kiddy ride!" He laughed.

"You ass! We could have died!" cried Ellen pounding her fist into his chest with all of her might.

'We weren't going to die, Ellen," Joe said with condescension.

Ellen's adrenaline-ridden fingers shook as she picked up their groceries and finished bailing.

When they reached the *Volante* Isabel kissed her hull. She was the floating womb of their safety.

The next morning the family decided to take themselves on a jungle ride of their own.

"I am only getting into that dinghy if you swear to me that when we need to come home, you will wait until the waves die down," Ellen told him, pointing a finger into his face.

"No problem, honey," he said.

"Seriously, Dad, no more excitement like that," said Isabel. She lowered her voice, "Seriously, Mom can't take it."

"Okay, kid, okay," Joe said as he shook his head and chuckled to himself.

The family got into their rowboat and explored the many little channels with all their twists and turns of the river and its tributaries. Some were completely overgrown by limbs and lush vegetation so thick that one could not see through them. Others became too shallow for even the small keel of the dinghy and Joe had to brace the oars in the mud and push them back the way they came.

Mosquitoes swarmed around the family. Isabel was bitten until she looked like she had chicken pox. Ellen swatted and smacked at her face, slapping herself over and over. Ellen thanked her lucky stars she had started the family on the horrible tasting malaria medicine three months ago. Only Joe was unscathed. The mosquitoes diverted their flight path to avoid Joe. He rowed along in a blissful calm while his family sat in clouds of black, biting insects.

As they made yet another turn into the mangroves, the family saw a tall rusty building looming out of the bank in a clearing. It had been painted gray at some point in its life, but now it was a mottled rust orange. A long, metal shoot stuck out from the building and ended down by the river next to a short dock. Joe pulled the dinghy up to the dock and tied up. The family got out and explored the area. They walked around the building and called out, "Hola", but there was no response. They tried the door to the building and it swung open, revealing a mass of metal boxes, fuel tanks, flywheels and spark plugs, which had been constructed into a large machine of unknown purpose.

Joe and Ellen walked around the metallic colossus trying to decipher its use. There was a large vat on top of the machine that held no trace of what had been put into it, as it was remarkably clean. They looked for signs or markings on the machinery itself to find a clue as to its origin, but the could not find so much as a serial number.

In the dark of the metal shed that housed the mystery machine, they felt they had uncovered a covert experiment. They startled at the creaks and groans the rusted pieces made as they walked along the catwalk that went around the machine.

Baffled, they left the building, closing the door behind them. They headed back to the dock. No sooner had they departed the building than the machine slowly started to life. There was a slow drone, a squeak and a hiss, and then the machine was off and running with a rhythmic clanking. The family stared at the building in disbelief.

"I didn't see anyone, did you, Ellen?" asked Joe as he looked around.

"No, no one," said Ellen.

As they continued back to the dinghy there was the sound of something large and heavy hitting metal, and then that large something sliding. By the sound, it moved towards the family. They turned and saw a huge block of ice careen down the metal and shoot towards them. They watched as it spun past them and shot out into the water.

The family had not noticed that they were no longer alone. The water around the dock was now full of rafts, dug out canoes, and rowboats. Young children now argued with each other over the block of ice. They became human piranhas, beating each other off with makeshift paddles, kicking up water and yelling at each other. But there was a jovial tone to all this yelling. It was clear they all knew there would be enough ice to go around. The challenge and fun was to see who could get their ice first. In the dry heat of the blaring sun, the ice block sparkled, unaware that it was about to return to its original state of water vapor.

With a thick 'whoosh' and a 'splash' a new block of ice came swooping down the shoot and there was a mad scramble for the new prize. The ice blocks came in quicker succession; freezing, white missiles that melted in the blistering heat and hit the water half the size they had started. The family stood on the shore and watched with fascination at the native ritual of picking up the day's ice. They were relieved to be out of the way up on dry land.

As the water cleared of children and their boats, extra ice blocks floated in the water. One young man noticed the family standing up on the bank and assumed the white dinghy tied to the dock was theirs. He paddled to the dock and pulled a block of ice from the river. He made great efforts over the side of the boat, thrashing, splashing and losing his balance as he grabbed a huge block of ice off of his raft and fell over backwards as he tried to stand in the family's dinghy, lugging the block of ice.

They did not see the young man get up. Joe took off down the hill towards the dock. Ellen and

Isabel followed close behind. The young man sat up just in time to see three panicked strangers running at him. He sat still as he tried to calculate their intent, but his instincts told him to run when confronted by danger, so he jumped out of the family's rowboat and swam as fast as he could for his own raft. He looked back at the family from the safety of his own property. He looked at the family waiting for their response.

Joe smiled, Ellen waved, and Isabel laughed and yelled, "¡Gracias por el hielo!"

They saw an amazing transformation in the young man as his concern faded. He broke into a broad smile filled with large white teeth. He had large black eyes that filled with stars and twinkled. He rowed back to the family. He had two ice blocks on his raft. He spoke Spanish in an accent that required leaving the consonants off the ends of all his words. His name was Jesús. In that moment the family added him to the long list of Mexico's truly nice people who helped others for no apparent reason other than it was an integral part of his nature to be wonderful.

Jesús asked the family where they were from, and without hesitation he asked the family to dinner at his house.

Joe rowed along behind Jesús while Isabel rode with Jesús on his raft. As they wound their way through the mangrove swamp, they could see thatched roof houses that let out wisps of smoke and enticing aromas.

They pulled up onto a bank into the middle of Jesús' family compound. Old men and women sat in plastic folding chairs and directed the goings on about them with flicks of their wrists and flutters of their fingers. Young people carried wood and water into the houses. Young girls in aprons washed dishes and clothes on the banks of the river. No one seemed surprised to see Jesús with random strangers. He walked past five people without making introductions while Joe and Ellen smiled and made friendly motions with their hands. Isabel, however, just followed behind Jesús as if she had been to this new place a hundred times.

Joe and Ellen stood out to them like two large neon signs in the middle of the darkness of the dense jungle. They were conspicuous in their shorts and bright t-shirts. Joe's phony leg was an object for deep scrutiny; one young man poked at it with a stick. When Joe stepped away from being prodded with a stick, the inhabitants of the mangrove swamp's jaws fell. They could not believe that a fiberglass leg could feel. The young man pointed to Joe's leg and then to the center of the enclave.

Jesús pried them from the visual interrogation by his family and led them to the center of the enclave. With all eyes upon Joe and Ellen, Jesús pulled back a cloth door and revealed a young man, perhaps thirteen years old, lying in a bed with six pillows set up so six people could sleep in the bed like sardines.

Jesús pulled the blanket off the young man's legs and the young man slammed the covers back down in anger. For the briefest second, Joe saw what he needed to.

The young man was missing a foot just like Joe.

Joe's eyes swept the room in an attempt to not stare at the young man. He saw a crude crutch made from a tree branch and padded on the top with ripped cloth. Joe cringed. When he was in the hospital he thought he had everything taken from him, but he realized now that he he had so much more than he realized; opportunity. This poor kid had no opportunity at all.

Ellen nudged Joe and they walked out of the doorway. Jesús pointed at Joe's leg and then back at the thatched house. Joe understood what Jesús was asking, but Joe did not need Jesús to ask. The instant

Joe had seen the young man with the missing foot, Joe knew what he had to do.

The family returned to the *Volante* and Joe got to work. He searched the boat for materials and found wood, fiberglass, resin and the necessary tools. He shaved a piece of foam from the extra bunk's cushion for padding. The family piled into the dinghy and made their way back to the enclave in the mangrove swamp. When they walked up to the young man's house Jesús motioned for them to wait outside.

He went into the house with caution, like a cat-burglar. A few moments later there was the sound of a few muffled words, a scuffle, a loud thud, and then the young man appeared behind Jesús, dragged out upon the sheet upon which he had been lying.

Jesús dropped the sheet and gave the young man a hard stare. The young man glared at him in turn.

Joe walked between the stare war and took measurements of the young man's leg. He put one of his own clean stump socks onto the young man's leg. Joe then took the foam and held it up to the leg and shaped the foam with a good, sharp knife. He would pare a little of the foam away, and then hold the foam up to the young man's leg to check for fit.

Then he carefully attached the foam to his leg with masking tape and covered the leg with fiberglass soaked in resin. He carefully molded and shaped the phony leg around what remained of his calf, careful to leave enough room for the young man to be able to bend his knee.

Joe fashioned a basic foot shape at the bottom, that would allow the young man to walk. As the fiberglass hardened, Joe removed the leg and gave the young man a sad smile. He hated to have to make a prosthetic limb for someone so young, but he was happy to have the expertise to enable this young man to be able to get up out of bed. He took the leg with him back to the *Volante* for finishing touches.

Joe made sure the prosthetic limb fully cured. He carefully inspected every millimeter with loving scrutiny. He filed and smoothed the pieces of fiberglass that stuck out and removed the runs in the resin. He searched the paint locker and mixed shade after shade until he found one he thought was a reasonable proximity to the young man's skin tone. He went to his sock drawer and pulled out the three best stump socks he owned.

Two days later, Joe got back into the dinghy without Ellen or Isabel and rowed back to the enclave. He walked up the bank and was greeted by

Jesús who led him to the young man's house without a word. This time, the rest of Jesús' family followed him as if he were a beloved holy man instead of a stranger. Joe stopped Jesús from opening the curtain to the young man's house. Joe pulled the curtain back himself and shooed the others away.

The young man eyed him with hostility. Joe ignored it.

Joe ignored the young man when he kicked out at him. Joe grabbed his leg with a gentle force. He shoved a sock onto the young man's leg, and then pushed the phony leg onto the stump. He used gentle coercion to swing the young man out of bed and stood him upright, pulling him tight to his side. With firm movements he steadied the young man and forced him to take a few steps. The young man walked in a halting manner back and forth in the tiny space. He looked at Joe. A tiny smile moved across his face.

He extended his hand to Joe and said, "Me llamo José Angel."

Joe shook José's hand and walked out of the small house. The people looked past Joe and at José. Jesús was the only one who noticed Joe get into his dinghy and row away from the enclave.

As soon as Joe reached the *Volante* he started up the engine, which brought his family to the deck. He winched up the anchor and they set off from San Blas.

Joe wanted to give José the perfection of independence without having to show gratitude. He did not want the young man, who had locked himself in a dark room of depression, to feel the necessity to thank him. He did not want any attention. He wanted to get as far away from San Blas as possible.

He remembered the intense claustrophobia he had endured while in the Stanford Medical Center's burn unit. He imagined he must have looked just like José Angel, the covers pulled over his head so tight he hoped he would suffocate to death just to have the opportunity to escape the room. He wanted José Angel to get up and walk out of that room of depression and breathe real fresh air, just like he had been able to do by coming to Mexico.

Ellen watched her husband at the helm. He was back on track to being the decent, wonderful person she had imagined when she married him. From his knowledge of materials, and his own boat building experience, Joe had fashioned a leg that some men took eight years of medical and engineering school to be able to create.

Joe set their course for Mazatlán, and left San Blas before José Angel or anyone from the village could do more to thank him. He saw Ellen looking at him and he gave her a tiny smile.

"I have taken so much, Ellen, I just needed to pay into another's life. I just needed to do one good thing for this country before we left."

She snuggled into him, and watched the stars on the way to Mazatlán.

Mazatlán

Mazatlán loomed ahead of them. A bay with beaches lined with swarms of bodies playing in the surf. Isabel could not see the sand for all the of the arms and legs. T-shirts and dresses full of water made up the majority of swimwear. However, in front of the large hotels, the swarms were filled with large flesh colored places where skin slipped out of tiny bikinis and Speedo trunks. Free hands held drinks in large glasses filled with fruit-based drinks lots of alcohol.

At the other end of the beach fresh fish barbequed on a stick, and cups of fresh fruit lightly covered in salt filled the towels spread out on the beige sand. But as the family set anchor, Isabel realized that the water was a terrible dirty brown. It was not the healthy brown of a muddy river. It was a chemical brown with grimy foam, a filth that did not wash off and was insidious, like being covered in Vaseline. People played in the water, but Isabel was disgusted. She looked at the brown goo and gagged. She could not fathom how people could allow themselves to swim in such pollution. She averted her eyes from the beach and searched for the blue of her beloved ocean.

Before they went ashore, Joe and Ellen sat Isabel down to talk.

"This is it, kid. We will be going back to the States from here," Joe told her.

"The money is running low and your dad needs to have another operation," Ellen joined in.

Isabel looked down.

"There is no need to be sad, kiddo," said Joe.

"OK," said Isabel, but she never looked up.

***

On land, Isabel found the open air market to be full of the usual colorful fruits lying in their rainbow array in stalls next to a pile of fish that let off an odor of old age. The blankets and silver jewelry for the tourists all sat in their usual places waiting for the throngs of sunburned, scantily clad, loud people to find them and take them over the border. She saw nothing wonderful in Mazatlán. Mazatlán to her was a poor copy of places she had already been.

There was one new sight Isabel saw from which she could not avert her eyes. Gathered outside the walls, outside the market, were women and children. They sat on little blankets or right on the cement of the sidewalk. Some had wares spread before them, like the lady who sold chipped brown coffee cups displayed on a crumpled pink rag. Ellen bought two cups. Some women were of Huichol descent, as judged by their clothes, and sold dolls in native Huichol dress around them.

Isabel walked past a fat lady with a skeletal child collapsed against her chest. His tiny ribs pushed in and out as he labored with every breath to provide his body with the air he needed to support himself, for the air was his only source of nourishment and had been since he was born. Isabel took the popsicle she was eating out of her mouth and gave it to the woman for her son. Isabel did not know what else to do. She watched as the lady stuck the popsicle in her own mouth and the tiny boy looked at Isabel with hollow eyes. Isabel stumbled away in shock.

Isabel continued on her walk through this strange city, a city that distinguished itself to her by its lack of color and laughter, by its people who reflected all of their lost hopes and dreams. Isabel could hear their guttural disgust as her parents walked past without buying any of their wares. She could feel the glares of the hungry, the poor and the mistreated pierce her skin. They looked at her with hate because she was who they wanted to be and saw in her family their own demise. This hate was pure, and bitter, and held with it the wish to murder Isabel and rip her limb from limb. Being the object of such intense, unspoken hatred was a defining moment of her young life. Until this point every person she had met, except for one, had treated her in the universal manner one should treat all children, with care and understanding. She had been exposed to a variety of people, some of whom were strangers, others had known her since before she was born, but every person had looked upon her with the love that a child inherently pulls from a human's nature. In this very instant, however, she realized for the first time that her very presence was enough to invoke jealousy and make people hate. She was no longer comfortable in her own skin. Utter helplessness invaded Isabel, the feeling of seeing something that needs to be fixed and that one knows is morally wrong, but not being able to do a damn thing about it. In the mere flit of an instant, she realized she had lost the time of her youth when every moment was a source of joy and she was an endearing angel to all she encountered. She knew then that becoming an adult would be a terrible and painful process.

Joe did not say much as they walked through the town. But back aboard the *Volante*, he downed a handful of pain relievers and opened the hard alcohol. Isabel awoke at midnight to the sound of her father puking his guts out in the head. Ellen would not let him get into in his bunk with her. He ended up passed out on the cabin sole next to the head.

When he awoke late the next day, Ellen was pulling out all of Isabel's clothes, trying to see which ones fit.

"I am sorry, Ellen" Joe said sheepishly.

Ellen stopped folding the shirt she had in her hands.

They took another trip ashore to find the laundromat and to get Isabel ready for school back in the States. Ellen wanted to be sure that Isabel did not show up at their friend's house, the Gunnersons, smelling like mildew. They asked a person on the street where to find the laundromat, and in the typical manner with lots of pointing of the arms, they were told, "One block to the right then go for a ways, and then go one block to the right and you will see it on the left after about seven or eight blocks."

"So you mean it is just up the street?" Ellen asked.

"Exactly."

In the perfectly modern laundromat Isabel sat and watched the people walk past; the old man in his straw hat with holes, the young women in tight clothes and bright lipstick, the business people in their suits, the short, round ladies with the smocks over their dresses, the babies all bundled up and covered despite the heat, the man who sold toys that hung from a stick over his shoulder, the little boy with a popsicle trailing after his mother, all of them brown and beautiful. Isabel looked at her own pale complexion and lamented once again that she lacked such mahogany tones.

"Remember, Isabel" said her mother, jolting her back to reality, "take the Air Porter to the Sausalito exit and the Gunnersons will pick you up."

Isabel was excited to go to school with other children, and to see the house they had left behind. She wanted to see her grandparents, because as everyone knows grandparents are the magical fairy godparents of little children. Isabel did not concern herself with what she was leaving behind in Mexico. She did not grasp that this was a trip of no return. She had no idea that she was leaving her magical land forever.

The States

Isabel had just turned ten years old. She walked in to a new school to start the fifth grade alone. The Gunnersons offered to take her, but she insisted on taking the bus by herself; she had taken the bus many times before. She did not want them to spend their time on her.

She walked into her classroom and was happy to see a few familiar faces.

"Hey! Collette," a large girl turned and rolled her eyes at Isabel, obviously more interested in getting something out of her back pack than in seeing an old playmate.

"Hey, Jennifer," Isabel waved. Jennifer waved back.

"Hi, I remember you," Jennifer said. Just then another girl approached.

"That is *my* friend," she said and grabbed Jennifer by the arm and pulled her away from Isabel.

What is the matter with these people? thought Isabel. These kids were a far cry from the children with merry black eyes and kind words she was used to. She looked around the room and saw the gray walls haphazardly hidden by construction paper art projects and posters. The gray desks suddenly became all too apparent. Isabel felt her vision blur. She steadied herself on the the shelf next to her.

Oh, my God. I remember now. The gray. I have been sent back to the dreaded Gray Zone. She sat down and stared down at her gray desk top until recess.

Isabel perked up a little at the sound of the bell. She remembered recess as the one fun moment of school. Out she went to have some fun. But the girls in her grade made it impossible for Isabel to do anything, because Isabel did not have an ESPRIT sweatshirt. Apparently not having an ESPRIT sweatshirt that year was paramount to having contagious leprosy.

They made fun of her accent. They laughed at her because she did not know what a video game was. They tripped her when she tried to join in a game of soccer at recess. As she lay flat on her face, all the children in the recess yard laughed at her. Not a single one helped her up or asked if she was OK.

She retreated to her classroom to read a book. The teacher walked past and told Isabel to go play outside. Isabel picked up her book and ducked into the bathroom. She sat on the toilet and pulled her feet up so no one would see her and read.

She knew she could not call her parents in the middle of the Pacific Ocean to tell them about her bad experience.

She left school that day utterly disappointed. She had looked forward to all she thought the States had to offer, in particular friends, and sleepovers. All she found was cruelty. She would have taken the bus home, but too many of her fellow students waited at the bus stop and she did not want to deal with them. She set out to walk the four miles to the house where she was a guest.

Unbeknownst to her, however, there was a school just up the road. These students walked towards her in a pack. Twenty kids ranging in age from ten to thirteen descended upon her; Lord of the Flies, the urban version.

They saw her walking in her clothes that were foreign to them and they shouted cruel words to cut her down before her features even came into focus. They shoved and pulled at her. They knocked her backpack off her shoulders and tore the contents out of her bag and threw it around. They yelled at her that she was ugly. They pulled her frizzy hair. As she jostled past them with the remnants of her back pack clutched to her chest, some of the kids picked up rocks, and chunks of wood, and threw them after her, some hitting her in the head and back.

Isabel just kept walking.

An hour later she trudged in the front door of the house. She hid her tattered backpack by folding the rips over and holding the bag clamped to her chest. Mrs. Gunnerson asked her about her first day of school.

Isabel smiled and answered, "Fine."

She went to her room and tried to reconstruct her homework from memory. She ate dinner as normally as possible. She saw the bruises on her back as she got into her pajamas.

Isabel did not cry. She made every effort to appear normal. She was not going to let those kids make her cry. She went to bed and slept the heavy sleep of one preparing for battle.

The next four days continued the same—the name calling, the beating, the tearing of clothes, the berating. The weekend was spent in the relative calm and maternal comfort of running errands with the mother of the house, but the following week brought more beating, yelling and name calling. Isabel was exhausted from running away, finding new places to hide, and making up new lies to tell her host family about how great school was going.

She took to writing her fears and anger down on the backs of scrap pieces of paper, afraid her precious journal would be torn from her. She would write out her frustration in jagged stabs that tore the paper and made her words illegible. When the beaten piece of scrap was full of holes and covered in graphite, she would take the tattered remains and tear them into tiny little shreds and flush them down the Gunnersons' toilet. She did this all in secret, every night, waiting for her parents to come and rescue her. Writing away her anger kept her tears at bay.

The waiting seemed endless.

Isabel continued living in patient desperation for her parents to return and change her situation. Finally, after a month and a half, they came for her. The *Volante* stood docked at the Corinthian Yacht Club in Tiburon. Isabel was so happy to see her parents. She ran to them and gave them huge hugs. Before she had a chance to speak, they told her about the awful beating they took to get up the coast. The word beating has a very different meaning in the nautical world. Beating to a sailor means going against the wind and waves. They told of the pounding waves that impeded their progress and the freezing cold that fought them every inch of the way. They told her how lucky she was to have been safe and warm in a friend's home in Sausalito. They stood in front of her exhausted and worn.

Isabel went to open her mouth to tell her mother and father how wrong they were, that she had not felt safe. But there was something amiss between her parents. Isabel could tell that there was an even greater distance than usual between her between them. She watched them closely, scrutinizing their every move. There was something different.

Finally, after yet another day of exclusion, bumping, jostling and name-calling, Isabel tried to tell her parents.

"Look," she began, not really sure where to start, "I am having a really hard time here, ever since I was at the Gunnersons…"

"You should be grateful you were here enjoying the hospitality of friends," her mother interrupted.

"But, Mom, I am getting beat up every day just because I don't wear the clothes that they think I should," Isabel persisted. "They are calling me names, and knocking me down. One girl is even throwing two by fours at my head!" She pointing vehemently at her own head.

Her mother looked her daughter up and down and said, "Well, it is true you don't dress well."

Isabel stopped her story right there, index fingers still pointed at her own temples. All air left her body. This was not what a mother was supposed to say to a daughter who has spent the last six weeks being threatened and maimed. In particular, such a comment was not to be made by a parent about something as superficial as clothes. They had spent the last three years in an environment where the labels on one's clothing were the last thing anyone would have given any importance.

Isabel looked to her father for a show of support of some kind. Anything would have sufficed at that moment; a gesture, a squeeze, a kind word. He had not heard any of her story. Preoccupied, he instead said, "Isabel, your mother and I love you very much. We are getting divorced."

Isabel looked from her mother to her father. There are moments when so many thoughts and words flood into the mind that it paralyzes the mouth and appendages. This was such moment for Isabel.

Isabel looked at her parents, her head twitching left and right so fast as she looked from one to the other that her vision blurred. *No one cares we moved back to a place that is not safe? No one gives a shit. Not a single shit. No shits given. Not one shit*, she thought.

After a long pause during which her parents scanned her face for a verbal reaction, but were too blinded by their own sorrow to see one, she simply said, "Whatever."

She looked at them. They were clearly disappointed that she was not saddened by the news of their divorce. What did they expect from her? How is a ten year old kid supposed to know the depth of pain a divorce brings? Or realize from that moment that she will never have her two parents occupy the same space again?

Isabel had her own more immediate problems, like being able to get to and from school safely. The two people in the world who were supposed to make safety happen for her were too wrapped up in their own minds to help. She stared at them, disbelieving their lack of interest in their only child's plight.

All of her flight feathers fell in a ring around her feet. She left the *Volante*. She stomped down the dock, a young, featherless bird, without parents.

She went out to the main street. There was a cute candy store on the corner that, before their trip, Joe had always taken Isabel after he won a sailing race. Isabel went to the familiar store. She looked for something to build her confidence, like a few well placed words from a best friend, but the store only sold tangible items. It smelled like her secure childhood in there, with the scent of chocolate and candied apples, but there was no actual comfort to be found. She bought a packet of gummy cherries, a pen, and a new journal. She sat down on the curb right in front of the store and began to do the one thing that had brought her peace in the past six weeks.

She opened the little, cobalt blue journal and wrote, *The Volante was in the act of flight…* and a little speck of a feather sprouted on the back of her neck.

The End

Glossary of Terms

Acacia plants with pretty pink flowers that can grown between six and eight feet tall, and have strong long, black thorns.

Alcohol de caña cane alcohol. Was sold in pharmacies as rubbing alcohol, but some of our cruising friends liked to drink it.

Bandidos bandits

Bilge where the water collects in the bottom of a boat, under the floorboards.

Boatswain's Chair a sort of fabric chair meant to be hoisted up and down the mast for repairs

Bolillo Mexican sandwich roll, kind of chewy

Bow front of the boat, usually pointy.

Caballero gentleman, or horseman

Cabin sole the interior flooring of a boat

Carnicería butcher shop

Chart table a small table to keep charts and also a place to lay charts out when needed to take measurements to plot a course.

Chicharrones deep fried noodles or pork skins

Chicle Chiclets gum

Cockpit exterior area where the steering and sitting happens

Coaming a curved piece of wood that is a a good hand hold.

Companionway small ladder leading from the cockpit to the inside of a boat

Conasupo Mexican supermarket

Crossing to go from one port to another, or can be used more specifically, to cross a large body of water.

Cruisers / Yachties what people who travel on boats call themselves instead of nautical nomads

Depósito the place where one can buy bottled drinks and they take a deposit for the bottles.

Deck the exterior, flat walkway of a boat

Dodger a large piece of canvas with plastic windows that is typically installed on top of the cabin and protects people in the cockpit from waves breaking over the bow.

Fathom there are seven feet in a fathom.

Forepeak the storage area in the bow. On the *Volante* the forepeak was full of sails and chain from the anchor. It was accessed by an exterior hatch.

Galley kitchen

Gates what the old ship building piers and dock areas are referred to in Sausalito

Gracias por el hielo 'Thank you for the ice'

Guayabera Mexican, short sleeved men's shirt with pockets and embroidery down the front

Gunwale the top edge of the hull

¿Hablas español? 'Do you speak Spanish?'

Head bathroom

Hanging locker tiny clothing closet

Hola 'Hi' in Spanish

Huanacaxtle a type of hardwood that looks a lot like teak

Huichol name of one of the many indigenous tribes in Mexico

Jib smaller sail that hangs on front of the main sail, closer to the bow

Lee Protected from the wind

Limber holes small holes in the dividers between the compartments in the bilge that allow for water to travel from the highest point to the lowest point of the boat. The lowest point of the boat is where the bilge pump is located.

Luchador Mexican wrestler

malecón a sea wall that has a walkway on top of it.

Main s'l main sail, also the largest sail. Hang over the center of the boat.

'Me llamo José Angel' 'My name is Joe Angel' in Spanish

Palapa thatched roof made from palm fronds, common roofing material in many places the *Volante* traveled

Paleta popsicle in Spanish

Peyote used by the Huicholes for ceremonial visions

Ponga a narrow, approximately eighteen foot long and five foot wide motor boat, usually made out of fiberglass, without a cabin, that are used all over Mexico as fishing boats and water taxis.

Port left Side

'¿Que pasa?' 'What's up' or 'What happened' in Spanish

Reef (as in 'put a reef in the mains'l') a folding of the sail, and the subsequent tying in place of the fold, thereby making the sail smaller.

Salon usually the widest part of the boat where the table and settees, and in the case of the *Volante* some bunks, are located

Settee a place to sit that is built into the boat. The ones on the *Volante* were long enough to serve as extra sleeping berths when needed.

Seat locker usually found in the cockpit, the part of the cockpit where one sits. This sitting area is often on hinges and one can store items in there, such as jib sheets, winch handles, etc.

Settee a small built-in bench. The ones on the Volante pulled out to make a wider berth to sleep upon.

Starboard right side

Señor Sir or Mister in Spanish

Stern back of the Boat

Tamarinds a tree fruit that comes inside a pod. The fruit is very tart. The seeds are pretty.

'Te amo, mi reina' 'I love you, my queen.'

Tiller the piece of wood that attaches to the keel and allows for steering. Boats usually have a round wheel, or a long-straight piece of wood known as a tiller for steering. The *Volante* had a tiller.

Thwart the small seat in the middle of a rowboat.

Winch a large spool shaped contraption that allows one to let the sails in and out easily

Windlass s large winch that lets chain in and out

Yachties / Cruisers what people who travel on boats call themselves instead of nautical nomads

About the Author

Christian has always had a passion for writing and started at the tender age of 7. She grew up in Sausalito CA, on her family's sail boat from the age of 5 until she left for college. When she was 7, she and her family lived off the coast of Mexico for three years where she learned to speak Spanish. Several years later, Christian would write her novel *In The Act of Flight* based on her life growing up on a sailboat.

Christian attended Barnard College in New York and graduated with a B.A. in Latin American Studies.

Christian now lives in Eureka, California with her husband, two children, and a menagerie of pets. When she's not writing, Chris spends her time at her day job as a Registered Veterinary Technician.

To contact Christian and keep up to date with other literary works and releases, please visit:

http://www.christianpitts.net

https://www.facebook.com/authorchristianpitts

Her next novel, *Living Luciano*, based on her great-grandfather's role in the trial that ultimately brought down the infamous gangster, Lucky Luciano, in the 1930's, will be out in summer 2019.